THE COMING STORM

THE LION'S DEN SERIES BOOK 5

EOIN DEMPSEY

This book is for my family.

1

Saturday, May 22, 1937: Montreuil, outside the city of Paris, France

Michael Ritter pulled at the collar of the shirt his father had bought him the day before. He pushed out a breath, trying to comprehend what was about to happen and how his life would surely never be the same again. But all nervous ruminations disappeared when Monika materialized at the end of the aisle. Resplendent in her simple wedding dress, she beamed at him from the chapel door, and Michael's father took her arm. When he and the rest of the family traveled from Berlin to Paris at the last minute, she insisted that he escort her down the aisle. With no living close relatives of her own, Monika had taken on Michael's as if they were a life raft on a raging ocean. His father was happy to oblige and radiated happiness as she whispered something in his ear.

The tiny chapel was empty save for his family and the young priest waiting at the altar. Michael's stepmother Lisa looked magnificent, as always, in a sky-blue dress. His 15-year-old sister Fiona and 12-year-old brother Conor looked ready to explode with excitement, and Hannah, his seven-year-old step-sister, sprinkled flowers in the bride's path. It was evident how proud she was of her role by the care she took in dropping the red and pink rose petals in perfect lines along the marble floor.

Maureen stood beside him, where the best man usually would have been. She was the perfect person for the job. He owed her everything, so asking her to be by his side was one of the greatest honors of his life.

A thousand thoughts floated to the surface of Michael's mind as his beautiful bride began the short stroll toward him. It was hard to believe he'd known Monika less than a year, meeting her at a lavish party thrown by Joseph Goebbels before the Olympic Games in Berlin. Meeting her opened the door to another part of himself that he'd never known.

It was no surprise to his family when he told them—in the code they used in their letters—that she had been the one to initiate the conversation about marriage. She left the timing to him and was open to whatever he wanted as long as it was soon. Monika saw no point in delaying what they both wanted. And this beautiful day in this tiny chapel in a far-flung suburb of Paris was the culmination of the intense love they shared.

It was true that they'd only known each other for ten months, but they'd experienced more in that time than many couples could in a lifetime together. She held him in her arms after the policeman in Marzahn shot him in the gut. She and Maureen worked together to save his life and found the surgeon who agreed to operate on him without telling the authorities. And somehow, he survived. The scars from that bullet were as much a part of him as the memories. The pain was gone, but something within him was lost that night. The desire for speed—the overarching obsession that had driven him these last few years—was diluted now, and he'd not been training in earnest since that bullet tore into him. What he lost that night was little compared to the joy Monika brought him, and he took her hand as his father presented her.

His father took a moment to embrace him before returning to Lisa and the children, then the priest began. After their father had arranged for them to be smuggled out of Germany, he, Monika, and Maureen had not stayed in Denmark long. With plenty of money in their pockets, they moved to Basel in Switzerland, a place the family visited from time to time. But Maureen and Monika soon grew tired of the slower pace of life there, and the lure of Paris proved too much. After six months in Basel, they moved to Paris, the most beautiful place he could ever have dreamed of.

This was the first time he'd seen his siblings since the trio fled Germany, and only the second chance to see Lisa. It was worth the risk for the family to travel for their wedding, even for Fiona and Conor, who must have imagined their sister and Monika had something to do with the policeman's death after seeing their likenesses in the newspaper afterward. If they did suspect anything, they had the good sense to keep their mouths shut. Michael would have throttled either of them for ruining Monika's big day.

Even if his siblings could be trusted, who knew how far the Gestapo's tentacles reached? The Berlin police hadn't given up searching for the person who killed one of their own outside the Roma concentration camp in Marzahn on the last night of the games. Perhaps they never would. Each of the three young people reckoned with the possibility of never seeing Berlin again, and though they'd come to terms with that, it didn't mean they'd given up the fight they began there.

The time came to exchange vows, and Michael took Monika's hands, staring into her eyes as he repeated the Latin words after the priest. It was hard to know exactly what he was saying, but if those words bonded him to Monika forever, he would repeat them a thousand times in any language. Monika took her turn next, and once finished, she turned to the priest to ensure she had said them right. He nodded with a handsome smile.

"You may kiss the bride," he said in German, and Monika threw her arms around Michael's neck.

His family erupted in applause as Michael drew back from his new wife. Lisa was dabbing her eyes with a handkerchief, and his father was clapping. Hannah ran to them and threw her arms around Michael's legs. The priest shooed her back to her seat before leading the newly married couple into the bright sunlight outside. They embraced each family member again, but stopped short of posing for a photograph.

The car they'd hired pulled up, and Michael held the door for his new wife. They sped off, waving out the back window to the small wedding party, even though they'd be meeting them for lunch in minutes. His father insisted they mark the occasion, which was why they were out here in the far suburbs of Paris, where he deemed it safer. Conor and Fiona would have little to report back to their Hitler Youth leaders about if they didn't see where their siblings lived or worked. Keeping secrets from them, and particularly Fiona, was a necessary agony. It was hard to know who to trust these days.

~

Saturday, June 5, 1937

The faith Michael once had in his body was gone. The one thing he could rely on in life had disappeared into nothing, fading away like ripples in water. The sun was high in the blue sky above, but the sweat on his hands and forehead was out of proportion to the day's warmth. Several other athletes were running laps, but he was alone at the start of the 100 meters. Monika was at the finish line and waved to him. Michael could make out the smile on her face and the words of encouragement she shouted. The singlet he wore was devoid of the swastikas that had adorned his Olympic uniform, and there wasn't a Nazi flag to be seen anywhere. Only a single French flag flew on a flagpole at the end of the track. He reached down to his abdomen and touched where the Nazi policeman shot him. The Roma family they freed that night were safe, living in Sweden, but he still bore the scars. He thought that being so close to death would have given him more focus on what he wanted in life, but the opposite seemed true. He stood up from his squatting position to wave to Monika.

"Come on," he muttered. He kicked out his legs as if that could somehow bring back who he was before the bullet hit him. He'd thought about the 100-meter Olympic final every day this past year. Falling halfway with a torn hamstring seemed like a bump in the road of his career then. Success in the following games, or perhaps the ones after, seemed inevitable. Jesse Owens's words about looking forward to running with him in the next games ran through his mind so many times that they were like a mantra to him.

He said "with," not "against."

It had taken several months to get back in training after nearly dying in Maureen's friend's house on the night the Olympic Games ended. By Christmas he was back jogging and running long distances by March, but sprinting was too much, until now. Perhaps it was fear that held him back. What would his life be if he couldn't do this anymore? He'd been an Olympic finalist—one of the fastest men in the world—soaking in the roar of the crowd. What could fill the void of silence now? His father's plan—to get an athletics scholarship and move back to America to go to college—depended on his sprinting ability. Just ten months before, he could run 100 meters better than almost anyone else.

Monika walked up the track to him. He heard her voice before he saw her, as his eyes were trained on the dirt.

"You ready?" she asked in English. She wanted to speak it all the time with him now. Her ability to learn languages was one of many things that amazed him about her. The sun was behind her and illuminated her auburn hair so that it shone like fire. "If you don't think today is the day...."

"I've been putting this off for months," he said with a mirthless laugh. "I can do this."

"You're not going to be as quick as you were when you were in the Olympics." She switched to German. "Don't be too hard on yourself."

"I know." But they were only words. Eleven seconds was the result he'd be happy with. It wasn't a time to frighten his opponents—Jesse Owens could run half a second better—but at least at that result, he knew that getting faster was still in him. He could be what he'd once been again.

Monika took the hint. "I'll see you at the finish line." She held up the silver-plated stopwatch she had bought him for Christmas. This would be the first time he used it. He watched his wife walk to the end, beautiful as ever, in a swishing white dress. Once she reached the finish line, he knew it would be time to run and wished in his heart that she'd never get there. But she did.

He crouched into the starting position and imagined he was back in the Olympiastadion, Jesse Owens on one side, Ralph Metcalfe on the other, and the crowd's cheers echoing in his ears. He could almost hear that noise and people calling out his name. Michael closed his eyes, let the sound of the crowd wash over him, and leaped from the starting blocks.

Monika was screaming, jumping up and down, but something was wrong as Michael pumped his legs. A weight seemed to drag behind him, or the track was sticky, and his previous routine speed eluded him. His body couldn't create what it once had. His abdomen didn't hurt—no dramatic agony brought him down. His fitness wasn't in question, and he wasn't panting as he crossed the finish line. It was far worse than that: The injury had rendered him mediocre.

His wife's face left him in little doubt about what he already knew. He let his legs go and ran on a few yards after the line, coming to a halt in front of some empty wooden bleachers. It seemed fitting.

She waited for him with the stopwatch in hand. The watery smile on her face was easy to see through, but he loved her all the more for trying to spare his feelings and hide the truth.

Monika threw her arms around his neck and kissed him.

"Is it that bad?" he asked.

"I'm so proud of you."

"What's the time?"

She looked at the watch and held it up in front of his face. "Eleven point nine seconds." His heart dropped like a stone. "You can't expect to get back to Olympic standards after being out for so long. A few months of training and you'll be back to your best."

"Maybe."

He didn't want her to see the tears in his eyes, so he turned away, pretending he was going to jog around the track. Her voice cut through the air.

"I don't care."

He whirled around, indignant. "What did you say?"

"Slow, fast, I don't care. I want you—that's all. You can run every day or never again. As long as I'm by your side, it doesn't matter to me."

The strength seemed to return to his body, and he walked back to her.

"You've already achieved so much," she said. "More than most in a lifetime. And what you did for me, when that bullet hit you... You saved me. That's more important than any Olympic medal ever could be."

A smile blossomed across his face, and he kissed her again.

2

Thursday, September 9: Paris

The cafés and restaurants of Paris were full once more after the August hiatus. Among the many things Maureen had learned about the Parisian lifestyle in her time here was that the people loved their country vacations and took them in the heat of late summer. Many businesses in the city shut down for much of that month. Now that the warm weather had faded a little, the people of Paris returned, and the streets were heaving once more with the slim, serious, beautifully styled individuals who inhabited this marvelous city.

Switzerland was the first stop in her escape from Germany, but if her exile from Berlin was to continue, she, Michael, and Monika decided to spend it here. Paris was a magnet for anti-Fascists of every stripe, all plotting Hitler's overthrow. It felt good to be among fellow travelers.

She undid her waitressing apron and washed her hands. Armand, the restaurant's manager, waved to her as she said goodbye. The feeling of freedom at the end of her shift doubled when she saw who was waiting outside on the street. Hans

Richter was one of her favorite people in her new home city. She didn't know much about him, apart from he was from Dusseldorf and had fled the city to escape Nazi oppression. But perhaps knowing he was earnest and dedicated to the cause was enough. She smiled as she greeted him with the traditional kiss on each cheek.

"What are you doing here?"

"I have someone I want to introduce you to," he said. "He's the son of a Luftwaffe general."

"And is he someone we can trust?"

"Meet him and judge for yourself. I left him with Monika and Michael at the Café Royal and came to fetch you."

They strolled along Place de la Republique. Dozens of people sat outside the cafés dotting the square, basking in the warm evening sun. She wondered whether she would have ever believed, five years before, that she'd be here, an American in Paris, speaking German to a political co-conspirator. She had grown up in New Jersey but spent the last five years in Berlin, where she and her family had moved back in '32 when her father received a job offer from Uncle Helmut. Her father and Helmut's daughter, Helga, inherited the factory when he died, and what was once a mediocre metalworks was now a thriving munitions producer. Maureen owed her father a lot and wasn't ashamed of what he did for a living. She understood his motivations and knew they extended far beyond those of the other fat cats filling their pockets with the riches heaped upon them by the Nazis.

The paranoia that gripped the citizens of Germany was foreign here, and people were free to discuss ideas that would see them jailed in Berlin. Maureen had been talking to Hans for several weeks now, and loved how curious he was to hear everything she thought and knew. Still, she didn't speak to him about Seamus Ritter. In the circles she ran in, her father's business was an embarrassment, at best.

They continued down Rue du Temple and crossed over to the narrow street of Rue Chapon.

Michael and his new wife were sitting outside the Café Royal with the outsider Hans had mentioned. It was strange to have Michael and a girl he'd never met a year before be such a massive part of her life, but they were the only family here. She and Michael were always close, but never like this. His new wife was also unknown to her a year ago, but they bonded quickly. First through Monika's desire to help the cause, and then in saving Michael's life after the policeman shot him. The same policeman's face had haunted her dreams for weeks after. It took her a while to come to terms with the fact that she had ended his life, but after a few weeks of guilt, she realized that the world was better off without one more rapist. She didn't choose to kill him. He chose to attack Monika; all she had done was defend her brother and her friend. The dreams faded to nothing.

The young man, the general's son, was sitting beside her brother, smoking a cigarette. Though seated, she could tell he was tall. He was well-built and had deep brown eyes and thick muscular shoulders that bulged under his shirt.

"This is my friend and new comrade, Gerhard Engel," said Hans, and Maureen greeted him with a handshake.

"*Bonjour*, Gerhard." She could understand and speak some French now.

"Good to meet you," Gerhard replied in German. "I met Hans at a meeting last week, and again last night, over beers."

"We realized we had a lot in common in that short time," Hans said. "Politics and beer."

"What else is there?" Michael asked.

Sitting here with these men made her wonder about her love life. She and Thomas were still together—technically, at least—though she hadn't heard from him in months. Not since she moved to Paris. Was he afraid to contact her, or was it something else? It was hard to say, but the questions about his thinking weren't as frequent as they were a few months before.

"You look like a local," Maureen said to Monika, sitting beside her. Her brother's 19-year-old bride was dressed in a stylish beige dress with a black beret.

"We've taken to this place," she answered. "I mean, how could you not?"

"The only thing it's missing are Nazi flags plastered all over every building," Michael said.

The whole table smiled at the thought of Paris being a National Socialist city when it was completely the opposite—the center of so many anti-Fascist plots.

The waiter came and took their order. Hans selected the house red wine for the table before focusing his attention on Michael. "How is the training going?"

"Good. Good."

Maureen wondered if anyone else noticed the sadness in her brother's demeanor.

Gerhard's eyes suddenly widened.

"I think I recognize you." He pointed at Michael. "Yes, I knew it was you!" He stubbed out his cigarette in the ashtray in the middle of the table. "I was in the Olympic Stadium for the 100-meter final last year. You are the man who got injured during the race."

"Remembered for coming last," Michael said with a wry smile.

"Not at all! You had every person in the stadium on their feet.'

"Living under the pasty dictator was causing us more stress than we were prepared to deal with," Michael said.

"Why didn't you return to America after the Olympics if you were so fed up with the Nazis?"

"We decided to try Paris for a while first. Maureen was the one who suggested we follow her to Paris a couple of month ago."

"I read an article in the newspaper about you last year before the games. You were the young hope of the Reich."

"And look at me now."

"You ran a courageous race," Hans said. "I saw it too, and I think I read the same article. You weren't mentioned in it, Maureen, but your father was. He's an important man...to the Nazi regime."

Michael nodded. "He has many considerations to take into account. It's easy to judge a man trying to make a living—"

Maureen interrupted her brother. "Michael's being polite, but the truth is, we don't speak to him anymore. We can't abide by what he does."

"I know what it's like to not approve of a parent's actions," Gerhard said. "Not everyone is like their father."

The men around the table seemed to accept what she said. She waited for one of them to change the subject and was pleased when Hans spoke up.

"Gerhard fought in Spain, killing for his beliefs. But how do I know you're serious, Maureen? People never follow through. You'll probably get bored of all this and move back to Berlin in a few weeks...."

"Don't talk to her like that. She doesn't have to prove herself to you," Michael said.

Maureen drank some wine, waiting a few seconds to speak. "I can't go back to Germany. I killed a policeman in a suburb of Berlin called Marzahn last year."

"I've never heard of it," Hans said.

"A lot of people in Berlin haven't either. That's why they set up a concentration camp there—for the Roma they snatched from their beds. The government decided to 'clean up' the city by interning hundreds of innocent people before the games."

"And you killed a policeman?"

"Yes."

Hans said, "I didn't realize that—"

"My father died in a concentration camp," Monika said. "I've no more use for a country that kills a man because he is a trade union leader. And Hans, what about you, while you're questioning us?"

"I escaped from a concentration camp," he said.

It was the first Maureen had heard of this. "Where?"

"From a godforsaken hole called Buchenwald, near Weimar. It's brand new. I was one of the first prisoners."

"Enough of this suspicion of each other. We've all suffered at the hands of the Nazis. We're bound by that," Michael said in his American-accented German. "I'm surprised by the attitudes of some French toward Hitler. I assumed that they'd be universally opposed."

"If only!" Gerhard said and lit up another cigarette. "The French upper classes are more supportive than most would imagine."

"Supportive?"

"I spoke with a man last week—a rich man—who asserted that Hitler is the lesser of two evils in Europe today. He argued that the French shouldn't let themselves be used as pawns by the English in their policy of keeping the continent divided, and that it might be easier to shake hands across the Rhine rather than across the Channel."

"Have they forgotten the war? It was only 20 years ago!" Maureen said.

Hans stood up and pretended to fluff a nonexistent mustache. He pressed out his belly and spoke in a guttural faux-French tone. "France and Germany represent the two highest cultures in the world, and why should they not unite?

And why should Frenchmen of breeding and social position permit themselves to be ruled by demagogues and Jews, the dregs of this world? Hitler solved the problem of labor unionism, and his solution is good for all countries. Hitler is the one enemy of Bolshevism who really means business."

Maureen would have laughed at the impersonation of the upper-class Frenchman had it not been so accurate and frightening.

"Many French would take Hitler over Stalin," Gerhard said.

"Other than the Reds, of course. Will they be so fond of Hitler once his tanks roll into Paris?" Maureen asked.

"You think that's a possibility?" Monika asked. "You think he means to conquer all of Europe?"

"He's spending more than double on building up the military as Britain or France. Why? He'd have you believe that those billions of Reichsmarks are to counter the threat from the east, but that's a bluff. He's been writing about expanding the Reich since the '20s," Gerhard said. "A lot of my friends don't believe it, but someone explained it to me once like this. Imagine a poor man who starves himself but puts all his resources and time into building a boat. What do you think his intentions are? To play music? To fly? No. Someone who spends everything they have on building a boat has only one thing in mind—to set it to sea. That's what a boat's for. It's not good for anything else."

Hans sat back in his chair and picked up Gerhard's cigarette lighter. It was tinted gold and shone in the evening sun. "Look at these people." He pointed to the Parisians shuffling past in their chic dresses and suits. "They're convinced nothing like the Great War could ever happen again. Living in denial is key to the French and British governments' appeasement tactics. They say they're not ready for war. When Hitler sent his men into the Ruhr, they weren't prepared. But as the Nazis are pumping billions into tanks, bullets, and bombs, France and Great

Britain are falling further behind. When are they going to be ready to stop this madman?"

"What's the attitude to Hitler and the Nazis in America?" Gerhard asked.

Maureen shrugged. "I haven't been there for a few years, but as far as I understand, the vast majority of the people are of one mind about Europe: They don't want any part of the mess they perceive in this place. They have no interest in what happens over here...as long as it doesn't affect their lives."

"But it will," Gerhard said. "Surely they recognize that once the Nazis taste military victory, they aren't going to stop."

"The American people will believe it when they see it, and until then, there's no point in trying to point that out. Roosevelt seems to have given up."

"The world's most powerful ostrich, with its head in the sand," Gerhard said.

"But with an army fit for a nation the size of Panama," Michael pointed out. "Not for the richest country in the world with a population of almost 130 million."

"Isolation can lead to complacency," Maureen said.

"When will it begin—this war we're all talking about as if it's inevitable as the sun rising in the east tomorrow morning?" asked Monika.

"When they're ready," Gerhard said. "Guns rust, powder deteriorates, and planes get out of date. They won't wait a day longer than when their machinery is set to go."

"What can we do to stop this impending disaster?"

"It's clear the British and French governments aren't about to swoop to the rescue," Gerhard said. "The only chance we have is the German people themselves."

"You've thought about this?" Michael asked. "When was the last time you were in the Reich?"

"I left last year, and spent some time in Spain."

"You fought in the war?"

"For a while. It's awful down there. People call it a civil war, but believe me, it's nothing of the sort. It's an invasion of a free people by the Italian and German dictators. It's a dress rehearsal—practice in the use of their new tanks and airplanes, and to establish landing fields and submarine bases to attack the shipping of free nations when the real war begins. I fought for six months before I'd had enough. I came here to get away from the fighting, and to attempt to form some sort of resistance so what I saw in Valencia doesn't spread to the streets of Paris."

Gerhard downed the remainder of his wine and poured himself another from the carafe the waiter left on the table. "The German war machine is being tested in Spain as we sit here. Hitler is sending his tankmen, his artillerymen, and above all, his airmen there, in relays. For three or four months—just long enough to learn the new techniques of mechanized war. Then those men go back to Germany and explain what worked to their superior officers. Soon Hitler will have the best-equipped, most battle-hardened army in the world. And they'll run the other bungling amateurs, the British and the French, into the ground."

Electricity flowed through Maureen's veins as she looked around at the young people at the table. The fire lit within her by the Subversives, the group of freethinkers she'd met with every week in Berlin, was still raging.

The Subversives were nearly all in their 40s or older, and we are all so young, she marveled. *Neither Hans nor Gerhard are older than 25, and I'm only 21. Yet we're the ones working to save the world.*

The waiter returned to the table with a charcuterie board of cured meats and a variety of delicious cheeses—all rare items in Germany these days.

"The way to save Spain, and the rest of Europe, is to somehow persuade the French—or better yet, Neville Chamberlain and the rest of the British government—to end their nonintervention policy. We have to show the Western powers that this is their fight, and that the plight of the Jews, and everyone else the Nazis have subjugated since they got into power, will be the fate of all Europe soon," Hans said.

"And how do you plan to do that?" Monika asked. "How do you plan to budge the stagnant Western powers?"

Hans shook his head and gazed at the street for a few seconds. "We need money for printing presses. Once we have a few, we can publish the truth and distribute materials on the streets of Paris and London. Then people will put pressure on their governments. I have friends in England...."

Gerhard didn't speak. He seemed removed from the discussion. Maureen looked at the veteran of the war in Spain across the table from her.

It took her a few minutes to rejoin the conversation. Her new sister-in-law was the one speaking.

"What about Hitler? I can't fathom where his thoughts originate. I think to fully comprehend what's happening in Europe today, we need to understand him, and how he thinks. Five years ago he was a joke, and today he's the most powerful man in the world."

The sun was fading over the city, and the streetlights flashed on. Gerhard lit a cigarette and began speaking as the smoke lingered around his face.

"Hitler was a neglected stepchild. He wanted to be an artist, but never got any training, except in killing his fellow men. He experienced abject poverty, unemployment, and the life of a wastrel in a shelter for bums. Then in the trenches, he lived in the freezing cold winter rains and mud, and in the scorching dust of summer; bitten by lice, blasted and shot at. He was wounded and infected with terror. Year after year it went on, and it ended in his country's defeat and humiliation."

His voice was low, and he stared into the air as he spoke, making eye contact with no one.

"That was his training," he continued. "His university. No surprise that he's a neurotic and has to take drugs to put himself to sleep, with moods of exaltation followed by others of suicidal depression. It's said that the only love he ever felt was for his half-niece, but his jealous rages pushed her so hard that she committed suicide. Or more likely, he killed her. Who knows which? He doesn't have a wife or family, and rumor has it that he's not interested in either. His only goal, his obsession, is returning Germany to greatness by conquering his enemies inside and outside the country. He can't be reasoned with or bargained with when it comes to what he wants, because there's nothing else he craves. He doesn't pay himself a salary. Göring is a millionaire, like his friend Goebbels, who beds every beautiful starlet Germany produces these days, but not Hitler. His only interest is his legacy, making Germany the most powerful nation in the world, and he will not stop until he achieves it."

No one spoke for a few seconds. The waiter returned to the table to break the silence. The carafe of wine was drained, and he asked if they wanted another.

"Not for me. I think I've said enough on this fine evening." Gerhard stood up and threw down more than enough money for his part of the bill. "Tell me when you agree to the next meeting time," he said and left.

The others resumed the conversation, but Maureen wasn't listening, just watching him as he strolled toward the river.

"Give me a minute," she said and jumped up. Hans grabbed her hand as she squeezed past him, but she extricated herself. "I'll be back in a few minutes."

She caught Gerhard outside a boulangerie, and he whirled around to face her with a puzzled look. He checked for his wallet. "Did I forget something?"

"You think we're just talkers, don't you?"

He regarded her for a few seconds with amused eyes. "You should get back to your boyfriend and the rest of the group."

"Hans isn't my boyfriend. Do I need to repeat my question?"

He laughed and shook his head, walking off. She followed him. "So, what should we do apart from talk?"

He glanced at her with a smile. "I'm not going to get rid of you, am I?"

"Not until you tell me what you think we should be doing."

"Seriously? I've no idea."

"I don't believe that."

They strolled across a bridge. She refused the cigarette he offered, and he told her he was from a small town near Hamburg. His two brothers were both committed Nazis.

"Why did you leave Germany? You never said."

"I fought with my father. I couldn't understand why he took an oath to Hitler when it was contrary to everything he believed. I thought I could do some good down in Spain, but then I realized that the war down there is only a precursor, and I had more important things to take care of."

"Why here?"

"Because conversations such as the one we had tonight are illegal in the new Germany. I've been working on something. Do you want to see?"

Rue de la Cité took them south of the river and into the Latin Quarter. The city's lights shone on the black surface of the Seine, and Notre Dame extended high into the night sky.

"This is home," he said as they came to a door. He drew a key from his pocket and led her through to a courtyard, where he greeted several people, in passable French, who were sitting out enjoying the night air.

"Just up these stairs." The staircase was solid granite, and the paint on the walls was flaking and streaked with dirt. His apartment was on the second floor, and he opened the door to let her in first.

"Please excuse the mess," he said, although the studio with a small kitchen looked spotless. His bed was in the corner by the window, made with military precision.

The thought that she was alone in a strange man's apartment struck her like a needle. It was time to get to the point. "So, what is it that you've been working on?"

"This." He brought her to the desk by the window. He took a key from his pocket, opened the drawer, drew out a sheet of paper, and handed it to her. It was a printed page, and she read it aloud.

Our country has fallen into the hands of the Prince of Lies. Every falsehood Hitler spews is engineered to devolve the Reich into war. Have we not learned our lesson from the incredible waste of 1914–18 that extinguished so many lives and robbed the German people of the greatest generation they ever knew? Everything the Nazi Party does is to further its own means, not those of the German people they feast off. The Wehrmacht is the greatest army in the world, but who wishes to see the flower of German youth destroyed in the mud and filth of France and Belgium once more? The Weimar disaster is behind us, and that history cannot be changed. To return to greatness, the Reich must return to its roots: the Kaiser must be reinstated, with a powerful president to back him up. The rights of all and the lives of millions depend on our actions. A few men in the right positions have the power to do this. Only they can halt the madness our great nation has succumbed to.

Maureen handed the sheet back to him. "You want to bring back the Kaiser? That's hardly democratic."

"But it may be the best we can get at this stage. My father is a general in the Luftwaffe. He is one of the few men who has the power to depose Hitler and the Nazis and end this nightmare. And he is a fan of the Kaiser."

Maureen stared. "So this is for him?"

"Perhaps. We haven't spoken in five years. He has no idea that I'm here in Paris."

"So what makes you think he'll listen to you now?"

"Because he's a patriot. He took that oath to Hitler along with the rest of the armed forces, but I know him. His true allegiances lie with the German people, not some jumped-up failed Austrian artist."

"Why are you telling me this, and not Hans?"

"Hans doesn't agree about the Kaiser. He wants to flood the world with revolutionary leaflets."

"I'm a social democrat and not fond of the Kaiser either."

He reached into his pocket for another cigarette. "I know, but... I can tell, you wouldn't sacrifice lives for ideals. You don't just want to talk. You want to do something, even if it's not perfect."

Maureen didn't quite know how to take that compliment. She kept her distance but wasn't walking away yet. "So, you want him to read this...letter? And you think it will convince him?" She couldn't keep the doubt out of her voice.

Gerhard lit the cigarette, shaking out the match with his other hand. "I'm sorry... I haven't thought that far yet. My grand plan to upend the most powerful regime in Europe is still in the embryonic stage." He spoke sarcastically.

"You're not kidding. Don't try to con me."

"All I have to offer is that I know my father's heart and where his loyalties lie. He's a powerful man—enough that he could effect real change. He and his peers might be able to remove Hitler and the rest of his sick brigade."

"If only they could be convinced that doing so would serve the German people best?"

"Exactly."

"You think these men would risk their lives if they believed it was the right thing to do?"

"They will if we point out the disaster about to befall the people they're meant to be stewarding under Hitler." A stiff, determined look came across the young man's face.

"What's the prevailing attitude of the generals? They once referred to Hitler as 'the Austrian corporal.'"

"I don't know. It's been too long since I sat down with my father, but they're a conservative bunch—obsessed with the old order."

"Would democracy be a step too far for the likes of those men?"

"Yes. There are certain things they'll accept, and then others they won't. The return to the days of the Kaiser is the best we can hope for. They won't usher in the age of democracy again. Asking them to do that would scupper any chance we have of ousting Hitler."

"Would the Kaiser join with them in any coup attempt?"

That made him smile again. "You think I've spoken to him down at his mansion in Corfu? But if the military did overthrow Hitler, I'm sure the Kaiser, or his son, would get on the first train back to Berlin. Their palace is still sitting there."

"You need a way to communicate these ideas to your father."

He held up the sheet. "That's what I thought I was doing."

"Well, you're not." She took the paper from his hand again, reading it over. "You need to speak to him as a son...touch his heart. Reach out to him in a personal way."

"You don't know my father." Gerhard shook his head. "He... blames me for a lot of things." His eyes wandered as if he were peering into the past. "He's more likely to do the exact opposite of what I tell him. Stubbornness is a trait that runs right through my family. It doesn't make for easy reconciliations."

Maureen thought of her own father. The anger she bore toward him as a younger girl had faded now. Sometime in the last few years, it dissipated like smoke in the wind.

"Gerhard, nothing is impossible. I'm sure your father would be open to reconciling. His feelings for you haven't changed."

"You think so?"

She thought of her father, the arms manufacturer, in the mansion he inherited in Berlin. "Yes, I do."

3

Friday, September 17: Berlin

Seamus Ritter gazed down from the balcony of his new factory. A few months ago, this site had been home to a mosquito-breeding marsh, but now it was ready to begin production of the most state-of-the-art war weapons ever devised—those that would rule the skies. A jungle of complex machines lay below him, each one beating and pounding out its own individual tune and placed precisely on a spot that engineers had measured to the hundredth of an inch. The motions of those machines were determined, in some cases, to the hundred-thousandth of an inch. The finest watch had never been built with such care as the steel, aluminum, and magnesium pieces that were stamped, ground, or polished here. The factory produced such a cacophony of sounds that it all became one, an immense racket which, he was assured, the ears of the workers would soon cease to hear at all. Down a long line appeared, in the process of growth, a row of swift and deadly fighter planes that would be able to hurl themselves through the air at the rate of a mile every 15 seconds or less. There weren't nearly as many on that assembly line as he hoped to see, and the line wasn't moving fast enough to please him, but this was only the beginning. His peers—the other armaments manufacturers—saw this magic happen at the end of July 1914 and spoke in giddy tones about this particular gold rush dwarfing those times.

Germany had become what every munitions manufacturer in the world dreamed about all their lives. The country was putting everything it had into armaments: reducing the wages and lengthening the hours of all its workers and bidding its captains of industry to build all the plants they could. They were promised they would receive all the orders they could fill and keep their machines going at full speed 24 hours every day, Sundays and holidays included.

All German science, discipline, and wealth were being directed to this end. When the day of reckoning came along, the army on the ground would have air cover to protect it—first to drive its enemy out of the skies and then to crush its defenses and enable the Wehrmacht to march anywhere it so pleased.

Helga, the cousin with whom he shared ownership of this business, stood beside him. The smile on her face seemed tattooed on these days. Nothing, in her mind, could be greater than extending her father's legacy by helping Germany regain her greatness among the world's nations. The Nazi pin on her chest was set in solid gold and likely cost more than many of the workers toiling below made in a month.

She seemed content to split ownership of the company with Seamus, someone who didn't share her sympathies with the Nazis. Were their bond of blood and her undoubted love for his children enough to trust her? Denouncing him to the Gestapo would have been the simplest thing in the world—half of Germany seemed to be doing it these days. With him out of the way, she'd be free to run the company herself... Or would she? Was her status as a woman standing in her way?

He was more than prepared to work side by side with a woman in a country that valued females less and less. The Nazis they received their orders from tolerated her, but those requests always went to him. He was the face of the company, not because of his brilliance as a businessman, but because he was a man. Perhaps that was the only thing keeping him in the role, and his talented, Nazi-supporting cousin had to keep him in place to retain her own position. But more likely, it was a little of each reason. He wondered how long the house of cards they'd built together could stay upright.

Seamus was dubious about what her father, his late Uncle Helmut, would have thought about all the Nazi banners hanging from the ceiling of the factory. His uncle didn't bring him over from America back in '32 for this. Although, how could the old man have known how much German life would change in the five short years after his death? Seamus's promise to the elderly factory owner was intact—the workers still had jobs, and the Jews and the foreigners remained employed at the old factory in the city. But this workforce was different. Every man here was a German, and loyal to the regime. Seamus felt alone among them, cast adrift on an ocean of subservience to the Führer. Hitler's face was plastered all over the walls. Helga and the members of the Trustee Council—a Nazi-approved panel of workers to replace the now-illegal trade unions—said the posters were good for morale. Maybe so, but for all except him. For Seamus Ritter, the sight of the despot's visage had quite the opposite effect.

Helga either didn't see through Seamus or didn't care to. He suspected the latter, as his cousin was no fool. He consoled himself with the knowledge that he was undertaking this vile mission for reasons opposite to hers.

"Those dive-bombers will be a fearsome sight," she said almost gleefully.

"The sirens the designers installed are an interesting touch."

"Anything to demoralize and terrify the enemy. Can you imagine crouching in the dirt, hearing that horrific high-pitched whistling sound hurtling down at you?" She was smiling as she spoke. "It doesn't bear thinking about."

Seamus wanted to ask her what she knew about huddling in the dirt while bombs flew. During the last war, he'd lived what she spoke of with a devilish smile. Would she be so excited if she'd felt that fear she spoke of, or seen what those bombs would do to human flesh?

"Let's hope they never get used."

"That would be the ideal result, wouldn't it?" She was still grinning. "But it's an imperfect world, and we need to place our trust in the Führer. He knows best."

Seamus couldn't take any more. He retreated to his office and picked up a ledger. The orders were massive, resulting in millions of Reichsmarks. It was obscene. No one asked why they had to produce so much in peacetime.

He picked up a framed photograph of his family taken at the beach at Wannsee two summers before. He focused on Maureen and Michael and wondered what they were doing. Berlin was far too dangerous for them, and likely would be for years to come.

Fiona stood behind her older siblings in the snapshot with a bright, beautiful smile. It was rare he saw her happy these days. The Nazis had infected her with their sickness. What chance did an impressionable 15-year-old stand against the onslaught of propaganda the government subjected her to? The Nazis controlled and monitored everything in her life—her school, after-school activities, and every book and newspaper article she cared to read. All her friends were in the Hitler Youth or the League of German Girls. Not joining them would have marked her as a pariah. She stated with pride that performing for the Führer during the Olympics was the greatest day of her life. The propaganda was effective—she was a true believer.

He focused on 12-year-old Conor. Was he going to be the next one to fall for Nazi propaganda? He was much quieter than Fiona and didn't seem that interested in politics. But perhaps it was only a matter of time.

He imagined his first wife, Marie, sitting across the desk from him. What would she say about what had happened to her children? How would he explain what happened in the years since her death?

Thinking about Marie didn't feel like a betrayal to his second wife, Lisa. It was nothing more than remembering a part of his life that vanished when Marie succumbed to tuberculosis. After all, what was a human being if not the sum of their past experiences, the places they'd been, and the people they'd met? And no one person had shaped him more than his first wife. He had little doubt they'd still live in America, settled and happy, had she not died so young. But life had a habit of laughing at his best-laid plans.

Was it just five years since they came here from New Jersey with the promise of a job offer from Uncle Helmut? It seemed longer—like he'd lived a thousand lifetimes here already.

His eyes fell on Hannah, Lisa's daughter. That sweet eight-year-old girl would never know who her real father was...and that her mother had killed him and her stepfather helped her to bury him in the Grunewald Forest.

Seamus put the photograph down and attempted to get back to work. The noise from the factory floor forced him from his seat to close the door. But even with less sound from the machines below, the chatter inside his mind continued unabated. Getting out was the only solution.

He tidied his desk and left. Helga was in her office

surveying the orders they'd received for fighters and bombers with a stern look.

"I need to go to the other factory."

"Of course. You haven't forgotten about your jaunt to the country tomorrow?"

"Forgotten about my invitation to Göring's estate? No, that didn't slip my mind."

"Just checking," his cousin said with a rueful smile.

Seamus knew she wanted to be the one to go. But a woman at a hunt with the other masters of the new German gold rush? The Nazis would never permit such a thing. Women were for producing the soldiers for the Nazi war machine, not the planes and bullets those men would use. Helga thought she was lucky to have the privileged position she did in a society where women were forbidden to be judges, lawyers, or work in the civil service. Hitler also banned them from jury duty because he argued they could not think logically or reason objectively. In a country where young girls—like Seamus's own daughters—were trained to be housewives and discouraged from further education, the role Helga enjoyed was a rarity. Even her slim figure was discouraged by the National Socialists, as thin women were thought to be less likely to give birth.

In a world where she was seen as equal, Helga would have run this place alone, and likely have done a better job than any man he knew, himself included. Except then the Jews and foreign workers would all have been fired long ago.

"I'll let you know how it goes with Göring tomorrow," was all he said.

His cousin waved goodbye, and he left. A phalanx of middle managers passed him on the stairs between the floor and the offices.

"Can we talk?" one of the men asked.

"Helga's in her office. I have somewhere to be."

The man shrugged and turned to go back downstairs. Nobody in this country answered to a woman nowadays.

The drive north to the factory in the city took 40 minutes, and Seamus felt a sense of relief when Uncle Helmut's old facility came into view. He parked in the lot and walked inside. By no means were all the workers here opposed to the cause of the Nazis, but pockets of skepticism of the National Socialists still existed.

His Jewish manager was at his desk as Seamus pushed the door open.

"How are things over at the new factory?" Gert Bernheim asked. Seamus took a seat opposite him.

"Nazi-fied."

"What do you expect? We're producing warplanes and ammunition, not fruit and flowers."

"You don't think the Führer would install the most loyal Nazis into positions of power in the food and floral industries?"

"I expect he'd want to control them, as he does everything else in Germany." Gert dropped his pen and took off his reading glasses. "It's getting worse, Seamus. Benz and Borst are threatening the Jewish workers."

Gunther Benz, the head of the Trustee Council, and Artur Borst, one of his cronies, were nothing but trouble. To control every facet of German culture, the Nazi government had organized Trustee Councils in all businesses. The members were elected from among the workforce...from a Nazi-approved list.

"Physically?"

"No, but they say they'll be fired any day, and Benz told Leonard Greenberg that he'd make sure his family was shipped off to concentration camps before long, and that the factory would soon be cleansed of Jewish vermin."

Seamus let his friend's words sink in. It was getting more dangerous by the day to be Jewish on the street, but this factory was supposed to be a safe haven. He had sworn to Uncle Helmut before the old man died that he'd protect his workers, no matter what creed they followed.

"Did you speak to Benz or Borst?"

"I thought it best to leave that to you."

"Sorry, yes. I don't know why I asked you that. I'll deal with those two idiots." Seamus stood up and turned to his friend as he reached the door. "Have you got time for Fiona to see you tomorrow?"

He had been making Fiona spend one afternoon a month with Gert and his wife Lil this past year in return for allowing her to attend League of German Girls meetings and rallies. She was sulky about it, but she needed to see that Jews weren't the evil, depraved caricatures the Nazis portrayed them to be.

"She could join us for Saturday lunch."

"Thank you. Lisa will drop her over."

"Lisa? Oh, of course. You're Herr Göring's guest tomorrow."

"Unfortunately. There are no weekends for any of us when it comes to arming soldiers of the Reich!"

Also, he thought, *no holidays, or even in some cases, no nights.* And that was precisely how the government and the captains of industry wanted it. The Nazis got the weapons they craved, and in return, the factory owners got richer and richer. The workers' wages were capped.

Bernheim smiled slightly. "Enjoy the trappings of luxury, and represent us well."

"I'll do my best."

Ten minutes later, Benz was sitting in Seamus's office. His face showed his defiance, his lapel, his Nazi Party badge. As the original member of the Nazi Trustee Council within the factory, he knew that Seamus was powerless to fire him.

"What did you say to Greenberg?" Seamus asked in a razor-sharp tone.

"Nothing more than the truth."

Benz had been a nondescript metal polisher before the National Socialists came to power. Here sat a prime example of the Nazi policy of elevating the dregs of society to positions of power.

"You don't have the authority to fire anyone, and if you make any threats against my workers again—"

"What will you do?" Benz asked with a yellow-toothed smile.

"It's not good for business." Seamus slammed his fist down on the table. The other man's facial expression didn't change. "Greenberg is one of the most skilled workers we have. He's been employed by my family for 25 years."

"He won't be here another 25 months. If you cared about those animals—and it seems like you do—you'd tell them to get out of this country while they still can. They're not wanted."

"Greenberg and the other Jewish workers aren't going anywhere. As long as I'm running things, they'll have jobs. I'd get used to that notion, if I were you."

"As long as you're running things," Benz said and stood up. "I'll remember that."

Seamus waited a few minutes, taking the time to drink a whiskey and cool off before he went down to Greenberg. He and the other Jews worked on a different production line from most of the other Nazi-sympathizing workers—of whom there were more and more these days.

"I'm sorry," Seamus said to him.

Greenberg was a few years older than Seamus's 42 years, but the lines on his face portrayed him as a much older man. "Did you speak to Benz?"

"Yes." *For all the good it did, I may as well not have.* "I'll keep him away from you and the other Jews."

"That's all he gets for threatening my family?"

"He has the government on his side—you know that. If I had my way, he would have been out the door years ago. My hands are tied."

"So say all weak men," Greenberg said and turned away. He returned to his station, working the press that churned out dozens of helmets daily.

Seamus let the man have his moment and went back to his office. His regular Friday afternoon was looming. He tried to dismiss their conversation as the price to pay for the mission he was trying to achieve, but Greenberg's tone of resignation and disgust lingered like a foul stench in his consciousness. A stifling sense of powerlessness overcame him for a few seconds, and he went to his office window with another drink in his hand. He knocked it back and walked to the safe in the corner. Doing something to undermine the madness all around him was the only cure for his malaise. The safe opened with a metallic clunk, and he reached for some documents inside.

His friend—the American diplomat, or spy, or whatever he was—should find some use for these. He shoved the envelope of documents into a briefcase and was outside in his car in two minutes.

4

Friday, September 17

He and Hayden never met like regular citizens anymore. No one was to be trusted.

The Gestapo tolerated the American diplomat, as the Americans tolerated the German agents organizing Fascist rallies in New York and Washington, DC. Still, neither he nor Seamus wanted to bring attention to their relationship.

Seamus parked his car, then strolled through the Tiergarten, the massive public park in the middle of the city, a short drive from the factory. It was a sunny afternoon, and couples with children were strolling through the park. He scanned all the faces he passed. Just as Hitler said, there were enemies everywhere in the new Reich, but Seamus wasn't worried about the ones the Führer referred to.

The Gestapo came in more forms than the tall, muscular Aryan man in a trench coat of the popular imagination. The real enemies were not just the Gestapo, which had its tentacles in every aspect of German life, but also the average citizen. The authorities had convinced the public that reporting anything they deemed as suspicious was their patriotic duty. Denouncements seemed to be at an all-time high, but most were made out of malicious, petty intent. Most people who were reported and dragged into Gestapo headquarters on Prinz-Albrecht-Strasse, now the most feared address in Berlin, were there because they made too much noise at night, or their children had broken a neighbor's window. It had become the one-stop destination for those trying to bring ill will to bear on others... just as Petra Wagner had denounced Lisa to steal her part in the movie they were making. Many people used the repressive system to their own advantage.

Seamus walked the perimeter of the park's block and then entered a cheap hotel that Hayden had specified in his coded note, delivered the day before by an orderly from the American embassy.

The carpet was threadbare and worn, and the curtains blocking out the daylight seemed dusty and old. Being here reminded him of where he'd been just five years ago. Memories of riding the rails from one worksite to the next filled his mind. The life of luxury he led now felt only borrowed. Nothing more. As if it could be pulled out from underneath him like a tablecloth from a table, and the fine china of his life would come crashing to the hard floor.

He passed the front desk and turned into the bathroom. The key was in the second stall, and Seamus took it and went to the washbasin. An SA man in his early 30s emerged from the other stall and came to the mirror. Seamus nodded a wordless greeting to him, dried his hands off, and left. After looking around the lobby again, he climbed the stairs to the second floor, confident the man wasn't tailing him. He knocked before entering.

His old friend from the war was by the window, peering down at the street as Seamus pushed the door open.

"These hotels are getting worse. I ran into a dung shirt in the washroom."

"Those guys are too dumb to suspect anything. I wouldn't worry."

"I'm not—I'm just complaining about the filth. We've got to arrange a better way to meet."

"You want to take chances?" asked Hayden. "The Gestapo is everywhere. Rumor has it they've bugged every decent hotel room in the city. So we can only use the indecent ones."

Seamus walked over and sat in the chair his old friend had set up for him. "I see your logic. What important people would lower themselves to meet in a hole like this?"

A piercing female scream bled through the wall, followed in quick succession by a male retort. A shouting match ensued. Seamus couldn't make out all the details, but the female voice seemed sure that the man was having an affair.

"You think they can hear us as clearly as we can them?"

"We'll be a little more discreet," Hayden said. "You want a drink?" He pulled a bottle of whiskey from his bag and poured them each a glass. Seamus sipped the bitter liquid as the other man began.

"What do you have for me?"

Seamus reached into the briefcase and handed over the packet he took from his office safe. "An enormous order for the new Messerschmitt Bf 109." Bill opened the envelope and scanned the documents as Seamus continued. "That's going to be one heck of a war plane. We also have some for the Junkers Ju 88 bombers to reduce London and Paris to rubble, and of course, our old favorite, the Stuka dive-bomber, to attack military targets and put the fear of God into the poor soldiers on the receiving end."

"You know anything about what your rivals are producing?"

"Just the idle boasting they engage in at cocktail parties. They're like kids on Christmas morning. It's as if the government is driving trucks of money to their houses every day and dumping it out on their front lawns. All they have to do is gather it up."

Hayden kept looking through the sheets.

"Some of those papers are from Roland Eidinger—the naval orders," Seamus said. "He's also moving a lot of arms and equipment with his fleet for Franco's Fascists in Spain. Do you ever want to meet him?"

Seamus's friend, Roland Eidinger, was one of the wealthiest men in Germany but had no love for the Nazi regime.

"The fewer people I meet, the safer we'll all be. How does Roland feel about churning out submarines and arming the Nationalists in Spain?"

"He's sick to his stomach about it. He wants to leave Germany, but I convinced him to stay the course for a bit longer. The upside of it all is the enormous amount of money he's making."

"And you?"

"We're getting our piece of an enormous pie. What Helga is going to do with her money, I have no idea."

"Probably give it all back to her Nazi masters."

"That wouldn't surprise me," Seamus said as the argument next door abated.

"When the noise stops, I get nervous," Bill said in a whisper. "Thanks. My superiors will be interested in this. Roosevelt himself will see these figures. I met him once—did I ever tell you that?"

"FDR?"

"Yes, at his house in Hyde Park in upstate New York. You ever spend any time in that part of the country?"

"No."

"He's a good man. Insisted I called him 'Governor,' said it put him at ease. He's fascinated by the German rearmaments program. He's the main reason we're sitting in this dingy hotel room drinking fine scotch right now."

"Is he aware of the emergency situation developing?"

"Well aware, but the American people don't want to hear it. The isolationists, the New Dealers, the Catholics. None of them are interested."

"Even the Catholics?"

"Yeah. The president's hamstrung without them. They decide elections. Their priests told them the Reds are the mortal enemies of their religion, and the enemy of my enemy is my friend, and all that stuff. That's why FDR can't help out in Spain. They'd vote him out for arming the atheistic Reds against the courageous, and Catholic, General Franco."

"But is he going to increase defense spending in line with what the Nazis are doing?"

Bill shook his head.

"Why not?"

"His domestic agenda is top priority for him, and he couldn't get the additional spending through Congress anyway, even if he wanted to."

"What do they expect Hitler to do with all this weaponry he's stockpiling? Stuff it under his mattress?"

"They don't care. Europe is far away, and the way America sees it, the governments over here change their leaders more often than their socks. Maybe they assume Hitler will be gone in a year or two, and the next man will take over?"

"What about the British and the French? All of my contracts are with the Reich government, but some of my rivals sell to them. I heard Otto Milch was in Paris last month."

Otto Milch was one of Seamus's bitterest business rivals. Unbeknownst to the rich old man, he was the natural grandfather of Hannah, Lisa's daughter. It was Ernst Milch, Otto's son, who had tried to murder Lisa, and it was he they'd buried in an unmarked grave in the Grunewald Forest after she fought back.

"The British Royal Air Force is good, what there is of it, but the generals are stuck back in the last war," Bill answered. "These are men who've never flown, and who see airplanes as a convenient but uncertain way for army commanders to find out what the enemy ground forces are doing. The attitude in the Royal Navy is stuck back in the 19th century. The British admirals seem to rate mastery of the air above the seas as ungentlemanly, or something ridiculously English like that. And if you think the British are bad, it's far worse in France. Their air capability is pitiful, and their program of nationalization in the face of the German threat is lunacy. As for America—don't ask. We have an air force fitting for a small Central American republic."

Seamus slumped back in his seat and finished the scotch he needed now. "So, what's the good news?"

"You and your buddies are getting rich. Is there any sign of a Resistance?"

"If there is, I don't know about it."

"Someone will have to take action at some stage," Bill replied. They were silent for a few seconds as the shouting resumed next door. "Last time I use this place."

"What if Hitler pushes too far?" Seamus asked. "You don't think the Allies will step in?"

"With what armies? Hitler will make his move when he's ready, and with the British and French falling further behind every day, the Wehrmacht will roll right over them."

"What about the Soviets?"

"The 'Red hordes in the east,' you mean?" Bill finished his whiskey and picked up the bottle to pour himself another. "Stalin's doing his best to kneecap his own military. The man's a paranoid nightmare. Word is that he's killing off most of his senior military commanders, and carrying out Hitler's work for him. No, it's up to the German people, or possibly the generals in the Wehrmacht. They're a conservative bunch and won't want to launch into a new war. No one's forgotten the last one, at least."

"Are you working on any of them?"

"I don't have access to those men, and wouldn't know who to speak to even if I did. I can't go into some upper-class party and walk up to a crusty old Prussian general with a glass of champagne in my hand and ask him to depose the Führer."

"You're right—I can't see it happening...."

"Well, if you ever get the chance yourself... Are you prepared for your day with Göring and the other masters of the universe tomorrow?"

"As much as I'll ever be, I suppose. This will be my first time meeting the Reich Minister of Aviation. Do you have any experience with the man?"

"I've been introduced. My advice would be not to underestimate him. To my mind, he's the most important of all Hitler's lackeys. He might look like a comic book character—and dress like one, too—but he's one of the most competent executives you'll ever meet. He drives his subordinates with a lash and gets the orders of his Führer carried out with utter loyalty, and without the inconvenience of scruples. I'll be interested to hear what your impressions are."

"I'll do my best to earn his trust, and of the others I meet tomorrow."

"Do you know many people going?"

"My old friend Otto Milch will be there, as well as the representatives of Farben and Krupp and all the giants of the industry."

"Fertile ground indeed."

"I'll see what I can garner about production, and the direction in which the Nazis are heading from here."

"Just be careful. You're no use to me locked up in a concentration camp."

"Duly noted."

He poured another finger into Seamus's glass. "Is there anything else? You look like you've something on your mind."

"Perhaps. What do you think Hitler's plans for France are? Is it safe there?"

"The Führer hasn't shared his plans with me, but I'd say he has his eyes fixed on France. His mind seems to be dominated by irrational phobias. It's no secret he hates the Jews the most, and after that the Russians, then the Poles. Then, I think, the French." Bill paused to place his glass down before continuing. "He said in his book that the annihilation of France is essential to the safety of Germany, and he means it. I believe everything in that diatribe of hatred he and Hess wrote together."

"I haven't read it."

"You should. Just hold your nose the whole time and keep a stiff drink close at hand."

"Thanks for the advice."

"Yes, Hitler tells the truth, knowing that what he says is the last thing anybody will expect or believe. He has one faith and one idea, and that is the Germans as the master race, destined to conquer the world under him as Führer. That is the magnetic pole to which his being turns, and the one thing you can count upon in dealing with him."

Seamus sat back in his seat and took a drink from his glass. He felt like he needed it at that moment.

"So, who are you worried about in Paris?"

"Nobody. I don't know anyone there."

Hayden smiled. "Of course you don't. However, please tell Maureen and Michael to be careful. Paris isn't as far from here as many people seem to think."

"What do you know?"

"Paris is full of people who fled the Nazis, and from Mussolini too. One of their favorite activities is smuggling their newspapers, pamphlets, and leaflets back into the Reich to enlighten the masses here. But the powers that be aren't taking it lying down. The Nazis have their little Gestapo in Paris, and Mussolini his little OVRA. Dr. Goebbels has his Personal Department B, and the SS their Braunes Haus, just like in Munich. German agents come in every conceivable shape and size: scientists and journalists, teachers, students, traveling salesmen, importers, laborers, and refugees. I hear agents are trained to pose as leftists, even being sent to concentration camps in Germany and beaten there so that the other prisoners see them, and word goes out to the underground that they're on the level. Then they 'escape' to Paris, and collect names and addresses of the 'comrades,' both at home and abroad."

"Maureen's an idealist."

"Don't let her get in above her head. The Nazis don't take kindly to being challenged."

"What do the Parisian police think of this foreign civil war going on under their noses?"

"They represent the status quo, just as they do in any country in the world. The head of the Paris police, Chiappe—pretty much a Fascist himself—is in open sympathy with the nativist organizations the Nazis are helping to subsidize in France. It's a mess."

"And this is the country meant to curb Hitler's ambitions in Europe...."

"It doesn't seem they would, even if they were able."

"Thanks for the advice." Seamus felt sick to his stomach, drinking more whiskey to quench his nausea.

"On a more amusing note, I hear Goebbels is thinking of dumping that film star who informed on your wife...."

"Petra Wagner? May she rot in hell."

"Maybe being scorned will make her turn on her Nazi bosses. She'd be a useful insider."

"Don't even think of approaching her. She's not someone to be trusted."

"Trust, eh? Remember that?" Bill said.

"In fleeting memories."

The two men sat back and enjoyed the whiskey for another hour before they stood up, shook hands, and left separately.

5

Saturday, September 18

A black Mercedes with Nazi flags above each headlight pulled up outside the house just after ten in the morning. Lisa adjusted Seamus's tie one last time and kissed him.

"Good luck today."

"I can't believe you're spending the day with Herr Göring!" Fifteen-year-old Fiona, wearing her League of German Girls uniform, was pink with jealousy. "A true hero of the Reich, and one of the Führer's closest confidants! Will you come and speak with my troop about your experiences? It would mean so much to me."

Lisa nodded with gusto. "Your father would be delighted to."

"Daddy?" She ignored her stepmother.

"Of course. So long as I don't embarrass myself too much." It was sickening the way he was forced to pander to the teen. She knew too much—suspecting Maureen and often disrespecting Lisa.

"You'll charm them like you charmed me," his wife said. "The car's waiting—"

Fiona interrupted. "Papa, can I skip the stupid Bernheim's today? There's a rally."

He kept smiling. "Darling, if I can take time to talk to your troop, then you can take the time to have lunch with my good friends the Bernheims. Now do you want to boast to your friends about your father knowing Göring or not?"

"Oh, all *right*." She flounced off.

The driver, wearing full SS uniform, held the door for him, and he sat in the back seat. They drove in silence to a new factory north of the city, where a dozen vehicles like the one he rode in were already parked outside as they pulled up. An adjutant greeted him as he stepped out of the Mercedes. The man checked his papers, and Seamus was escorted to a waiting area once he was given the all-clear.

His old adversary, Otto Milch, took the time to scowl at him as he entered the room where the industrialists were waiting for Göring to arrive. Seamus didn't return the gesture and moved to some men he knew, making small talk about business until Göring arrived.

The WWI flying ace who Hitler had assigned the task of building his air force showed up a few minutes later. True to form, he wore a sky-blue suit decorated with lines of medals so thick that Seamus wondered how he was able to move. Göring was a huge man, and beads of sweat covered his forehead. He put both hands on his hips and spoke with a bellowing voice.

"Welcome, gentlemen. For those of you I've not met, I'm pleased to make your acquaintance. I hope we'll have an illuminating and sociable day ahead of us."

Another man appeared beside him, dressed in a gray suit. It took Seamus a few seconds to recognize the man. He did so just before Göring introduced him to the group.

"The man on my left needs little introduction," the Air

Marshall began. "When he was younger, he performed an unorthodox and courageous action, stepping into a little Flivver on Long Island and heading out across the Atlantic. When he landed at Le Bourget Airport near Paris 34 hours later, he became the first man to make a solo flight across the ocean and was instantly one of the most famous men in the world. Gentlemen, I give you our special guest for the day, and my personal friend, Mr. Charles Lindbergh."

Seamus stayed back as his fellow dignitaries swarmed the man known as "Lucky Lindy" to congratulate him and shake his hand. An interpreter at the American's shoulder translated everything said to him. Seamus was one of the last to shake his hand. Lindbergh was tall and slim with pale skin. He seemed taken aback when Seamus greeted him in English.

"Good to meet a fellow American this side of the pond," Seamus said.

"And you, old sport," Lindbergh answered with a smile. "What brings you to this part of the world?"

"A job offer that got better and better." Seamus thought to ask the man the same question but knew his back story already. His good friend Clayton Thomas, the *New York Times* reporter, had explained it to him only weeks before.

Lindbergh didn't enjoy the newfound fame the transatlantic flight brought him. He was repulsed when he found he couldn't walk on a street anywhere in America without being surrounded and mobbed. His irritation soon began to show in his gruff dealings with newspaper reporters. Then came the tragedy of the kidnapping and murder of his little child. The upheaval of the trial was too much, and after it, he fled to Europe. He had made a lot of money, and his conservative political views emerged. The Nazi ambassador to England saw an opportunity to use the naïve Midwestern Swedish-American for propaganda. It suited Hitler and Göring to have the world believe that Germany possessed overwhelming might in the air, and the tall, dignified, and honest young flier was picked as the trumpet to blow this news to the world. Lindy was invited to be General Göring's guest and, apparently, enjoyed visiting the Reich. He had already been several times. He was received with every honor and was even given a decoration. All doors were open to him in Nazi Germany.

Lindbergh cleared his throat to say a few words to the men. The translator kept pace with him.

"Thank you, gentlemen. I recently flew my lovely young wife in our small plane over the Reich, and saw that all along the Swiss and French borders, Herr Göring has built an airport every 20 miles. Germany is now the most technologically advanced country in the world, as regards aviation. And that's due in no small part to this man here, my friend, President Göring."

The large general loved titles and had at least a dozen of them, including President of the Reichstag.

"It's always a pleasure to have such a distinguished aviator as yourself in our midst," Göring said.

"I come here not to make a political statement, but to be present at the most exciting place in the world of aviation today. With further investment from visionaries such as yourselves, Germany can cement its place as the world leader for decades to come. With mastery of the skies comes peace and prosperity, for who would dare to challenge a country that rules the battlefield above their heads? And believe me—that is where the next war will be fought. The National Socialists' plan is to prevent that from ever occurring. I have been escorted through many giant factories, and it's estimated that Germany is building 20,000 planes a year. With the help of you men, that number can be doubled. Entrepreneurs like you will secure the prosperity and safety of this wonderful country. The future is in your hands."

A raucous round of applause followed. These men stood to

gain the most from producing 20,000 to 40,000 planes a year. They could fool themselves into believing that their planes wouldn't be used as weapons of war, and might even believe that, but one day, those planes would rain death down on the earth below. The bombers would drop their payloads on families asleep in their beds, and the fighters would strafe women and children fleeing on the ground, just as in Spain. It was as inevitable as the self-serving smile of magnanimity on almost every face in the room. The planes he and Helga now made, and the bullets they produced at the original factory in the city, were no less lethal than anything the other industrialists manufactured. His only comfort in being here was that Hayden would soon know every detail of what he saw, and that information would flow to the president of the United States himself.

"Won't you join us, gentlemen, as we take a tour of our new state-of-the-art factory?" Göring led the men through a door into a gargantuan facility.

Another man stood waiting for them at the door. He was older than his master, with gray hair and a thick mustache over a thin mouth. He was dressed in full military uniform with a row of medals on his chest to rival Göring's.

"Gentlemen, I'd like to introduce you to another distinguished servant of the Reich. This is General Horst Engel of the new Luftwaffe. He's in charge of much of the research that goes on in this facility."

General Engel greeted a few of the men standing near him, and then they all followed him into the depths of the factory. Great lines of bombers were moving along the production line, and hundreds of workers were hammering and smoothing out metal that would one day hurtle through the skies.

Lindbergh dropped back as they walked and fell in beside Seamus. They exchanged a few pleasantries in English about where each was from.

"It's an exciting time to be a flier," Lindbergh said.

"I don't fly planes. I've only just started making them."

"It's the most wonderful feeling—true freedom. It's what I dreamed of when I was a little boy, and the National Socialists recognize it as the revolutionary element it will be in any war."

"You think it'll come to war?"

Lindbergh paused a few seconds as if afraid of who was listening in. "That's not what the men I speak to want."

Seamus wondered if the aviator believed the words coming out of his mouth or whether he'd been trained to parrot them.

The general called them to a halt. Göring had disappeared. It seemed General Engel was their host now.

"Welcome to the new institute for aeronautical research." The assembled guests, who numbered about 20, fell silent. "Planes have to fly faster and higher, but also be stronger, and at the same time, lighter. The safety of the country, the mastery of the world, might depend upon a ten-mile-an-hour difference in speed, or a .50- instead of a .30-caliber machine gun."

The general led them into a hangar where a plane sat propped up on stilts, 20 feet off the floor. Aerodynamic steel shells that looked like speakers on a phonograph stood on either side of it as if they were about to suck the aircraft in.

"This is our wind tunnel testing area," the general said with no lack of pride. "Here we can test our models for speeds up to 400 miles an hour. We are also training our men in air-reduction chambers, and getting them accustomed to electrically heated suits and having oxygen pumped into their lungs. Why? So that fighter planes can get above enemy bombers, even those equipped with sealed cabins and superchargers. Air war is going to take to the stratosphere, and the nations that don't get there first will never get there—they'll be destroyed in the first hour of combat."

Several of the men laughed. Lindbergh stared on in wide-eyed wonder. No one asked about the likelihood of air combat, or even who this future war would be against. They all just stood and marveled. Seamus found himself staring too. All the Nazi talk seemed to have become real here.

This was one of the most technologically advanced facilities on the planet. Hitler and Göring, and all the others, were serious. The money they spent wasn't window dressing. They were determined to develop the most sophisticated killing machines human beings had ever known.

"We intend to turn the future into the present," Engel continued. "We can do this because our men at the top have the vision required. Herr Göring was, and is, a flier, and has gathered a crack team to propel us forward. These men know what air war is, and what it might be. If the day comes when we're forced to defend our country, the Wehrmacht will have air cover to protect it, and the Reich will drive any enemies out of the skies and then crush them on the ground."

Another round of applause followed. The masters of war stood clapping for a few seconds before Göring reappeared.

"Now you see why I'm here," Lindbergh whispered to Seamus. "It's incredible."

Seamus didn't have to pretend to agree, taken aback by the sights. German minds were indeed capable of anything. Encouraged to explore destructive technologies such as what he'd seen today, these researchers would produce the weapons to conquer anyone who stood in their path. He wished he had a camera but had been warned in advance against bringing such devices.

The visitors were allowed to stay in the wind tunnel area for a few minutes before they were brought to a window to watch the machines in action.

Göring addressed the assembly a few minutes after the demonstration ended. "It's a fine day outside, perfect for some hunting. I'd be honored if you'd accompany me to my estate for an afternoon of shooting, having good conversation, and creating new friendships. If you wouldn't mind sharing cars, you'll be at my estate within the hour."

"Ride with me?" Lindbergh asked. "I feel more comfortable with a fellow American who speaks my language."

Seamus agreed, and the men left the factory in the same car Seamus had arrived in. Half of the cars had disappeared, perhaps to pick up the next set of dignitaries.

"The Germans will have the world's finest air force within a few months," Lindbergh said.

"It doesn't seem that any of the other powers care to compete."

"Of course, it also means Herr Göring will soon be one of the richest men in the world."

Seamus decided to speak some of what was on his mind, to test Lindbergh's loyalties just a little bit. "I heard he set up the Hermann Göring Steel Works, the biggest of all time. It's privately owned, of course. Nationalization is for the Reds."

"The contacts we make today could see us through the rest of our lives," came the reply.

"Quite."

Seamus peered out at the countryside, knowing not to further test his fellow countryman's loyalties.

"German ingenuity is incredible," Seamus said. "It's amazing what Göring and the others have been able to achieve in such a short time."

"It's a stark contrast to America, isn't it? All the money wasted, and the endless talking. The country of our birth is falling behind. At this rate, it'll never catch up. The Nazis aren't perfect, but they have the strength of will to do something about their problems, and they're certainly not going to lie down and let the Soviets roll over them."

Lindbergh reached into his pocket for a silver-plated cigarette case. He offered Seamus one, and they both lit up.

Seamus rolled down the window, and the smoke escaped like thread unfurling from a spool.

"What are your thoughts on their treatment of the Jews?"

Was the aviator testing him now? Seamus chose his words carefully.

"The Jewish issue is something I've lost sleep over. I've cultivated enormous admiration for the Führer these last few years. God knows, I was dubious enough when he came to power. But I've seen what he's done for this country and reaped the benefits myself. I have supreme confidence in his program as the salvation of German culture, and how he'll use that to preserve order all over Europe. But I don't see the Jews as anything like the menace that some people do, and perhaps the Nazis have harmed their cause with the rest of the world by insisting on it. To my mind, the obsession they have needs to end. It's bad for business...along with everything else."

The driver flicked a glance at them in the rearview mirror.

Seamus fell silent, smoking his cigarette. The esteemed airman said, "The Führer seems convinced they *are* a menace to Germany."

They sped over the low, flat land of Brandenburg and came to the Schorfheide, with its forests and fenced game preserve. It belonged to the German government, but with no one to tell him "No," Göring took it for himself. The original hunting lodge was good enough for the Kaiser but not for Göring, who transformed it into a palace and named it Carinhall after his beloved Swedish first wife, Carin. Seamus wondered what his current wife thought of that, and of the fact that Carin's tomb was on the grounds. The idea that they had their wedding here amused Seamus. Emmy, Göring's second wife, would have to content herself with his other, smaller hunting lodge in Prussia named after her.

A long, graveled driveway brought the Mercedes to a wide,

concrete two-story building, with a doorway like an ancient castle, with elk's antlers above it.

A butler opened the door and greeted the two men with a bow. They were led to the foyer, where some other industrialists were already standing. All sorts of hunting trophies adorned the walls of the hall. Stags' and boars' heads jutted out from the walls, their dead eyes staring into nothing.

A special edition of *Mein Kampf*, as big as an atlas and with exquisite binding, had been set up on a table with a candle on each side, just as in a church. Behind it, on the wall, was a painting of a Madonna and Child. A few men were browsing through an album containing photographs of the Air Force Commander's past deeds. Candles also burned in the corner before a shrine to his first wife.

"Quite something, isn't it?" Lindbergh whispered to him. "And you haven't even seen the lion cub yet."

"The lion cub?"

"Wandering around the house."

Seamus hoped his compatriot was joking.

Their host arrived a few seconds later with a smile as grand as his hunting lodge. He welcomed them and spoke about a few of the artifacts in the room before leading them on a tour of the building.

Upstairs, their host showed them the most elaborate playroom they had ever seen—a floor made into a toy village with trees and hundreds of other accessories running around and through it, a triple railroad track with toy trains. The great man sat at a desk and pressed buttons, and the trains shot through tunnels and over bridges.

"One day these will be for my son," he said. "Emmy is expecting. We plan to announce it to the nation soon."

Another round of applause followed.

Lunch was served soon after at a table seating 24 guests. They dined on pheasant and drank the finest wine. Seamus seemed to be stuck with his fellow American, and the general who had given the tour of his factory sat on his other side. Once the conversation about how magnificent the house was and how powerful the Reich would soon be ended, there seemed little else to say. Everything seemed so overblown and fatuous, but Seamus told himself he must keep sociable. He had to cultivate Göring and see what he could learn. People were relying on him.

Another brief speech and a toast followed—to the greatness of the only man Göring would admit was superior to himself. All around the table engaged in the Hitler salute.

Someday all this will end. Seamus always said that to himself. If the other men around the table knew he was a spy, if they could read his thoughts, he'd die that very day.

General Engel downed a shot of schnapps and began talking again as the meal ended. "You go shooting much?"

"Almost never," Seamus replied.

"Stick with me—I do it all the time. The game on the reserve is outstanding. Your wife will thank you, believe me. You are married?"

"With five children. Are you?"

"My wife died a few years ago. A wonderful woman. I visit her grave every Wednesday."

"My first wife died in '29. You have kids?"

"I have three sons...." Engel's face dropped. "I mean, two."

"I'm sorry. He died?"

"As good as. I don't know where he is. I don't care to, either."

Seamus nodded, wondering what the third son had done. He concentrated on his food.

After lunch, the men were led out and given clothes for the hunt. Each was supplied with a shotgun and placed into a group. Seamus thought he and Milch were to be put together for one uncomfortable moment, but instead, Seamus was grouped with Lindbergh and Engel.

A gamekeeper in his early 20s led them to a platform 25 feet high with a ladder at the side. They climbed up and looked out at a sweeping forest of fir trees. It didn't take long for the animals to appear.

"The deer are fed from hayracks when grass isn't available. The hinds are never killed, and the stags only when fully grown," the gamekeeper whispered.

Engel had explained earlier that it was a great honor to have the first shot, and there was an accompanying significant fall in prestige if you missed. They drew lots to see who would take it, and Seamus won. He waited for a clear shot. A massive, elegant stag came into view through the trees, flanked by two females. Seamus held his fire. The men were tense with excitement, standing rigid. Seamus couldn't help his enthusiasm, too.

"Now's the time," whispered the keeper. The great beast had taken a couple of steps forward, exposing his front half.

Seamus brought his eye to the rifle and pulled the trigger. The report echoed in his ears, and the stag dropped. The hinds scattered. The other men cheered as if he'd achieved something of value.

"Good shot!" Lindbergh said.

Engel patted him on the back. "That wasn't your first time with a rifle in your hand."

"True." Seamus didn't reveal that he'd fought against the general's forces in the last war.

"You're a natural," the gamekeeper said.

The other men soon bagged their own animals, though not with the same skill as Seamus. Engel surprised him with his humility. He put his arm over Seamus's shoulder as they finished. "You should come out on my estate sometime. It's not as grand as this, but the hunting's a little more... authentic."

"I'd love to."

Sleds came, and the carcasses were taken back to the lodge. The gamekeepers laid them on the lawn in front of the house.

A few men built a bonfire of pine branches, and the hunters posed behind their trophies. An older gamekeeper read off the list of the kills and the names of the hunters who shot them. The keepers of the herd had a name for each stag, and Seamus learned that he had killed a stag known as Allie. The general made another brief speech, thanking the guests for coming, and then the keepers raised their horns and sounded the stags' deaths in musical notes. The day was succumbing to darkness, and the fading scene was so beautiful that Seamus almost forgot why he was here and who these people were.

Seamus returned to the car and found Lucky Lindy was coming with him on the drive back to the city.

The other American tried to make conversation on the road, but Seamus had little interest in getting to know the man. He was of little use, and his personality and character didn't entice Seamus to become his friend. He longed for a kindred spirit and knew he had that in his wife waiting at home. He knew what questions she'd ask him when he returned: Who did he meet, and what use could they be? Getting close to Göring proved difficult, and he only shared a few words with the second-most powerful man in the Reich. Perhaps the general was someone he could form a friendship with? Still, it was good to attend these gatherings and to be seen by the other masters of the German war machine. His role for Hayden was about nothing if not gaining the trust of the most powerful men in the Reich, and today he'd taken another critical step toward achieving that. Lindbergh was a figurehead, nothing more. The Nazis would extract the propaganda value they desired from him and send him back home.

The car sped on toward the city, and Seamus pretended to fall asleep on the back seat.

6

Saturday, September 18

Trying to fathom her father's motivations was a difficult task. Fiona stared out the car window as Lisa drove her to the Bernheims' house. It was embarrassing. No one else she knew was forced to fraternize with Jews. She dreaded to think what would happen if someone found out she'd been doing this for a year. The League would throw her out, and none of her friends would ever talk to her again. A life of isolation—and all because her father forced her to have lunch with his factory manager every month.

It was funny. There were plenty of Jews in Newark when she was a little girl, but she never gave them a second thought. They were just other kids in school, or other grown-ups in the store. It wasn't until she came to Germany that she realized the danger she'd been in all that time, and how insidious the Jews were as a race. She'd been blind before, but Hitler opened her eyes. That was all he wanted—to show people the truth. If some, like her father and his half-Jew wife, refused to accept that, then all the worse for them.

Lisa was talking about how she never knew she was half-Jewish until her mother blurted it out on her deathbed—a story she'd told so many times Fiona could almost recall it word for word.

"What difference would it have made if she hadn't converted because of the prejudices of other people?" Lisa asked. "Am I a better mother because I was born Lutheran? A better person?"

Fiona didn't answer. She didn't have the heart to tell her stepmother that although she had Jewish blood in her veins, she should have thanked her mother. At least the woman had the good sense to deny her illicit roots.

"Gert and Lil are wonderful people," Lisa continued as they pulled up behind a horse and cart. "You can see that, can't you?"

"Of course. But perhaps this country isn't for them."

Lisa didn't speak. Her knuckles were white on the steering wheel. The horse and cart turned off, and they sped on.

The Bernheims were in the front yard as they arrived. Lisa greeted them both with kisses on the cheek. Fiona approached it as she always did. This was about acting. If she placated her father long enough, he'd give up, and besides, she'd be 16 in December—old enough to get married. If Harald wanted to have babies for the Führer, her days of having to listen to the liberal ramblings of her father and stepmother might soon be at an end.

Lisa said goodbye and promised to come back for her in two hours. *Two hours!* Fiona did her best to hide her discomfort as Frau Bernheim led her inside. Her husband soon followed, and they sat at the table to eat a lunch of bread rolls and various meats and cheeses. The food was good, and after a little small talk, Fiona decided to ask a question she thought they'd like.

"Isn't today your Sabbath? Shouldn't you be at the synagogue?"

Herr Bernheim shifted in his seat and placed the half-eaten bread roll in his hand back on the plate.

"Attending isn't as easy as it used to be. Many synagogues have been defaced, or even burned to the ground. Those Jews that do go have to deal with the wrath of the SA men and the Hitler Youth, who picket just about every synagogue in the city."

"And beyond," Lil said. "We're not religious anyway, not the synagogue-going types, but that doesn't mean we aren't disgusted at the treatment of Jews who do attend."

"Those brave people," Herr Bernheim said. "Fiona, do you know anyone who pickets Jewish businesses or places of worship?"

Fiona hesitated, taking ample time to finish the food in her mouth. Telling the truth wouldn't serve her well here. "No. You must wonder why."

"Why what?" Lil asked.

"Why the SA and Hitler Youth picket those places. Why the Nazis want you and your kind out of the country."

Herr Bernheim laughed and lifted his cup to his mouth. He was just about to speak when his wife interrupted him.

"It's a strange thing to belong to a tiny minority of people that the masses seem terrified of. I do wonder why, every day. Why do the Nazis blame us for losing a war that we had nothing to do with ending? Why do they not trust us to hold any position of power or influence? Why won't they let us educate our children, or even marry Germans? What are they so scared of?"

"Their own inadequacies," Herr Bernheim said. "The easiest thing when faced with a difficult situation is to blame someone else, and the easiest people to blame are the traditional foes: 'the lazy poor' 'the dangerous foreigners,' and, of course, the Jews. People have been doing it for thousands of years."

Fiona took a few seconds to digest what Herr Bernheim said. He appeared so earnest and forthright, yet her troop leaders had warned her about believing the lies the Jews spouted. It was all so confusing. How could the Führer be wrong? It didn't make sense that he could be. It seemed a simple choice—trust these people or trust Adolf Hitler, the greatest man on the planet.

"If you hate it here in the Reich so much, why don't you leave? Why stay in a country that doesn't want you?"

Herr Bernheim's face tightened. His wife put a gentle hand on his forearm, and he seemed to relent.

"First of all, we don't hate the Reich. That's their word, their emotion," Lil said. "We just want to live in a place where we have as much chance to succeed as anyone else."

"It's not easy to leave," her husband said. "It's ironic that a government that seems to want to get rid of the Jews makes that action so difficult for us."

"I don't understand," Fiona said.

"Have you heard of the Reich Flight Tax?"

"No, I haven't."

"It's a tax the National Socialists impose upon the Jews when they try to emigrate."

"And only the Jews," Lil added.

"The tax rate rises every year. Currently it's set at 81 percent," Herr Bernheim said.

Fiona looked around the room for a few seconds. This didn't seem like the house of a rich family. It was much smaller than hers. But all Jews were wealthy, weren't they? The Bernheims must have hidden their money somewhere. The government obviously just wanted the money that the Jews had stolen from the German people.

"That can't be," she said. "The government has encouraged all Jews to leave."

"While making it almost impossible for most of us to do so," Lil answered.

"How can we when the Nazis tax us at 81 percent when we leave?" Herr Bernheim asked. "We can't go to another country to be destitute."

"You can hide your money, maybe," Fiona said.

Lil shook her head. "The Reich Postal Service keeps tabs on us for the Gestapo. It tells them when we change addresses. Real estate agents inform them when we want to sell our houses, and notaries when we sign legal forms. Life insurance companies are required to tell the government when Jews opt to cancel policies. They get every early indicator that we're planning on emigrating. If we drop our fork at dinner, they'll know the size of the stain we left on the carpet."

Fiona was surprised. "How many of you would leave Germany tomorrow if no restrictions existed?"

"Very many of us. According to the Reich Flight Tax, anyone with assets of 50,000 Reichsmarks or more is subject to pay more than 80 percent to the government upon emigrating."

"So why don't the people under the threshold leave?"

"Because they would have little to nothing anywhere else. It takes money to move to a new country."

"So the people who can afford to move will have their assets stolen by the Nazis, and those who don't qualify for the tax can't afford to emigrate," Lil said.

"Can't you sell your houses, old heirlooms, your diamond earrings—even your cars?"

"And what do we do with the money? The banks will report the lodgments to the Gestapo, and they'll take their cut."

"I believe in the National Socialist cause and the decisions Herr Hitler makes. There must be a good reason for the tax."

That was about the most polite thing she could say on the subject. Once again, Lil put her hand on her husband's arm to calm him. Anger flashed in his eyes. He took a sip of water from the mug in front of him and began again.

"And that's not to mention the issue of obtaining visas to get into other countries. The British are slashing the number of Jewish visas allowing people to move into Palestine, and getting to America isn't much easier. You have to buy your way there, and if you've just given 81 percent of your wealth to the government in Germany...."

"Hitler doesn't want us here, and we don't want to be here," Lil said. "The Nazis have poisoned the well of this country for us. We were so happy just a few years ago, but everything's changed now." She dabbed her eyes with a handkerchief as her husband put his arm around her.

"I'm sorry." Fiona's words were genuine. Perhaps she was being drawn in by their lies, but she couldn't help feeling sympathy for the people across the table from her. "What are you going to do?"

"I really don't know," Herr Bernheim said.

Perhaps Father was right to send me here, Fiona thought as she walked out to the car with Lisa when her time with the Bernheims was done. She had learned something from being with them that day. How could a working man move away when the government took 81 percent of his wealth upon departing? The Germans wanted the Jews gone but made it hard for them to leave. It didn't make any sense. Maybe she needed to find out more about the problem. She resolved to ask the people she trusted most—her troop leaders in the League of German Girls.

Lisa thanked Herr and Frau Bernheim but didn't speak to Fiona as the two women walked to the car.

"We have one more stop to make before we go home," Lisa said.

"Where?" Fiona asked as they sat in the Mercedes.

"I want you to meet someone."

She pulled out of the driveway without another word, and they drove east across the city. Twenty minutes of tense silence later they were in Kreuzberg, a neighborhood she'd never visited.

"If you're eager to show me the poor areas of the city, save yourself the trouble. I spent two years sharing a room with my siblings in my aunt's house."

"I'm not here to illuminate you on the poverty in our city," Lisa responded and parked the car. The street looked dangerous. Two men in ragged clothes were sitting on a stoop a few feet from them and were eyeing the car with voracious eyes. Lisa didn't seem to care and jumped out of the driver's seat.

"Are you sure this is safe?" Fiona asked under her breath, but her companion either didn't hear or didn't care to. With no other apparent choice, the young girl stepped out of the car. The sour stench of trash filled her nostrils. Two onlookers whistled as she got out.

Lisa quieted them with a few harsh words. "This is it."

Lisa strode to the front door of an old gray apartment block and up a dark unpainted stairwell to an apartment on the second floor. Fiona hurried after her.

A middle-aged woman answered with a dull smile.

"Judith, how are you?" Lisa asked. "Can we come in?"

"Of course." The woman held the door open for them.

The apartment was neat and furnished for comfort rather than style. It had been a while since Fiona was in a place like this. Memories of her former life in America flooded her mind. The woman, moving with a noticeable limp, offered them tea. Lisa accepted on behalf of both of them. The two guests sat on a threadbare couch opposite a fireplace, unused at this time of year. Their host reappeared two minutes later to break the silence that had descended.

"Judith, I'd like to introduce you to my stepdaughter, Fiona. She loves going to the movies with her friends."

The woman offered a weak, awkward handshake. Did Lisa bring her here to embarrass her?

"I don't go to the cinema. I'm not allowed by law," she said and took a seat perpendicular to them. Fiona began to understand—Jews were barred from movie theaters these days.

"How is your health?" Lisa asked.

"I have good days and bad."

Lisa turned to Fiona. "Judith works for your father. She's been there many years."

"And for his uncle before him. Your father is a good man, just like Helmut." She drank some tea and grimaced in what seemed like pain as she sat back. She didn't look much older than Lisa—perhaps 40 at most—yet she moved like an elderly woman. Old photos of her with a man that seemed to be her husband sat above the fireplace.

"I brought Fiona here today to listen to your story—what happened to you, and why. I thought she could benefit from hearing it."

Judith looked at Lisa as if to ask if she were sure. A nod was enough for the woman to sit forward and begin. "My religion wasn't something that mattered much to me growing up. I knew lots of devout Jews—I just wasn't one of them. Things were bad when the Nazis first came to power. Lots of Jews thought that once Hitler hobbled the SA on the Night of the Long Knives, things would settle down. It seemed to make sense that once the bullies of the Brownshirts were killed off that Hitler and the Nazis would have more pressing matters to deal with than subjugating Jews."

"Like governing the country?" Lisa asked.

"Exactly. Things were better for a while, but after the Olympics, the Gestapo and the Brownshirts came after us with a vengeance."

Fiona almost couldn't bear to sit and listen.

"I don't know why they chose us, but several Hitler Youth

boys took to following my husband and me through the streets. They'd shout at us and dance around us as we tried to go about our daily business, before growing bored and running off to harass someone else. One day we came back from a walk in the park to find our door smeared with paint, and then the week after, they broke it down and ransacked our apartment. We had no one to report the crime to. The police laughed at us, so the abuse escalated. We stopped going anywhere but to work for fear of the Brownshirts and the Hitler Youth, but we had to leave sometimes for food. Uli, my husband, insisted I stay home except when I went to work. He took it upon himself to get our daily necessities."

The woman stopped. Tears welled in her eyes. Lisa reached forward and took her hand, urging her to go on. "One day in August, we decided enough was enough and went out for a walk along the river. The boy downstairs was watching us. He must have run and told his friends. They caught us on Köpenicker Strasse. I counted 12 young men who attacked us. They beat Uli and dragged him out on the street, dumping trash on him and spitting on him as they kicked and kicked. He died. And then they came for me."

"Show her," Lisa said.

Judith stood and turned around. She lifted up her sweater to reveal a dozen or more angry red lashes on her back. "They had canes with them and took turns in beating me. I passed out from the pain, never thinking I'd open my eyes again."

"That's monstrous," Fiona said. "I'm so sorry about your husband."

"No charges were ever brought against any of the boys who murdered him. I still see that one on the stairwell sometimes when I dare to venture out, but that's a rare occurrence these days. Seamus and Lisa have been so good to me, even though I haven't been able to work since."

"We should go," Lisa said and stood up. Judith rose also,

and the two women shared a gentle embrace. "You have everything you need?" The Jewish woman nodded. "I'll be back in a few days."

"Are the lessons over for the day?" Fiona asked as they returned to the car. Her stepmother didn't answer—just glared back at her with angry eyes.

7

Friday, October 1

Petra Wagner, star of the silver screen, opened her eyes. The first thing she felt was pain—not of the emotional variety that peppered her existence these days, but physical agony. She reached for water on the bedside table but found only empty glasses, which last night had held schnapps. The covers fell away, and she realized her state of undress. Pulling them back over herself, she lay still to listen. No noise. He'd already gone—likely to one of his morning meetings with Berlin's newspaper editors. Once, they had decided what stories their publications would cover, but now the pronouncements on what the public read about over breakfast rested with Joseph Goebbels. Freedom of the press was a memory. The media was a conduit to convey the messages the Nazis wanted the public to believe and nothing more. Germany's newspapers were like searchlights now, controlled from a common center and all focused upon the same spot at the same moment.

Just now, the lights were on the chancellor of Austria. The Nazis disapproved of his resistance to a possible merger of his country with Germany. No doubt, the man she'd shared this bed with the night before was currently dictating the most advantageous editorials possible to show the manifest magnificence and just nature of what the Nazis were trying to achieve.

Her parched throat drove her out of bed, and she found a dressing gown on a chair in the corner. The apartment was still littered with glasses and empty bottles from the party the Reich Minister for Propaganda had thrown the night before. The stench of stale beer and cigarette smoke almost turned her fragile stomach. She paced across Goebbels' bachelor pad and found a jug of water in the refrigerator. The liquid felt like heaven sliding down her throat, and she finished several glasses before placing the jug back into the otherwise bare appliance.

The apartment felt like an empty shell with the stylish and glamorous guests she'd rubbed shoulders with the night before gone. All the pretty birds had flown. The silence haunted her, though she was glad Goebbels wasn't here. She was all alone.

A mirror above the dresser revealed the truth. Her makeup, which the Nazis officially disapproved of, was smudged. Her eyeliner gave her the appearance of a raccoon. She wiped it off, taking a few seconds to grimace as the hammers began inside her head. Her eyes were bloodshot but revealed more than her hangover. A tear formed and broke down her cheek. This feeling inside her was ridiculous.

Her legs ached, and she pulled up a chair. "You've got everything you ever wanted," she said to the mess staring back at her in the mirror. "Can't you just be happy?"

Her new movie was premiering in the city in a few weeks, and all the most influential people in Germany would be there —Goebbels, Göring, and perhaps even the Führer himself. Himmler didn't love such things, but she had little time for the man herself and wouldn't miss him. She was on her way to becoming the biggest star in German cinema—the next

Marlene Dietrich—with her family reaping the benefits of her newfound wealth. She'd been able to buy her parents a new house, which was the most gratifying experience of her life. Then why did she feel so empty? Why did this pit of pain rest in her chest like a stone?

The truth was, her films were appalling. They were nothing more than a voice for Nazi ideology, with little or no artistic merit. They were for keeping the masses in line and roaring approval at Nazi rallies—nothing more. It was embarrassing.

"Enough," she said aloud and pushed herself off the chair. *This is ridiculous. I have lines to learn and commitments to honor.* Her clothes were strewn on the bedroom floor, and she had nothing to change into other than the evening dress she had worn the night before. A dagger of guilt plunged into her heart. The window offered some refuge, and she stared down at Rankestrasse for a few moments. The morning traffic had a hypnotic effect and dulled her pain, but thoughts of Magda Goebbels and her four children tore at her and dragged her back into her mind's maelstrom.

It seemed determined to torture her, and in deflecting from the Reich minister's wife and children, it settled on Lisa Ritter. Petra let her head rest against the smooth, cool surface of the window. Lisa's words, which she'd played in her mind a thousand times since she ran into her by chance in Lido's during the Olympics, echoed in her ears. But it wasn't her former friend's words that hurt so much—it was the look in her eyes, somewhere between resentment and terrible disappointment. Lisa got her the job on the movie that Petra had her fired from. In a moment of weakness, Lisa revealed her deepest secret, and Petra used it against her. She didn't care that Lisa was a Jew, half-Jew, or whatever she was, but the Reich Chamber of Culture did. With no one to stand in her way, Petra was cast in the lead role that Lisa was fired from.

Her career was built on betrayal and propped up by the act

of prostituting herself out to that ugly wretch she'd spent the night with. She tried to comfort herself with the notion that she was improving her family's lives. Her parents were staunch National Socialists and were proud of the propaganda films she made for the government that millions flocked to see. She knew her work on behalf of the Reich Chamber of Culture was utter tripe, but this was her dream—and it had come true.

"I have to get out of here," she said. "I have lines to learn."

Perhaps getting back to work would paper over the multitude of cracks in her soul. She called downstairs and had the doorman call a car.

Five minutes later, she was in the only clothing she had, her face wiped clean. A pair of sunglasses in her bag would serve to cover her bloodshot eyes. The call from the doorman interrupted her thoughts, and she left the messy apartment and descended the two flights of stairs from the penthouse to the street.

The sun was high in the morning sky, and she was grateful to not suffer from its glare. She thanked the doorman without looking at him and got straight into the waiting car. The driver nodded as she barked out her address, and he drove off. Ensuring there would be no eye contact, Petra stared out the window for the duration of the five-minute drive to Fasanenstrasse. She handed the driver a generous tip and got out without a word. A synagogue, closed by the Nazis the year before, loomed across the street from her apartment as if to remind her of her transgressions.

She picked up the newspaper from her mailbox without looking at it and carried on upstairs to her apartment. Walking past the elevator operator, she took the stairs.

The solace she'd hoped to find in familiar surroundings didn't materialize. The flaming dagger in her chest only grew more agonizing. She went to the mirror above her dresser but saw Lisa's face beside her. A bath didn't do anything more than clean her skin—her soul remained the same. The script she had to learn—about a German maiden beset by poverty until renewed by motherhood and National Socialism—remained unopened on her coffee table.

Lacking the motivation to open another ridiculous screenplay about the wonders of National Socialism, she picked up the newspaper instead. The headline was about the political situation in Austria—the latest Nazi land grab. For no particular reason, she let her eyes drift down to the bottom of the page. The story was in the bottom corner. The headline read:

SA Men Inspired by Movie Torch Jewish Businesses

Petra's blood ran cold. After watching one of her movies, a group of Stormtroopers in Lichtenberg burned down several Jewish-owned stores in the Berlin neighborhood. One man was killed in the fire, and a woman was in hospital. The perpetrators were charged with reckless endangerment and would no doubt get off with a slap on the wrist. She reread the story. *After watching one of my movies.* She remembered the scene where she led a mob to burn down the Jewish moneylender's house. Tears welled in her eyes and burst down her cheeks. The strength seemed to fade from her body, and she suddenly had to sit down. The anti-Jewish hatred in the Reich couldn't exist without the propaganda machine that sustained it, and she was a vital cog in that machine. She'd sold her soul and had already been consigned to live in hell.

It was hard to tell how long she sat there. Perhaps it was ten or fifteen minutes before she got up. A thought occurred to her as she picked up the newspaper again. The surviving woman was named Ethel Rosen, and she was recovering in Charité Hospital. Perhaps this was an opportunity to cleanse just a sliver of her conscience.

An urge like no other gripped her now, and she readied herself to go out in minutes. She knew what she had to do, but did she have the courage to follow through? She reached for her sunglasses once more, and a chic hat sent from Paris the month before. A car was waiting when she arrived on the street.

She called out the address, and the driver pulled away from her apartment building toward the hustle and bustle of Kurfürstendamm. Petra sat back in her seat, steeling herself for what she knew had to come. This was something she needed to do to calm her soul. Something was broken within her, and perhaps this was a way to fix some small part of it.

They knew her at the hospital. She often visited sick children, or people injured in train wrecks or other accidents. It was part of her job as a movie star, and it was something she enjoyed. Seeing the looks on the children's faces as she arrived at their bedsides was one of the few joys of this so-called "dream career" of hers. Getting in to see the woman from the story in the newspaper wouldn't be difficult. Perhaps Ethel Rosen might accept her apology, and gain some comfort from the fact that Petra wasn't an ardent Nazi herself.

The traffic in the city was sparse, and she had little time to think her actions through before the driver let her off in front of the hospital. She closed the door behind her. Striding toward the old stone building, she felt a surge of energy in her tired body.

The young nurse at the reception desk smiled as Petra took off her sunglasses. "I'm here to visit a patient—Ethel Rosen."

"Of course," the nurse answered. "I saw your last movie in the cinema a few weeks ago. It was so moving."

"Thanks," Petra replied with a watery smile.

"Rosen..." the nurse said as she flipped through the pages of a ledger. "She's in Room 362. It's just—"

"I know where it is."

Petra thanked the young nurse for her help before setting off toward the room. Several people stood back to stare at her as she passed. Was it because they recognized her, or was it for the same reason men always stared? It was hard to know. She was almost at the room when she realized she hadn't brought flowers. Perhaps she could come back with them later.

The door came into view. It was ajar, and she pushed it open with one hand while knocking with the other. Four women were lying in bed, two on one side, two on the other.

"I'm here to see Ethel Rosen," Petra said.

The woman nearest the door turned her head. She was in her late 40s, with thin brown hair that went to her shoulders. Her arms were bandaged all the way up to her elbows, and her face was scorched red from the fire.

"Who are you?" she asked in a dull voice.

"My name is Petra. I came to see if you were feeling better. Can I sit?"

Ethel nodded, though the quizzical look never left her face. Petra pulled up a wooden stool and sat by the bed.

"I'm so sorry about what happened to you," Petra said. "And about your husband."

The woman in the bed nodded as her eyes began to well with tears. "It's a disgrace. I can't believe what's happening to this country."

It was obvious Ethel didn't recognize her, but one of the other women spoke up. "Aren't you that actress?" came a voice from across the room. The other woman looked ten years younger than Ethel, with no visible injuries.

Petra turned her head to the other woman. "Yes, I'm an actress. I read about what happened in the newspaper," she said to Ethel. "I came in to offer my condolences."

She wanted to reach for the injured woman's hand, but didn't deem it appropriate.

"Thank you," Ethel said.

"Wait," the younger patient said. "She is the star of the movie those SA thugs watched. Ethel, she's the one in the picture they watched."

"What?" Ethel asked.

"Before they burned down your husband's store! She's the one from the film!"

Ethel turned to the movie star with a horrific cloud of rage and sadness in her eyes. "You're the one from the movie that inspired them to burn down my husband's store?"

"I had nothing to do with what happened. I came here to—"

Ethel was crying now. "You were part of this!" she cried. "Those men who killed my husband said you were their inspiration."

"I never meant that," Petra said. The atmosphere had changed. This wasn't how this was meant to go at all. "I wanted to come here to tell you how sorry I am. What happened to you was just awful. I'm so—"

"Get out, you Nazi cow!" Ethel snarled.

"No, I'm here to tell you that I'm not one of them, that—"

"You heard her!" the younger woman shouted.

The other two patients weren't speaking, but the looks on their faces said enough. Petra felt a tear roll down her face.

A nurse appeared at the door. "What's going on in here? What's the shouting about?"

"Our famous visitor was just leaving," the younger patient said.

"My husband burned to death. I hope you're happy with what you've created," Ethel said as Petra walked to the door. The bereaved woman's words were the final dagger to destroy what was left of her heart. She left the hospital with her head down, her sunglasses over her eyes to hide her tears.

8

Saturday, October 9

Fiona wiped the sweat from her brow as she scanned the mass of young girls for her friends. Amalia and Inge were already sitting together, and motioned her to come over. She squeezed in beside Amalia, who had saved her a spot. Several hundred members of the League of German Girls sat on benches in the evening sun, waiting for their special guest speaker.

The day's hike had been long, and Fiona's shoes were covered in dust. But she wasn't tired. Her body was strong—just as her instructors intended. She and the girls were about five rows from the stage and the lectern set up on it. Fiona adjusted her black tie among the sea of white shirts surrounding her. It felt good to be part of something important. The instructors reminded them every day that they were vital to the future of humanity—that without them, civilization would collapse. The pressure from the Bolshevists and the Jews was almost at breaking point, and Fiona and the other members felt it. Girls broke down crying for fear of what the Communists and Jews would do to them if the Führer was overwhelmed. The easiest way to comfort the doubters was to remind them that the Führer was infallible, and that protecting the flower of German youth was his obsession. The thought that the most brilliant man on earth was watching over all of them gave Fiona comfort. Without him, the entire Reich would be lost.

Being here made her realize how much she hated going to the Bernheims' house. She wasn't frightened of them and just looked down on them with pity, but she was beginning to realize that you never knew when a Jew might turn. And they weren't worms; they were rats...with teeth.

Her father should know better. He was no traitor. He supplied the Wehrmacht and the Luftwaffe with the bullets and airplanes they needed to propel Germany to greatness. He rubbed shoulders with Göring and had spoken to her troop about it. He was a hero to the League and, indeed, to Conor's instructors in the Hitler Youth.

But at the same time, her father had spent too long in America and came to Germany with some ridiculous, sentimental ideas about "all men being equal." It wasn't his fault. He was raised in a different time, in a country obsessed with the failed policy of democracy.

It was strange to think she'd spent so much of her life in America. It seemed a peculiar, foreign place to her now. Her teachers pointed out how democracy and liberal ideas had destroyed what was once a great country. It was hard to argue with them when her own father had been forced to abandon her and the rest of his children for two years before they came to the Reich. Germany and the National Socialist Party had saved him, though he'd never admit as much. It had saved her too, and given her a purpose that nothing else ever could.

Her troop leaders always said that it was easier for the young to understand the new ideas Adolf Hitler espoused, and to be prepared for the sparkling future that brilliant man had in store for them. He understood the world in a way the older generations never could. His genius was that he knew young people were the key to the future, and he did everything he could to shape them into the best servants of the Reich they could be.

Everyone she knew had absolute faith in him and the direction in which he was leading the country. Most of the parents did too—except her own father. And her stepmother, of course. But she was partly a Jew, so she had no moral fiber.

Fiona's troop leader, Millie, took to the stage, receiving polite applause from the onlooking group of girls. She was 20, with idyllic Aryan looks and blond hair. She often boasted about her wide, child-bearing hips and was being paired with an SS man to begin the process of bearing children for the Führer in the next few months. She cleared her throat.

"Quiet down, girls," she said, though barely a sound could be heard. "We have a special guest speaker for you today. You've worked hard these past few weeks, as boot leather has been worn down and sewing fingers have been toughened. Most importantly, your love and admiration for the Führer has grown. As a reward, we have today the head of the League of German Girls, and someone who knows the Führer personally, Trude Mohr."

The thought of someone knowing Hitler in the flesh drove the crowd of girls into a frenzy, and a thin blond woman with glasses came to the lectern dressed as they were and bade them quiet down.

"I met with the Führer himself, just last week," she began.

Several girls in the audience screamed, and Inge, on Fiona's left, cried a little.

"We are asserting the natural order that he spoke of to me. The German Reich will be built upon the foundation of family. Men have always been the head of the family, and will protect their wives, sons, and daughters. It is the job of the wife to serve and nurture her husband and children. This is a role just as vital as soldiers on the front line, or even the politicians enforcing the Führer's will. We, together, are the future of the Reich. Our *Volk* [people] needs a generation of girls, healthy in body and mind, and free of sentimental emotions and other ridiculous distractions. It is up to us to carry the values of National Socialism into the next generation as a bulwark for the German people."

Several girls stood up to applaud. The troop leaders, watching the crowd of girls like leopards circling their prey, shouted at them to sit down, and the speaker continued.

"Who here has already dropped out of school?" Mohr smiled as she surveyed the dozens of hands that flew into the air. Fiona felt almost ashamed that she and her friends hadn't left school yet.

"Excellent. We need to realize how we can best serve the Führer, and that is by producing strong, healthy Aryan children. Only that way will we protect our people against the myriad of threats we face. Where is Mila Bürkner, your former troop leader?"

Mila raised her hand, her pregnant belly jutting out.

"Look at her, girls—an example to us all. She'll soon receive the gold motherhood cross from our dear Führer for her eighth child." Rapturous applause erupted among the crowd of young women. "And at the tender age of 29," Mohr said. "A true inspiration to us all."

Exultation filled Fiona's soul like water. To be here among so many heroes of the Reich was incredible.

"In that vein, I'll soon be resigning as head of the League of German Girls. I'm getting married to an Obersturmführer in the SS, and thus, as the Führer demands, will step down from my job. I'll be concentrating on getting my own motherhood cross, although I've quite the task in front of me to catch the likes of Mila."

"Trude's almost 37, too," Inge whispered in Fiona's ear.

Mohr spoke for a few more minutes, thrilling the crowd with stories of personal meetings with the Führer. She stressed the importance of the task again ahead of them and departed to more applause.

"Now, the question remains, with whom shall we bear children for the Führer?" Amalia asked as they got up to leave.

"Fiona already knows!" Inge said.

Fiona blushed. She'd thought about marrying Harald. The idea sat well with her. After the stirring speech she had just heard, she was ready to start married life today. She could see herself staying home to raise strong children while Harald set out to do the Führer's good work. It seemed like a satisfying future—fit for any loyal German woman.

"I'm meeting him and Georg and a few others in the park after the rally. Why don't you come? Maybe we can all find fathers for our beautiful German babies."

The three girls dodged through the crowd, wanting to exit the small stadium first and get a head start on meeting the Hitler Youth boys.

"Harald's 18 now," Inge said once they were free of the crowd. "Perhaps he'll want to marry you before he joins the SS."

"I hope so," Fiona answered. She was only 15. Both she and Harald would have to get a dispensation to marry, because the age was set at 16 for girls and 21 for boys. But getting it would be easy—the Reich needed babies.

The girls took a tram across the city. Harald and his friends, Georg and Manfred, were waiting outside the Haus Vaterland on Potsdamer Platz. Evening was drawing in, and for the first time that day, Fiona felt a chill in the air. Harald smiled at her as she and the rest of the girls jumped off the tram.

"You taking us in there?" Amalia asked, referring to the massive pleasure palace behind him.

"You're a little young for that. Maybe in a year or two. We have something else special planned for tonight."

Harald, like the others, was in Hitler Youth uniform, and his toned arms bulged under the fabric. He was the most handsome boy she'd ever seen.

"So, what do you have planned for us tonight?" Fiona asked, trying to keep her heart from jumping out of her chest in front of him.

"It wouldn't be a surprise if we just came out and told you, would it?" Harald replied.

He took her arm and led her up the street past the Haus Vaterland. She nearly told him that her stepmother used to work in the nightclub upstairs, and that her father met her there, but she thought better of it. Lisa was a *Mischling*, after all. Half-Jewish. Not worth mentioning.

"What are your plans?" she asked Harald. "Are you determined to join the SS?" They were a few steps ahead of the others.

"And why shouldn't I be? Can you imagine it? I'd be a part of the most elite fighting force in the world—the Führer's personal guard. I'll be working for the Reich as a part of the Labor Service first. But that six months will fly. Then I can join up. How about you?"

She had to speak. It wasn't hard to imagine this being the last time they were ever together.

"I want to get married as soon as possible—this year, if I can —and have a thousand babies for the Führer. I can't imagine anything more honorable."

"And who's the lucky fellow?"

"I... I...don't know." Sadness descended upon her. The

desire to express her feelings to him was hard to suppress, but she remembered Frau Mohr's words about excluding frivolous emotional responses from their lives and walked on.

"I thought this would be a fun end to our day," Harald said as they came upon a group of Hitler Youth outside a Jewish department store. About ten of them were outside, yelling insults. The can of paint they'd used to daub a star of David on the window was spilled on the sidewalk.

Harald and his friends linked arms and stood in front of the door to bar customers from entering the store. Harald took it upon himself to stop several people emerging with shopping bags.

"Are you a loyal Aryan?" he asked one woman, who scuttled off without answering.

The girls stood watching the protest. "Don't you think it would be better if the Führer encouraged the Jews to move out of our country?" Fiona asked.

"He does. Are you questioning his methods?" Inge asked. Both her parents were ardent Nazi supporters. She often boasted of never reading anything Dr. Goebbels disapproved of.

"I'd never question the Führer. I just don't understand the taxes the government imposes upon the Jews trying to leave the Reich," Fiona said. "It seems more sensible to make it easy for them to leave."

"With all they've stolen from the German *Volk*?" Amalia asked. "You don't give criminals back the money they robbed when you release them from prison. That's what these protests are all about—cleansing our society. If young people like us make life impossible for the Jews, they'll leave anyway and be forced to return their ill-gotten gains to the people they stole them from."

"But if their blood and their presence is the biggest threat...."

"Why do you have to ask so many questions?" Inge said.

"What would our group leader in the League say if you asked them that?" Amalia stared at Fiona. "They'd tell you to stop thinking so much, and that the Führer already has all of these details worked out. All we have to do is follow his guidance."

"It just doesn't make sense to me," Fiona said.

"It doesn't have to make sense to us. We're 15-year-old girls," Amalia replied with a testy look. "We learn sewing and cooking —the important things for women. When was the last philosophy or management class we had?"

"Never, but we learn about politics all the time."

"Learning the Führer's teachings is above anything else," Amalia said. "What would we do without his guidance? We'd be lost."

A large man in a gray trench coat and a matching hat tried to push his way into the store. "Don't you children have better things to do than harass honest customers?" he asked.

Georg tipped his hat off his head and kicked him in the backside as he reached down to get it. The man realized he was overmatched and walked away. Fiona couldn't help but feel embarrassed for him. The boys were laughing in his face.

Harald looked over at her as if to gauge her reaction to the humiliation they put the man through. She returned an awkward smile. Who was to say that man wasn't a loyal German? Maybe he could buy what he wanted somewhere else. Sometimes she had to admit to herself that the teachings of the Führer were beyond her immature, female mind. Perhaps she was too influenced by the emotions the speaker warned against earlier. Amalia was right—it wasn't her place to question the Führer's teachings.

The girls watched for another hour as dozens of customers turned tail and headed off. A hardy few tried to get past the boys on duty but were not allowed. The store's management was conspicuous by its absence. They must have known better than to come out and question the Hitler Youth.

Harald and the others seemed to be in heaven and began singing some marching songs to extend their jovial mood. In an apparent sign that the boys couldn't be beaten, a middle-aged man emerged from the store and pulled down the shutters. The young men showered him with abuse but cheered as they heard the *click* of the lock. The store wasn't due to close for another hour—they had won!

Satisfied with their work, the Hitler Youth members congratulated each other before going their separate ways.

"I think we deserve a drink after that!" Georg said as he walked over to the waiting group of girls.

"I know somewhere up the street," Harald added.

Fiona had never been to a bar before, but wasn't about to admit that in front of them. "I don't have enough money for beer," she said, wondering what her father would say if she came home smelling of it.

"I have plenty," Harald said.

His father owned a chain of pharmacies in the city. Harald constantly had new clothes and always seemed to be able to afford to do whatever he wanted.

"Come on," Amalia said.

"Ok," she said with a smile. A couple of beers weren't going to hurt her.

Twenty minutes later, the group was standing in the corner of a smoke-filled bar, each with a beer.

"That was something earlier, wasn't it?" Georg asked.

Inge, his cousin, agreed. "Another important step in cleansing our city of parasites."

"The boycott of Jewish stores is important, but sometimes it doesn't seem like enough," Georg said. "If we're to rid the Reich of the Jewish vermin, we're going to have to do more than stop people from coming and going into their stores."

"What's it like living with a Jew, Fiona?" asked Inge.

Shocked by the suddenness of the question, Fiona lifted the beer to her mouth to give her a few extra seconds. All five were looking at her. She gulped down the foul-tasting liquid. "I can't do much about it." She wanted someone else to speak, but her friends stayed silent. They wanted more.

"My father didn't know when he married her," she said so all could hear. "He thought she was Aryan. It wasn't until later that he found out, but he didn't have the heart to kick her out. She's a *Mischling*—not a full Jew. So he thinks it's ok for her to be around in the house."

"But being Jewish is in the blood, isn't it?" Manfred asked. It was the first thing he'd said since they arrived. "It's like white paint. You get a splash of black in it... Well, it's unusable."

"You're right," she said. "And I'm sick of having to defend her."

"You know, talking about saving the Reich is one thing, but the Führer expects us to act upon his teachings," Harald said.

"I know, and I'm proud of what you did earlier," Fiona said.

"Yet you think the Jews should be allowed to keep their money," said Amalia.

Fiona went red. "Only to get them out of the country. I think more would go if they could."

"It's not up to a girl to think," said Harald. "The Führer will give us the direction we need. Keep faith in him."

"As we do," Georg said.

"Have you spent time with that family of Jews lately, Fiona?" Harald asked.

She had no idea how he knew about that. Keeping that other shameful secret from her friends had been an obsession with her this last year or so.

"What?" she replied with a smile. Once again, she used the beer as a prop to buy time. It wasn't good for much else.

"You didn't think we knew?" he asked with a handsome

smile. "Manfred here saw your stepmother dropping you off at their house. No one wanted to call you out on it. We know it wasn't your fault, or choice. What's it like to spend time with Jews?"

The moment she'd been dreading had come. It was all her father's fault. Beneath the surface, she was seething at him.

"It's been a nightmare," she said, searching for an explanation that wouldn't destroy her father's image as a hero of the Reich. "But I have no other option. My stepmother forces me to go—my father doesn't even know about it. I'm so scared they'll rape me, or even kill me."

"No one's blaming you," Amalia said and put her hand on Fiona's shoulder. "But why don't you tell your father?"

"I'm afraid of them," Fiona said. Tears welled in her eyes, and she almost felt as if what she was saying were true.

Harald put his beer down on a nearby table and turned to her. "Can I speak to you alone for a moment?"

She nodded tearfully and followed him out onto the street outside the bar. The cloak of night had fallen, and they stood illuminated under a streetlamp. He was six inches taller than her. She peered up at his blond hair, which looked like spun gold in the bright light.

"I can't believe what you've been going through. No wonder you think they should keep their money." She tried to answer, but he put a finger up. "It's not your fault. It's the influence those Jews have on you. My father's been talking about them my entire life. It's in their eyes—they hypnotize you with them. I'm not angry at you. You're to be pitied."

He put his massive arms around her in a soothing hug. As he pulled back, he hesitated to look into her eyes, and then his lips met hers. The touch of them against hers obliterated every other thought in her head. It was more wonderful than she ever could have imagined. She could have been anywhere in the world. Her head was spinning as he drew away from her.

"Do you really want to marry me, Fiona?"

"Oh..."

He laughed and stroked her face. "Then come with me."

"Now? Where?" With her heart beating like a hummingbird's wing, she imagined a church, a willing priest...

"Let's go back inside and see the others. Everyone's going to want to come along."

It was hard to know how to react. She'd just gotten her breath back from her first kiss, and now he was ready to marry her!

The boys had already finished their drinks. The girls were less keen on the beer, but had soldiered through half their glasses. Harald whispered to the girls and they oohed and clapped, beaming at Fiona where she hung in the background.

"Oh, Fiona, we're so happy for you!"

"Let's get out of here." Harald laughed, and he led them out onto the street.

"Where are we going?" Fiona asked.

"Just wait and see." Harald stuck out an arm and flagged down a taxi big enough to take all of them, and they piled into the back. "Close your eyes, Fiona," he said.

"I can't, I'm too excited."

"I have an idea," Inge said. She took the tie from her neck and put it around Fiona's eyes. The world went black. Her friends giggled as she felt Harald taking her hand. He urged patience and told her how much she'd enjoy their destination.

Fifteen minutes of driving later, the car stopped.

"Not yet. Keep the blindfold on her until we get out," Harald said with a chuckle.

Someone took her hand and helped her out of the cab. Not being able to see seemed to heighten her other senses, and she felt the encroaching cold of the night air and smelled freshly cut leaves.

Several of her friends had their hands on her now and positioned her in a deliberate spot. "Are you ready?" Harald said.

"Take off the blindfold!" she replied, her heart racing with joy.

Someone undid the tie and pulled it off her head. Her heart dropped to the cold ground as she saw they were on the pavement outside the Bernheim's house.

"What?"

"Don't worry. They're never going to hurt you again," Harald said.

Georg appeared with a bag containing several bricks from a house under construction a few doors down. Harald clapped him on the back and took one in his hand.

"Well done, Georg! You don't mind if I go first? Or would you like the honor?" he asked Fiona.

"Do what first?" Fiona felt her body stiffen.

Her friends laughed. "You'd better show her," Inge said.

The lights were on in the house. Curtains twitched, but no one appeared.

Manfred had a can of red paint, also from the building site, and he pried off the top with a screwdriver.

"Let's do this," Georg said with a brick in his hand. "You ready?"

Inge and Amalia stood with smiles on their faces.

"You want to watch?" Harald asked through heavy breaths. "This is about taking our country back."

Before Fiona could answer, he ran through the front gate with the other two boys behind him. He pitched the brick at the living room window, which splintered into a thousand pieces. The girls cheered them on as Georg threw his brick at the other front window, and Manfred tossed the paint onto the door in garish gashes. It looked like someone had been murdered there.

Harald's eyes were burning bright. He reached into the bag and handed Fiona a brick. "One window left—your turn."

Fiona took it. "We should get out of here."

"We will. Just time for one more. We have to show the Jews whose country this is."

"Do it," Amalia said. "Be quick!"

"We have to leave. What if they come out?"

"Jews are cowards," Georg said.

"We did this for you," Harald said. "Don't let us down."

The brick seemed to weigh a ton in her hand. She looked at each of her friends, who were nodding, urging her on.

"We set this all up for you. This is your chance to get revenge on the Jews who tried to sicken your mind and indoctrinate you," Harald said.

Her feet seemed to make the decision for her. Before she knew it, they were carrying her toward the front of the house.

One window remained intact. It was now or never, with her friends waiting. She kept the words of the Führer in her heart and tossed the brick. The glass shattered. Adrenaline rushed through Fiona's veins as she ran back.

Harald put his arm around her. The upstairs curtains trembled, and she knew Herr Bernheim was looking, but he didn't call out. No police would respond to his call, not for something as trivial as Jews getting their windows smashed. Yet the thought of him watching drove her to run. They all ran. She only stopped to look back when they were 100 yards down the street. Her future husband burst out in triumphant laughter and seized her in his arms. The other boys hugged each other as her two best friends jumped up and down.

"Imagine if the members of the troop could see us now!" Amalia said between heavy breaths.

Harald took her aside, his eyes alive with joy and excitement. He put his hands on her shoulders and spoke. "I'm so proud of you. I saw you wavering, but you did it. The Führer would be proud of you too." He kissed her again, and the magic from earlier came flooding back.

She was proud of what they achieved that night—taking a stand against the Jews. A certain part of her felt a tinge of shame, but mostly she was liberated and excited. She'd proved herself, and Harald would be hers!

9

Monday, October 9

The sun was rising above the city as Seamus pulled up to the factory just after seven. The workers would begin arriving in the next hour, but he liked to be here first, to be alone on the factory floor and enjoy the silence. Uncle Helmut, the man who brought him over from America back in '32 with the offer of a job here, came into his mind. His promise to Helmut to look after his workers had become a mantra to him during these last few years.

Many of the Eastern European workers his uncle harbored had returned home under the pressure the Nazis exerted on them. Communists were second only to the Jews in the National Socialist pantheon of evil, and anyone from Russia was assumed to be a card-carrying Red. In truth, many of them had been Reds before Hitler rose to power, but no place remained for them in the Reich. Before '33, Berlin was the city with the most Red residents outside of Russia, but Communists and Socialists were an endangered species these days. His last

Russian worker, Andrei Salnikov, returned to Leningrad a few months before. Only the Jews remained.

The mail was already in the box, and Seamus leafed through it. A postcard from Paris lay at the bottom of the pile, and he took it, leaving the rest for his secretary to sort. He breezed past the silent machinery on the factory floor and headed straight upstairs to his office. It was as well to send a postcard, as the censors read all foreign mail anyway. He sat down and feasted his eyes on the words from Maureen in Paris.

Dear Seamus,

Paris is wonderful. This place is a constant wonder. I'm happy, and so are my friends. We think of you all the time. I can't wait to visit my favorite restaurant once more.

Love,

Aunt Reba

The code he and his daughter established was simple but enough to fool the censors, who doubtless read all his and many other people's mail. Her letter was little more than an invitation to come to see her, but he knew from the wording that it was more urgent than usual. The mention of the restaurant told him she needed to discuss something important with him. He took a sheet of paper from his desk and a fountain pen and wrote back to her. The code in his letter made it clear that he would come at the end of next week. He folded the sheet of paper and readied it to go in that day's mail.

A sound from downstairs interrupted his thoughts. The clock on the wall read seven fifteen—still early for any workers to arrive. He went to his office window expecting to see his cousin but saw his best friend and office manager, Gert Bernheim.

"Everything ok?" Seamus asked as Gert opened his office door.

"Not really," the manager replied and sat down in front of his desk.

"We're not going to need to break out the whiskey at seven in the morning, are we?"

"If I thought it might do any good, I might."

Seamus sat at his desk, suddenly aware of his manager's almost frozen expression. "Are Lil and the boys all right?"

"They're fine. We got a letter from Ben a few days ago. He's enjoying university in Bern. It's not that. No, we had an incident on Saturday night at the house."

Seamus's heart sank. It was only a matter of time, as every Jew was a target. Judith Starobin had been the worst victim of the Jews who worked here so far, but where would it end?

"We were in the living room at about nine o'clock, listening to the radio, when we heard an almighty crash from the front of the house. Some kids—Hitler Youth and League of German Girls—threw bricks through our front windows and paint all over the door."

"No one was hurt?"

"Not this time."

"Why didn't you tell me about this yesterday? I would have at least come over to help you clean up."

"I was still processing what happened." Gert's voice was sharp and cold. Seamus waited. "I wrestled with telling you this for a while. After the first couple of bricks went through, I thought it was over and went upstairs to the front of the house to survey the damage. That's when I saw someone."

"Who?"

"A young girl, in League uniform. It was dark, but I got a decent view of her."

Ice cold, Seamus knew what his friend would say before the words came out of his mouth.

"It was Fiona."

Seamus brought his hands to his face. It took him a few seconds to speak. "I'm so sorry."

He fought past the instinct to deny it was her and pepper his friend with a dozen questions, because the news didn't surprise him. The only shock was that she'd betray her family's friends like that.

"I didn't have the courage to tell Lil and Joel. They think of her like family."

The words were like daggers in Seamus's heart. It was all his fault for bringing his family to Germany. Hitler's entire system was designed to ensnare children like Fiona. She wasn't equipped to stand up to it.

"I think we might need a drink after all," he said with an empty laugh.

"It's a little early for me."

"Who else was with her?"

"I didn't know them. Four or five others."

"I bet I could name them. I'd go to their parents, but they'd probably reward their kids for doing it. I will deal with Fiona, although, God knows, she barely listens to me... I'll go to her school."

"Her teachers won't listen if they know I'm a Jew."

"They're teachers, for crying out loud. They can't condone lawlessness."

"But they will."

He sank his head in his hands again. "What am I going to do?"

"Whatever you want, Seamus. You can just leave—unlike the rest of us. You have more than enough money now. You need never be poor again."

Seamus got up and walked to the window overlooking the factory floor. Didn't Gert realize how he'd been protecting the

Jewish workers here? His manager sounded dismissive, as if he didn't need him.

"Look, I'll deal with Fiona. Lisa and I need to sit down and work out what to do with her. This has gone far enough. Gert, I'm sorry."

"You're not the only one."

Seamus waited until his friend was gone to vent his frustration on the files on his desk, which tumbled to the ground with a *thud*. He balled his fingers into a fist, holding in a scream. A few deep breaths contained his rage, and he loosened his tie and went to the window again. He picked up his diary from the floor on the way and leafed to today's page.

He had an unmissable meeting at eight thirty with Horst Ressler, the head of Ressler Mining Corporation. Fiona would have to wait. "A stay of execution," he said aloud and threw the book down on his desk.

An hour later, the factory was in full swing, and the supplier he was meeting with was sitting in his office. It was difficult to maintain concentration, and he was glad Helga was there to fill in the gaps. It was also fortunate that Ressler was kind enough to at least pretend to listen to what Helga had to say. Many suppliers didn't let women in the room during meetings other than to serve coffee.

The time dragged on. Seamus's thoughts were with his daughter. He replayed the scene Bernheim had described to him in his mind over and over but still couldn't find an antidote to the poison in Fiona.

The meeting ended just before ten thirty. Seamus and Helga walked Ressler through the factory. He stopped to admire the machines for a few moments before stepping out into the parking lot. He shook the old miner's hand as Ressler made Seamus promise to meet later that night in Horcher's for dinner.

"I wouldn't miss it," he replied with all the enthusiasm he

could muster. He knew what kind of an evening the old man really wanted to indulge in and would take care to depart before the ladies of the night made their inevitable appearance.

The car was gone when Helga asked, "What's wrong? You seemed upset in there."

"It's Fiona. She's…having some problems."

"Anything I can help with? You know how fond of her I am. Maybe she'd like to come and stay with me a few days, if you're not getting on."

Seamus shook his head. "No, thank you. It's something I have to deal with. Now. I'll be back in a couple of hours."

Helga nodded and marched back inside, no doubt to sit below the signed portrait of Hitler she'd paid half the average worker's monthly salary for a few weeks before.

Seamus was sitting in the principal's office in Fiona's school 20 minutes later. The secretary showed him in while he waited for her to fetch the principal.

The desk was a mess of papers and sat in front of a window, outside which several classes of boys were engaged in their daily dose of physical education. Two hours a day were dedicated to fitness. Hundreds of boys in white sports shirts were lined up, performing synchronized star jumps while several teachers prowled around them with whistles at the ready.

Hitler stared down from the wall behind the principal's desk. His eyes seemed to be fixed on Seamus's face.

Principal Albrecht walked in with a Nazi Party membership badge on his lapel. He was a portly man with thinning hair, probably in his 50s. All teachers were required to be members of the Nazi Teacher's Association and were vetted for racial and ideological suitability. Only the most loyal were allowed to share their ideas with the youth of the Reich. Seamus wondered how Albrecht accepted the changes to his profession so readily. Maybe he was genuinely devoted. Even so, he was a school principal and could hardly agree with a student damaging property.

The two men shook hands. "Thank you for coming in, Herr Ritter."

"Thank you for seeing me on such short notice."

"Anything for one of the Führer's most important industrialists. What can I do for you, sir?" The principal leaned forward and clasped his hands together.

"I wanted to speak to my daughter, with you to back up my words."

The teacher looked startled. He went to the door, spoke to his secretary, and returned. "Nothing serious, I hope, Herr Ritter?"

"I think it so. We need to agree on a punishment for her." Seamus took a deep breath. "There was an incident on Saturday night. It was brought to my attention that Fiona and some of her friends—I don't know exactly who, so I won't venture to guess their names—vandalized a house. They threw bricks through the windows and caused hundreds of Reichsmarks of damage."

"Fiona? You're sure?" Albrecht said. "I'm surprised to hear that. She's one of our best students, known for both her dedication to her studies and the Führer himself. Let's see what she has to say."

Fiona's face dropped as she walked in five minutes later. She took a seat beside her father without speaking.

"Your father came in this morning with some shocking accusations."

She didn't speak, seemingly waiting for him to continue.

"Where were you on Saturday night?"

"With my friends."

"Did you throw bricks through Herr Bernheim's windows?" Seamus demanded.

"No."

Seamus's knuckles were white. "You're denying it?"

"I don't know what you're talking about."

"Bernheim, you say?" the principal said. "Is that a Jewish name?"

Hitler's eyes were on him. He knew he had to choose his words carefully here. "Herr Albrecht, whatever the name, a 15-year-old girl shouldn't be allowed to run around like a hooligan. I want you to give her a month of detention and forbid her from attending the school meetings of the League of German Girls."

Albrecht sat back in his seat. The boys outside were singing as they ran around the yard. They sounded like a battalion in the Wehrmacht.

"Jews make up lies all the time to get loyal young Aryans like Fiona in trouble. The girl denies any knowledge of what happened. It seems like it's the word of a Jew against that of your daughter. And the fact that the incident, if it occurred at all, happened on a weekend, means that it has little to do with the school."

"Herr Albrecht..." This wasn't what he expected upon coming here at all.

"Fiona is a thoroughly sensible young woman. She excels at her cooking and homemaking classes. She's a credit to her teachers and will soon be a fine wife and mother. You should be proud."

His daughter looked content.

He fought back his rage and grief. "Herr Bernheim saw you with a brick in your hand."

"I'm sorry that happened to him, but it wasn't me," she said with a grin at her principal, who smiled back at her.

"It doesn't seem there's much more to be said. I think young Fiona should return to class now."

"I'll see you later, Fiona," Seamus said. "We'll deal with this then."

She shrugged, stood up, and left.

Albrecht held out his hand, but Seamus didn't shake it.

Intense frustration ate at him like corrosive acid as he drove back to the factory. What use were money, cars, and mansions if his daughter was one of the screaming masses at Hitler's rallies?

He called Lisa from his desk, but she wasn't home. He slammed the receiver down and cursed out loud. Whiskey seemed the only refuge, so he went to the liquor cabinet. He was rolling the bitter liquid around in his glass when Lisa called back.

She wasn't in the least surprised at Principal Albrecht's attitude. "Attacking Jews is a part of Nazi philosophy now. The only reason he didn't praise her in front of you is because he knew how angry you were."

"I notice you aren't surprised about her behavior either."

"Seamus..."

He sighed. "What are we going to do about her?"

"Short of sending her out of the country, I really don't know."

"Once she hits 18, we won't be able to force her to leave...."

"Then send her to boarding school."

"Supposing she tells our friends in the Gestapo about certain past events?"

Lisa hesitated, but then said, "No. Seamus, she's a good girl. I can't see her doing that."

Their curt language was necessary when they didn't know who might be listening in.

Seamus said goodbye, put the phone down and poured himself another whiskey. Paris? No, Switzerland—the German part, where Fiona would know the language. Although maybe Paris first...just to see the others, quickly and quietly. Maybe Maureen could even talk some sense into her sister.

Yes, he'd take the entire family to Paris. Maureen needed to see him anyway.

With one small problem taken care of in his mind, he went to the window overlooking the factory floor. He spent a few minutes observing his employees when a flash of inspiration hit him. *Why didn't I think of this sooner?*

He rushed to Bernheim's office.

"Gert, I have an idea. I promised my uncle before he died that I'd take care of his workers. That was the most important thing to him, more than expansion or wealth. He never could have foretold how this country would change under Hitler and the Nazis, but my promise to him still stands. We have to do something different, to fight back."

His factory manager looked up at him, gray with tiredness. "What is it?"

"I was thinking that if the Jewish workers have any savings the government doesn't know about, I could smuggle the money out for them."

Gert looked at him in astonishment. "You're a good man, my friend, but do you expect the workers to trust you with any meager savings they might have?"

Seamus felt a rush of frustration. "Do you really think this is some elaborate scheme I've concocted to steal your money? To take advantage of the horrors the Nazis are inflicting on our people every day? I don't need your money!"

"I know you don't, Seamus."

"Look." He felt his friend was almost mocking him. "What if

each person sells everything they own. I collect the money and deposit it, either in cash or the equivalent in diamonds or gold, in a Swiss bank. I'll keep track of your deposits. That way we can avoid the ridiculous taxes they charge Jews to emigrate. Meanwhile, I'll figure out how to procure visas—most likely to Palestine, but perhaps France, or even America. I can't give you any specifics right now."

"The workers can't just turn our lives upside down based on your vague plans," Bernheim said in a calm voice. "They have families. Many have never left Berlin before. It's almost impossible to get visas for anywhere."

"Call a meeting with the Jewish employees," Seamus said. "I'll put my idea to them and we'll let them decide. Five o'clock, in my office."

"As you wish," his office manager said.

Seamus didn't voice his frustration at his friend's tone and left the office without another word.

Five o'clock came. Seamus said goodbye to Benz and the other Nazi workers. None of them seemed to know about the meeting he'd called with the Jews. Why would they when the two groups never interacted?

Bernheim and the 23 other Jewish workers, all of whom had been working for the company since before the Nazis ascended to power, piled into Seamus's office. Helga was at the other factory—marveling at the airplanes, no doubt—and all the other workers were gone.

The room was long enough that they could lay out three rows of folding chairs. Bernheim stood at the front with Seamus.

"What are we doing here?" Pamela Bernstein asked. She was the youngest person in the room at age 27.

"Thank you, Pamela, and to everyone for coming. Certain things have happened recently that gave me pause. It doesn't seem that anyone Jewish is safe in Germany anymore. My wife visited Judith Starobin recently. It's hard to believe what happened to her and her husband. It doesn't bear thinking about, but it's the reality for all Jews today."

"We have no one to turn to," said Leonard Greenberg, a man who'd been working in the factory since 1912. "We get assaulted on the street and the police laugh it off. We fight back and we're the ones who end up in jail."

"Or get sent to a KZ, like my brother," Pamela said.

"The situation is going to get worse before it gets better," Seamus said. "Many of us were hoping that the German people would wake up and oust the Nazis before they could do more damage, but that seems like a forlorn prospect. Hitler is more popular than ever."

"If we rose up, they'd slaughter us in the streets," Gert said. "It would make the pogroms we heard about in our youth seem like playtime."

A harsh silence fell on the room. Seamus knew he had to be the one to break it.

"Like many of you I've spoken to, I thought that Hitler getting more of what he wanted would detract from his obsession with the Jews, but that hasn't been the case. Herr Bernheim is the latest victim of violence that I know almost all of you have suffered."

A few of the workers asked Bernheim what happened. He played it down and didn't mention Fiona.

"No one was hurt this time, but what happens when they come again? Maybe with their big brothers in the SA? Where does all this hatred end?" Seamus asked.

"We know all this," Leonard said. "We live with it every day. With all due respect, Herr Ritter, you do not."

"You're right. My wife is half-Jewish, as you know, but in the Nazis' perverted view, she's somewhat acceptable. Somewhat." He looked around at the desperate faces in the room. "I know many of you have thought about leaving Germany."

"How can we when the Nazis tax us at 81 percent when we leave?" Pamela asked. "We can't go to another country to be destitute."

"I think I have a way around that."

A murmur circled the room.

"How do you plan to circumvent the authorities?" Leonard asked.

"How much does the Gestapo know about your lives?" Seamus asked. "What holes can we exploit?"

"What's your plan?" Pamela asked.

Seamus surveyed the faces waiting for him to speak. "How many of you would leave Germany tomorrow if no restrictions existed?" Almost every hand went up. One man at the back, a 15-year veteran of the metal polishing section, kept his arm by his side.

"Julius, why wouldn't you leave?"

"My mother is ill. I don't know how long she has left."

"What about your own wife and children? Have you considered leaving on their behalf?"

"Perhaps after my mother passes," he answered. "Is this plan you speak of happening soon?"

"I don't see how it can," Seamus said. "According to the Reich Flight Tax, anyone with assets of 50,000 Reichsmarks or more is subject to pay more than 80 percent to the government upon emigrating."

"Not all of your workers have assets that total that much."

Seamus asked for a show of hands. Less than half of the people in the room had enough assets if they sold all their possessions to be subject to the tax.

"So, the people who can afford to move will have their assets stolen by the Nazis, and those who don't qualify for the tax can't afford to emigrate," Seamus said, pushing out a breath. "I suggest everyone in this room starts the process of leaving

Germany. Sell your houses, old heirlooms, your wife's favorite diamond earrings, even your cars."

"And what do we do with the money? The banks will report the lodgments to the Gestapo, and they'll take their cut."

"Not if we don't use banks."

"And where do you suggest we hide our money? Under our mattresses?" Gert asked.

Several people in the crowd threw their hands up in disgust.

"No," Seamus said. "You give it to me."

People in the crowd were laughing now. "You're a good man, Herr Ritter, but do you expect us to trust you with our life savings?" Leonard asked.

Gert stepped forward. "Do you really think this is some elaborate scheme Herr Ritter has concocted to steal your money? To take advantage of the horrors the Nazis are inflicting on our people every day?"

Leonard paused to stare back at the factory manager and then shook his head.

"Before he died, I promised my uncle I'd take care of his workers."

"How would this system of yours work?" Pamela asked.

"Each person in this room commits to leaving Germany and sells everything they own. I collect the money and deposit it, either in cash or the equivalent in diamonds or gold, in a Swiss bank. I'll entrust Herr Bernheim to keep track of your deposits. Heaven knows if I kept the accounts, they'd have more holes in them than a pound of Swiss cheese. I think I can procure visas —most likely to Palestine, or even America. I don't have the specifics yet."

"A few of us have applied for US visas already. It's close to impossible. The Americans have their quota system and you could drown in the red tape. Palestine and the other countries aren't much better. We can't just turn our lives upside down based on your vague plans," Leonard said. "We have families."

"And who's going to take care of them if the Gestapo ships you off to a concentration camp?" Seamus asked. "Hitler's vitriol toward the Jews isn't just talk. We know that now. People are dying every day—people like Judith's husband. Who thinks that the Führer's plans stop here? I don't know what the future holds, but there's no law to protect any of you in Germany anymore. You're at the mercy of the Gestapo and the individual whims of the agents. Who's to say you won't all be in concentration camps soon?"

The two dozen people sitting in front of him seemed struck dumb. Gert shifted and sat back on the desk behind him.

"What about those of us who can't afford to leave?" Pamela asked. "You've discussed a way for half the people in this room to leave. What about the rest of us?"

"I suggest we pool our money. No one gets left behind, not because they can't afford it. I'll help out too. No one will be left short when they need money to emigrate, but those who don't have their own houses or cars to sell will find they do have the funds to emigrate."

Someone asked Bernheim if he knew about this in advance. The factory manager shook his head. "I only heard about this earlier today."

"If we move ahead, and I sincerely hope you all agree, we need to be unified in our mission. The money you give to me or Herr Bernheim will be there when you need it. You have my word of honor on that. But we tell no one. We cannot afford the slightest chance the Gestapo hears about this, because if we do, our next meeting will be in a concentration camp."

"Why are you doing this?" Pamela asked.

"Because I promised I would."

"Your uncle is dead," Gert said.

"Who said he was the only one I promised?"

"How are you going to get all that money to Switzerland?" Bernheim asked. "It's illegal."

"Leave that to me. You don't have to decide now—we'll reconvene. Think about what I said. It's the only way everyone gets out clean. There is a world where Stormtroopers don't rule the streets and you won't have to fear for your children's lives every time they leave the house. It's just a matter of reaching it."

The meeting ended, and the people in his office stood up and shuffled toward the door. Most seemed deep in thought. Almost all thanked him.

Fiona was in her room. She had rushed in and up the stairs without speaking to Lisa, but she was clearly upset about her father coming to the school. Lisa wasn't surprised that his intervention didn't temper her enthusiasm for the Nazis. She remembered being a girl her age and how the opinions of her peers meant everything. It seemed sending her away to boarding school in Switzerland or England was a more prudent option, but Seamus couldn't bear the thought of losing her. Perhaps it was time to choose the lesser of two evils.

Lisa knocked on her stepdaughter's door.

"What is it?"

"I just wanted to ask how school was."

"Worst day ever."

"Do you want to talk about it?"

"No! I don't want to see you or talk to you."

"Fiona, you don't mean that. We're family...."

"We're not family! You're not my mother. The Reich is my family. I'm going to marry Harald and have babies for the Führer and then I'll be rid of the lot of you."

Lisa, feeling sick, turned around and walked back downstairs.

Fiona was still in her room when Seamus arrived home two hours later. Needing some fresh air, Lisa motioned for him to follow her. They stood on the empty street outside the house.

"Fiona's upstairs, but she's in a foul mood and said she had the worst day ever in school. That's a quote."

"I knew what I was coming home to."

"She talked about a boy called Harald. She says she wants to marry him and have babies for Hitler."

"She's not even 16!" Seamus huffed and puffed for a few seconds until the sight of one of their neighbors forced him to bury his emotions.

"Hello, Frau Winder," Seamus said.

The old woman stopped. "How are the children?"

Her son was the local Blockwarte and reported directly to the Nazis about any suspicious behavior in the neighborhood.

The Nazi Party was present on every block and in every apartment house, wherever people lived in numbers. The Blockwarten were the lowest rung on the ladder of surveillance, but they were the ones in direct contact with the people. The Blockwarte were licensed snoops charged with keeping watch on their neighbors and reporting any breach in social discipline. He might note a failure to put out the swastika flag on gala occasions. He checked on how much each individual contributed to the latest Party collection, and observed if they did so willingly or reluctantly. And, of course, he was always alert to suspicious actions and careful to record any careless talk he might chance to overhear. An unfavorable report from a street warden could wreck a career or cost a life because behind their reports lurked the iron grip of the Gestapo. The Blockwarten weren't powerful people themselves —just gardeners, janitors, handymen—but they were everywhere. Collectively, they wielded formidable power.

"Why are you out on the street talking?" the old woman asked.

Lisa had seen Frau Winder's son out on the street the evening before, parading around in his uniform and throwing Hitler salutes around like confetti. Prior to being thrust into his role by the Nazis, he was an unemployed joiner with a drinking problem.

"Just out for a walk," Seamus said. "Anything to get away from the young ones for a few minutes."

"Those times are precious," she replied. "Don't waste them."

With nothing else to say, the older woman walked on.

"Nowhere's safe," Seamus said in a whisper once he was confident she couldn't hear them. "Let's get back inside."

He took her hand, waiting until they were at the front door to whisper again. "I haven't told her yet, but you are right. I'm sending her to a boarding school in Switzerland."

Lisa nodded. "Convincing her will be a herculean task. She won't want to leave her friends and this Harald boy."

"I'm not going to give her a choice."

"As hard as it will be, I think it's a good idea. You have to do something."

Seamus rubbed his hand through his hair. "I thought sending her to the Bernheim's house, showing they were human beings, would be enough."

"I'm sorry."

"I thought she'd see that they were good people, that they had dreams and goals and loved their families just like we do. I don't understand why it didn't work."

"Perhaps it isn't racial hatred driving her so much as peer pressure. What girl her age wants to be different? She's a foreigner here. All she wants is to be accepted."

"I can't lose her to the Nazis. I hardly recognize the person she's become. I think about the little girl she used to be all the time... And what about Conor? He's 13 now. He's not as outspoken or rebellious as his sister, but what's to stop him from falling down the same hole? The entire system is designed to gobble up vulnerable minds like theirs. Sometimes I feel like the boy sticking his thumb in the leaking dike. I cover one hole and another appears, and the water keeps gushing through."

"Let's speak to her together," Lisa said.

She almost made a joke about clearing the air before the secret police came for them, but even saying those words out loud would have been too much.

Hannah and Conor were in the living room playing checkers with the radio on in the background. It was on the station all transistors in Germany were automatically tuned to when sold —the one where the propagandists proclaimed the wonders of Nazism all day.

"Change that, Conor," Seamus said.

His son looked up in surprise, then did as he was told with a shrug. The sounds of Beethoven's "Fifth" swelled the air.

To Seamus, it felt like he was about to plug up another hole in the dike.

He stomped up the stairs, knowing the noise would alert Fiona. She needed to know he was coming. He rapped on her door with the knuckle of his middle finger.

No answer, just footsteps, and the door opened. She didn't speak.

"Tell me the truth. Did you toss that brick through our friend's window?"

"No, of course not." Her voice was dripping with indignation. It was as if she were the one being wronged for being falsely accused. "And anyway, he's not my friend."

He didn't push his way into her room, though the instinct to do so was hard to resist.

"Why would he come to me and tell me he saw you?"

"Didn't you hear what my principal said? The Jews are

constantly trying to shift the blame for their wrongdoings to loyal Germans."

"You're suggesting he made it up?"

"All I can tell you is that I didn't do what he's accusing me of."

"I've known Gert Bernheim for five years. He's one of the most decent men I've ever met. How could you betray him like that? His family took you into their home. You know them!"

Her eyes didn't waver. If anything, they became more defiant. "I have no idea who smashed his windows, but perhaps he brought it on himself."

"You're going to beg Herr and Frau Bernheim's forgiveness."

"Beg a Jew for forgiveness? I'd be thrown out of the League!"

"I don't care. I see you standing in front of me, Fiona, but I don't recognize you anymore. What happened to the smart, fun, caring little girl I used to know?"

"I'm still all those things, Father. You're just too blind to see what's happening in the world today. If people like me and my sisters in the League don't stand up for the Aryan race, our whole way of life will be lost. Can't you see that?"

Seamus stood in stunned silence for a few seconds. Memories of Fiona as a little girl flashed in front of his eyes.

"I'm so sorry," he whispered. It was difficult to hold back the tears, but he couldn't cry in front of her.

"Pull yourself together. Nature abhors a weakling."

He ignored her and continued. "I'm sorry for what they've done to you. This place has twisted your soul."

She shook her head. "There's nowhere I'd rather be than in the Reich. I've found myself here."

He tried one more time. "No meetings, no rallies, until you go back to the Bernheim's to admit what you did."

"What? You'd believe their lies over my word? It's just what my troop leaders said would happen. I'll tell them as well and I'll complain to the Blockwarte."

Her stare burned into him, but in a strange way, he saw her mother's eyes at that moment. What would Marie think about what her daughter was becoming? What would she do?

"I need you to think before you act. All your friends are Hitler Youth, but that doesn't mean you have to deny the voices in your heart telling you right from wrong. You're almost a woman, Fiona. I'm not going to be around to tell you what to do forever. Soon you'll be making decisions for yourself. You're the master of your life, not some political leader, no matter who they proclaim to be. I'll always be your father. Lisa and I are here for you, along with the rest of the family. We might not agree about everything, but I hope you'll realize that governments and leaders, no matter how great they seem at the time, come and go. Family is constant."

"The League of German Girls and the Hitler Youth are my family. My family is the Reich. I'm going to marry Harald and have babies for the Führer!"

"Over my dead body!" he snapped.

He turned and walked downstairs to where Lisa was waiting.

The other children were white-faced. He doubted they'd ever heard shouting like that in the house before. When he appeared in the living room, they ran upstairs to their bedrooms.

He poured himself a drink. "She won't admit a thing," he said to Lisa. "And it's all my fault. She's been searching for something ever since her mother died, and I suppose she's finally found it."

"It's not too late for her."

"I hope you're right." He wrapped his arms around his wife and kissed her. "I have to go out for dinner in Horcher's until about ten. We'll talk again when I get back."

His voice was weak. He felt defeated by the regime. No one could escape the clutches of the National Socialists. The idea that he could skate through life in Nazi Germany with children and come out unscathed was patently ridiculous, yet he'd somehow believed as much.

"She's not lost yet," Lisa whispered as he left. "But you're right to send her away."

He closed the door and trudged to the car, praying Lisa was right. Nothing he'd gained these last five years was worth losing his daughter's soul.

10

Monday, October 18

Lisa waited until the end of the meeting to ask the question. The once-weekly gathering of the Subversives was now twice a month, but the themes and format were still the same. Maureen's sudden departure after the Olympics created an opening at the table, which Lisa, at her stepdaughter's suggestion, was happy to fill. But without Maureen to spur them to action, the group had reverted to what it was before she joined—a talking shop.

Seamus joked that it was like the League of Nations in Herman's apartment. Still, it was comforting to know others thought the same way they did, and even better to have a free space to discuss ideas that would get one arrested on the street outside. The meetings always started with 20 minutes or so of general conversation, followed by sharp complaining about the Nazis and their effect on society. The faces were the same as when she first came to this apartment the year before. No one had left, though they often threatened to.

Lisa sat in her usual spot beside Thomas. Herman, who

owned the apartment they were sitting in, began by drawing attention to his new suit.

"I bought this last week. It's so ugly—made of Hitler fabric." The term was a reference to fake cloth made of fibers from trees. The Führer had announced plans to make the country independent of foreign imports. Elastic, margarine, gasoline, motor oil, rubber, and cloth were all now made from alternative materials found in Germany. The problem was the same with substitutes everywhere: They simply weren't very good, and people sometimes referred to them disparagingly as "Hitler" goods. But no one ever said anything like that in public. The Gestapo would come knocking for far less.

Herr Schultz said with sarcasm, "Those new fabrics are great. If you have a tear in your suit, water it and expose it to sunlight and the cloth will grow back."

Many things in the city were rationed now—in peacetime! It was as if Hitler were preparing the nation for the worst.

"It's been months since I've had a decent cup of coffee," Gilda Stein said.

Lisa agreed. Decent coffee beans were like gold dust these days.

Leon Gellert, a Jewish composer who'd been unable to work since the Nazis rose to power back in '33, began the more pointed political conversation by speaking about Austria's situation and how Hitler was determined to ingest every country surrounding the Reich.

"It's inevitable. Their technique of sending agents in, using them to organize sympathetic citizens, then agitating them against the sitting government is working wonders. When the government fights back, the agitators complain of being suppressed, and then they can call upon the almighty Führer in Berlin to swoop down and save them. He reluctantly agrees to rescue them from the oppression of the legal authorities who, of course, are just trying to contain the civil unrest the Nazis have stirred up."

Thomas nodded morosely. "Hitler's no fool. It's going to work in Austria, and then probably in the Sudetenland in Czechoslovakia."

"All under the guise of 'liberating' German peoples of Europe," Herman said.

The Tommy Dorsey record on the gramophone skipped. Like most of the albums Herman owned, it was banned by the Nazis. But it was an old one. Getting them into the country was more difficult than ever. It didn't seem worth risking a trip to a concentration camp to smuggle in a new jazz record anymore. Perhaps that same exhaustion of raging against the Nazi boa constrictor that had swallowed Germany whole had worn the Subversives down. They spoke in resigned tones about the Nazis now. The fire in their bellies, while not entirely extinguished, was a smoldering ember of what it once was.

Her glass of wine was empty, and it was almost time to leave. Lisa cleared her throat to speak.

"Is there any possibility Hitler could be deposed? Do you think the generals in the Wehrmacht or the Luftwaffe or the Kriegsmarine would rise up and do the right thing for Germany?"

"That's a difficult question to answer," Herman said. "You're asking us to judge the political will of men we don't know."

"Hypothetically," Lisa said.

Gilda sighed. "Anything's possible, but Hitler's a cunning swine. He had every member of the military swear an oath of allegiance to him. Whoever undertook this uprising would have to break it to do so."

"It seems like the only realistic hope Germany has," Lisa said.

"It's a remote one." Herman said. "Even if one of the generals were brave enough to risk speaking to his peers about organizing such an event, he'd have to get several of them to agree on a consensus. And if the uprising didn't work, the retribution would be brutal. If you corner a snake, you need to kill it."

"These are crusty old men you're referring to, most of them of Prussian stock. No one's more conservative. Revolution is the last thing on their minds," Gilda said.

"Perhaps their love for their country might trump those instincts. They know better than anyone that Hitler is leading us down the road to a war we can't possibly win."

"Says who?" Herman asked. "The Allies aren't exactly lining up to defeat him."

"And then there's the question of the soldiers themselves. Are they loyal to their generals, or to Hitler?" Gilda pounded the table in frustration. "This entire country is set up to worship at his feet. It stands to reason that most of the troops would question any orders to move against him."

"I refuse to believe that a core of the military doesn't have the best interests of the Reich at heart," Lisa said. "They are meant to protect it."

No one answered. It didn't seem like there was anything else to say.

Herman called an end to the meeting, and each person rose, shook hands, and said their goodbyes. With the Gestapo's eyes everywhere, it wasn't safe to exit the building as a group anymore, so they left one by one. Lisa crossed the room to Leon and caught his arm, motioning for Gilda to join them.

"Do you think it might be time to leave the country?"

"You trying to get rid of me?" he asked with a wry grin.

"I know how that must have sounded, but with everything going on...."

"It's something I think about every day," Gilda said.

"Come to the house this week. My husband might have a

way around the barriers the Nazis have erected to taking money out of the country."

"To emigrating?" Gilda asked.

Lisa nodded and reminded them of their address. Her Jewish friends agreed and promised to call.

She turned to Thomas as she waited for her turn to leave.

"Have you heard from Maureen lately?" he asked in a gentle tone.

Thomas and Maureen had been so sure their love could surmount any obstacle, but their enforced separation proved them wrong. His mother was still too ill for him to leave Germany, and Maureen was a fugitive, hiding from the law.

"We hope to see her soon."

"Please tell her I wish her well." His sad smile and words had the air of a last goodbye.

"It's heartbreaking what happened to you two. I'm so sorry."

"Thank you, but I don't suppose there's anything to be done."

The young man peered out the window. Lisa didn't say it was time to move on. He already knew.

When her turn came, she kissed Herman goodbye and walked down the stairs alone. She kept her head down as she exited the building through the basement door at the back and hurried to the adjacent street. The U-Bahn station was only a few minutes away. She stood alone once she got there, even though several of her fellow Subversives were on the platform waiting for the same train. Each got on in silence and stood apart from the rest.

Lisa arrived home at nine o'clock. She left the house key on the rack by the door and called out that she was home. Seamus appeared around the corner of the foyer with a strange look.

"What's going on?"

"There's someone here to see you."

Lisa didn't ask who; she just followed her husband through the house to the dining room, where Petra Wagner was sitting. She looked up with a humble smile.

"I'll leave you to talk...." Seamus walked away. "...and I'll make coffee."

Lisa felt rage rising within her. "What are you doing here?"

"I'm sorry to disturb you. I should have called—I wanted to apologize."

"What took you so long?"

The actress paused, flustered, as if searching for answers. "I've had a lot of work. I'm in a play on—"

"I'm not interested in the latest Nazi tripe you're spewing."

Petra nodded and sat back. "I get that. I'm here to try to make amends for what I did to you."

"I thought I could trust you before, but I made one of the biggest mistakes of my life. Why should I now?"

"I denounced you to the Gestapo." Her voice broke, but Lisa wasn't buying it. "I'm not here to manipulate you or act, just to beg your forgiveness."

"What brought me into your mind? Did someone denounce you for their personal gain?"

"I wanted to offer my sincere apology for what I did." Petra stared through dewy eyes, her voice leaden and dull as she spoke.

Lisa's jawline hardened. "Well, you apologized. Congratulations, you cleared your conscience. You can get out of my house now, and back to whatever claptrap you're working on."

Petra didn't move. "What I did to you was unforgivable."

"Yet you want me to forgive you?"

"The life I gained through betraying you is a fitting reward for my actions."

"The glamourous lifestyle of the sweetheart of the Reich?"

"I've woken up hungover in Joseph Goebbels' bed more times than I care to mention. That horrific little troll has the whole stage and cinema world at his mercy. I just took it as something I had to endure. Every young actress has to come to his apartment on Rankestrasse and submit to whatever indignities he cares to inflict. That's the price I had to pay."

"Along with destroying my career and my dreams. If you're looking for pity, you've come to the wrong house."

"I just want to explain why I denounced you."

"Why? You think I'm an idiot? Seems to me your plan worked to perfection."

"I see your face every time I sit in front of the mirror. I'm so sorry for what I did to you. My life is a misery. I feel so empty."

"And my forgiveness is what you need to make you whole again?"

Lisa's feelings were hardening even more. She wanted to punish this woman here and now for what she'd done.

"I don't know. All I can tell you is I had an uncontrollable urge to come and apologize to you when I woke up this morning. I understand if you can't accept it. All I can do is offer."

Lisa wasn't convinced of her sincerity. She thought she was acting.

"I have no reason to show up here other than to make things better. Why would I come otherwise?"

Seamus returned with two mugs of what was supposed to be coffee and placed them on the table before leaving again.

Lisa drank, and her face contorted at the taste. "This is disgusting. Your Nazi friends have even destroyed my daily coffee. Can you sleep with someone to fix that?"

"I want to help you. You hate the Nazis. I thought you might know some way to fight back."

Lisa ignored the remark. "You must have known how I'd receive you, or did you think I'd fall at your feet, incredulous that Petra Wagner, the 'great movie star,' would lower herself to visit my home?"

"You know I didn't think that. I want to apologize again, and reiterate how serious I am about helping you."

"How do I know you're not here to trick me into saying something about our beloved Führer, and then go straight to Gestapo headquarters on Prinz-Albrecht-Strasse?"

Petra reached across and took Lisa's hands. "Please believe me—I'm sick to death of those vile toads. I can't believe I ever let Goebbels touch me. I'm resigning from my next film if you don't let me help you."

Lisa peered into her former friend's blue eyes. It was so hard to tell with actors. All emotions could be simulated, but someone like her could be vital to Maureen's plans. Perhaps there was a principled human being lurking behind the stunning façade.

"The question of trust still remains."

Petra reached into her bag. "I brought something to prove myself." She pushed a piece of paper across the table with the Nazi eagle emblazoned at the top.

Lisa took the paper, marked Top Secret. It was a letter to the head of the Austrian Resistance, a man named Ernst Rolfing, detailing the funds being sent to fund his band of political agitators in Vienna. A paragraph at the bottom praised him for his work done to date and promised that the day of liberation was almost at hand. It was signed by Heinrich Himmler.

"Where did you get this?"

"From Goebbels' desk."

"You could be shot for—"

"You think I don't know that? I had to prove I was serious, didn't I? It's been a week since I took it, and nothing's happened. There were several copies. He won't miss it."

"What do you expect me to do with this?"

"Whatever you want. Bring it to Clayton—it'd be a big story.

The proof that the Nazis are deliberately stirring up political agitation in Austria is right there on that sheet."

"His editor would never publish this."

"Another journalist, then."

Lisa placed the piece of paper on the table, undecided on whether to destroy it or not. It was probably a trick.

"Why would you risk everything for the chance to redeem yourself to me, someone you'd never otherwise see again? You have stardom, money... Everything you've ever wanted."

"But at what price? Being up close with Hitler and his minions has shown me who they truly are, and they're ugly people, driven by hatred. It breaks my heart to know they wield so much power."

"And now you want to use your position to fight back?"

"I'll do anything I can, and it's not just about you. It's about the German people. I get hundreds of letters every week, from all over the country. Cobblers in Essen, housewives in Mainz, and hairdressers in Bonn. They all tell me that through my movies, I cemented their love for the Führer and his ideals. Thinking about what I've done makes me sick to my stomach. And then I read about hoodlums who burned down some Jewish businesses after watching one of my movies. I just want to atone for what I've done."

Lisa hesitated a few seconds, but the anger surging through her boiled to the surface. "Just leave now. The sight of you makes me sick to my stomach. Get out and take this letter with you."

"But—"

"I don't trust you, and it's probably a forgery. No one will touch it. I never want to see you again."

Petra stood up in slow motion, moving as if she was in shock.

"Get out of my house!" Lisa repeated.

"I'm sorry," Petra said through a swath of tears and ran to the door.

It took a few minutes for Lisa to calm down, and when she did, she noticed the piece of paper still on the table. There was little point in bringing it to Clayton, as Petra had suggested, and it was probably all lies anyway. But Seamus advised that they keep it and deposited it in the safe in their bedroom.

11

Friday, October 22

Maureen stood with her brother and sister-in-law as the train from Berlin steamed into Gare du Nord station in Paris. Hannah was first off, and all three smiled as the eight-year-old girl ran to them. It was strange that she looked so little like her mother. Her sparkling blue eyes were singular in the family. She embraced each of them. Conor wore a gray suit and looked like he'd become a young man while she was away. Her father and sister were off the train last. Fiona was as jovial as the rest of the family. The surly 15-year-old her father had warned her about in his curt letters, edited for the eyes of the Gestapo, was nowhere to be seen. Monika stood back to give the family time to reconnect, but Lisa dragged her into the circle, insisting without saying so that she was as much a Ritter as any of them. Maureen noticed the smile on her brother's wife's face but didn't draw attention to it.

Michael helped his father and brother with the suitcases, and Lisa took Monika's arm in hers. They walked out of the station together. Evening was falling on the city, and they arched their necks to admire the neoclassical architecture of the building they had just emerged from.

"Even the train stations are works of art here," Lisa said with a giggle.

"Where are you staying?" Michael asked.

"The Hotel d'Angleterre in Saint-Germain-des-Prés," his father replied.

"I heard it was one of Hemingway's favorites back in the 20s," Maureen said.

"Maybe we should go bullfighting or fishing afterward, then." Lisa's excitement was infectious. International travel was new to her, and she relished it.

"It was a long train ride," Seamus said. "But come back to the hotel with us. I have something for you."

Michael and Conor were dispatched to get two taxis. While they were gone, Maureen's father walked over to her. "Can I speak to you a moment?"

They were on the street. This was no place to discuss what was anything secretive, even in a free city like Paris. They stood by a newsstand, and once she was sure no one was listening, she began.

"It's Fiona." The look on his face, somewhere on the border between anger and despair, betrayed what was on his mind. "She's getting in too deep with the League of German Girls. She's changing. A couple of weeks ago, Herr Bernheim told me she and a group of other Hitler Youth threw bricks through the windows of his house."

"He's sure it was her?"

"Would you put it past her these days?"

Her father's words, hurtful as they were to contemplate, weren't without reason. "I didn't think she'd stoop to that level."

"Things have gotten worse since you were forced into exile last year. Can you talk to her? Maybe she'll listen to you. She repeatedly denies the whole incident ever happened when I ask her."

Her father spoke for another two minutes, echoing how worried he was and puzzling over what to do.

"She hasn't been to a League meeting or rally since, but I can't keep her out forever—that's what all her friends do. The Nazis have organized life for young people, and control how they see their friends."

"Which is the most important thing in the world to someone of that age," Maureen said.

Michael appeared. "We have a taxi."

"I'd like you to meet some people after dinner," Maureen said to her father. "And I have a proposition for you."

"All right. The others will be tired. I'll ask Lisa to take them home early."

"You can make it up to her tomorrow night."

"I'll have to." He walked back to where the others were.

The boys loaded the suitcases into the back of the cars, and the entire family set off south along Boulevard de Sébastopol.

The sun was still visible as they reached the hotel, though it had changed from its earlier yellow to dark orange, bathing the magnificent rooftops of Paris in amber. The taxis pulled up outside the old hotel, and the Ritter family spilled out. Just five years before, Seamus was in Ohio digging ditches while the rest were living with Aunt Maeve in Newark. Most days, Maureen reminded herself of how far they'd come. It offered perspective on the problems she faced.

"Monika, will you help the young ones get set up in their room?" Maureen's father asked when they'd checked in.

"Of course. Come on, troops," she said to the children. Fiona didn't respond as well to her faux orders as the other two and lagged a few feet behind.

Seamus led the rest to their room, and Michael shut the door once they were all inside. He laid the suitcases on the white sheets of the four-poster bed, which sat opposite a delightful stone fireplace.

"We have something for you," Lisa said.

"In the cases?" Maureen asked.

"No. They'd find anything we tried to hide in there. We're getting more creative as we grow more experienced at this international smuggling caper." Lisa went to the mirror and pushed back her hair to reveal diamond earrings.

"It's the best way to move wealth these days." She took them off and placed them on the dresser. "There's more."

Her husband opened the suitcase and took a black velvet cloth from on top of the clothes. He spread it out on the bed.

"Watch this," he said as his wife came to his side. He removed the chic black hat she was still wearing to reveal her hair tied in a thick bun. She reached up and drew out several pins holding it in place. Then she dug her fingers in and shook the bun. Diamonds began dropping like snowflakes onto the black velvet cloth. Maureen couldn't help laughing.

It took a few seconds to get them all out. Lisa said as she shook her hair, "You'll never guess who paid me a visit a couple of weeks ago."

"I'd be scared to even try," Maureen said.

"Petra Wagner, the star of German cinema."

"What on earth did she want?" Michael asked.

"Forgiveness. She wants to make up for her mistakes of the past, or so she said, at least." Lisa plucked out one last diamond.

"She could be valuable if you can turn her," Maureen said. "From what I've seen in the German social pages, she rubs shoulders with the highest of the Nazis, and the generals too."

"No way," Lisa snapped. "We can't trust her, so I sent her on her way. There's something else your father is working on."

Lisa explained a scheme Seamus had come up with to help the Jews from Ritter Metalworks avoid the taxes the Nazis imposed.

"You think it'll work?" Maureen asked.

"If they get on board," her father replied. "I don't see why not. The question will be whether they trust me enough with their life savings."

Maureen smiled. "That's a great idea. Paris is full of German Jews—I'm sure a lot of them will end up here."

"Seamus is encouraging them to go to Palestine or America. He's convinced Paris will be draped in Nazi flags soon," Lisa said.

"It's up to the rest of us to make sure that doesn't come to be," Maureen said. She stooped over the diamonds again as her father scraped them into a little pile. He folded up the velvet cloth with 20 diamonds in it.

"I have a contact in the city who can turn these into cash. He'll be in contact over the next few days. Don't worry—he's trustworthy. My man in Switzerland recommended him. He'll set up an account for you to draw from."

"We have jobs," Michael said.

"Just until you find your feet. Consider it a wedding gift. We'll buy an apartment here in the city in my name, where you can all stay. And if you decide to leave, so be it."

"Thank you," Michael said.

At the risk of sounding ungrateful, Maureen spoke up. "I'd rather use my share to rid our world of the scourge of Fascism."

"I have to look after my family above all else. Can you be a little more specific about your plans to liberate Europe?"

His flippant tone stirred anger inside her, but she hid it—for now. "I'm part of a group here in Paris working against the Nazis. We need money."

"You're still being vague." her father's frustration was evident, but she didn't care. This was about more than his feelings.

"We've been creating literature for weeks now. What we don't have is the money to buy the printing presses we need, and also to build the infrastructure to transport our writings to Germany and the rest of the world."

Seamus smiled and shook his head, infuriating her. "You think you're the first to try that? What effect have pamphlets had on the population so far?"

"The German people deserve the truth," Maureen said. Her father's attitude was embarrassing. She hadn't expected this—not at all. "All they read and hear are lies. Every day. Lies to service the Nazi regime that subjugates them. If they knew the truth...."

"And how do you plan to get this banned literature into the Reich?" he asked.

"It's also for Paris and London and Vienna and Rome, but there are ways. I saw enough smuggled literature when I was in Berlin."

He seemed to relent a little. "I appreciate what you're trying to do here, but how many printing presses are working in Paris tonight, churning out anti-Nazi literature?"

"I don't know," Maureen said, "but does that preclude us from doing what we can? It's up to every free person to combat the National Socialists. Because we're going to have to fight, one way or the other."

"I hear Paris is full of refugees, from both Germany and Italy. Lots of Jews, but also Socialists, Communists, democrats, liberals, pacifists. Every sort of idealist the Nazis hate, all fighting among themselves, like they do at home. All insisting that their way is the only way to fight Nazism. What are you?"

"Does it matter what label others affix to us? I see the evil, and I won't stop until it's defeated. Hitler is a cancer."

"The people in Germany reading those leaflets hate Hitler already! The papers don't do any good."

Maureen had thought Seamus was prepared to do anything to liberate his adopted homeland from the National Socialist scourge.

"I can't believe you're reacting like this." Frustration engulfed her like fire. "I've been working on this for weeks—we just need the money for the machines. We can't do anything without it. Please, Father."

He looked into her eyes for a few seconds. "Please," she said again.

His reluctance was plain to see, but he threw another diamond into the pile of 20. "That's all. I admire your passion, Maureen, but I'm here to deal with the practicalities in life. I need the rest of this money for my accounts in Switzerland. I'm calling at the bank in Basel on my way home. I'm setting up a fund for the Jews in the factory there."

"Thank you." The one diamond had to be worth a few thousand francs—enough to float their operation for a while.

"Now, let's forget about this, and get ready for dinner," Seamus said.

The anger within her dissipated. She nodded and left with her brother, the diamond in her pocket.

Maureen stood alone outside Les Deux Magots restaurant in Saint-Germain. A middle-aged man strolling by in a bowler hat looked her up and down with greedy eyes. Perhaps he was admiring the dress she bought on the Champs de Élysées the last time her father was in town. It was difficult to start from scratch, and she felt pressure to look good while living here. Leaving Berlin was difficult enough, but letting her entire closet go made it even harder. Paris wasn't a city where one could venture out in rags, no matter how inconsequential the journey might be.

Her brother and Monika showed up a few minutes later, hand in hand. The rest of the family soon followed. The restaurant was a short walk from their hotel, but they were still late.

The young maître d' greeted them like they were old friends and gave them the best table in the house. His stare rendered Maureen a little uneasy, and she was glad when he left.

They dined on a starter of wild burgundy snails and duck foie gras. The main course was even more splendid. Maureen's chicken supreme was exquisite, although Fiona gagged at the beef tartare her father ate.

When the main course was finished, her father made a quiet speech about how good it was to be together. He spoke in German for Hannah and Lisa's benefit.

"That's all I've ever wanted," he added.

They clinked wine glasses and settled down to order profiteroles for dessert.

Dinner ended just before ten o'clock. Conor and Hannah were fighting to stay awake, so Lisa stood up and offered to take the children home. Fiona protested that she wanted to stay, but she was yawning too.

The remaining four switched to English once Lisa and the children were gone. Somehow it felt more intimate.

They spoke about America and the people they still knew there. Michael was in regular contact with Aunt Maeve in Newark, while Maureen was more sporadic. Her brother had America in his mind yet, but it was a distant memory to her.

An hour passed before Maureen announced she had a meeting to attend. "What kind of a meeting goes on at eleven o'clock at night?" Seamus asked.

Maureen wiped her mouth with her napkin. "Just some friends."

"We're not in Germany. This is a free country," Michael said.

"Maybe not as free as you think," their father replied. He took a moment to explain a meeting he'd had with Hayden. His words sent a chill through Maureen's body. "My contact in Berlin told me the Nazis have positioned moles all over Europe. Some of them have spent time in camps, just to further their cover. How well do you know Gerhard and Hans?"

"Not well, but they're as committed to the cause as anyone I've ever met."

"It's just too risky for you to be involved with them with so many Nazi agents in Paris. I can't commit to backing anything long term. If the Gestapo got wind of this, you'd be beaten up and dragged back to Germany."

"We're not children, Father," Maureen said. "We're old enough to make our own choices."

"I know that, and I also know you will. I'm just asking you to be careful."

"This work is important. They're steadfast people."

"I'm sure your friends are good men, but we don't know anything about them."

"We'll find a way, with or without you."

"Let them find that way. You say this is a free city, but the Nazi tentacles are everywhere. We've been lucky so far, but I won't see you in a concentration camp."

"So, you want me to move back to America?"

"Is that something you've considered?"

"No. My life is here now. Thank you for dinner, Father. I'll see you tomorrow." Maureen stood up. The atmosphere was different, and a familiar sense of tension lingered.

"I'll stay a little longer," Michael said. "You want to?" he asked Monika, who nodded. They said goodbye to Maureen, who contained her disappointment as she strode out.

Maureen walked a few blocks until she came to an innocuous-looking basement door. She knocked once, then three times. Hans answered it and gestured for her to come inside with a casual flick of his head. The space inside was empty save for a long table in the middle and a writing desk in the corner. Several bare lightbulbs hung from the ceiling. Gerhard stood up from the desk as he saw her and greeted her with a kiss on each cheek. They made small talk about meeting her family for a moment or two before Hans asked what was on her mind.

"What's the problem? Did you eat a bad snail?"

"It's just some things my father said."

"Like what?" Gerhard asked.

"He said Paris is full of Nazi spies."

"What?" Hans asked, almost unable to keep the laugh in. "The Nazis are here, but when was the last time you saw a Brownshirt? This is a haven for those escaping the repressive regime back home."

"What do you think, Gerhard, about spies in Paris?" she asked.

"I don't know. I've only been here a few weeks. I've been to a few rallies, and I was at that march for democracy down the Champs-Élysées in September."

"I was too, with Monika and my brother."

"You think some of the people marching that day were Gestapo or SS?" Hans asked.

"Who knows? I'm just saying we need to be careful who we trust and who we talk to." She reached into her pocket and drew out the precious stone her stepmother had smuggled into Paris in her hair. "A contribution to the cause."

Hans took it in his hand. It shone in the light as he held it up.

"Thank your father from us, but this diamond by itself won't buy us a printing press. It's too small." He pocketed it. "I'll put it with the other funds we collected at the town hall meeting."

"You're an expert?" Gerhard asked.

"My uncle was a jeweler. I used to help him out in the store as a child. The skills I learned there are handy these days."

Maureen felt hurt at his reaction to the diamond but didn't show it. The desire to impress these men was unshakeable. It was like being 13 again.

Gerhard walked back to the desk and picked up a handwritten sheet of paper. "Hans, this latest pamphlet of yours... It's asking for a revolution. Who's going to read something that would get you thrown into a KZ just for possessing it?"

"Plenty of people," Hans replied.

"Yes, but they're the ones who think like we do already," Gerhard said. "We need to persuade the factory workers in Munich. The ship builders in Hamburg. The farmers in Lower Saxony. They're the ones who have the power to effect change if they rise up in numbers. But they'll never read something like this. The only people who read pamphlets this incendiary are revolutionaries like you."

"So, are you saying we do nothing? We should just talk about the evils of the regime destroying Germany and take no action?" Hans ran to the table and pushed the pile of papers onto the concrete floor. "Forgive me if I think Germany is worth fighting for," he said with venom. "I'll see you at the meeting next week. We'll be churning out these leaflets if I have to handwrite every single one."

He stormed out, slamming the door behind him.

"This isn't what I envisioned," Maureen said. She felt as if she'd just been beaten up.

"Perhaps there's another way," Gerhard said.

"What? Are we going to assassinate Adolf Hitler? I've had that thought a few times, but it's a tall order."

"Much as I'd like to see that rat on the end of a rope, I don't see that as a possibility—for now, anyway. Your father produces airplanes for the Nazis, doesn't he?"

"The latest bombers and fighters for the Luftwaffe so that one day, they'll rule the skies," she said with a dose of irony in her voice.

"Does he know Herr Göring?"

"Not personally, but he was at his estate a few weeks ago with some other masters of the universe."

"What about the generals in the Luftwaffe? Does he know them?"

"I couldn't say. What are you getting at here?"

"I need to get a letter to my father. Do you think you could help?"

"What do you want to say to him?"

He handed her the piece of paper.

Father,

I first want to say sorry because I know you blame me for Mother's death. The events surrounding her heart attack haunt me in my dreams. I wake up every morning wishing I could turn the clock back, but I can't, and I have to live with that.

I understand the position you were in, caught between Mother and me and the two boys. I've come to realize it's not their fault or yours, but the regime's itself. That's what tore our family apart, and it'll do the same to the entire continent if noble men like you let it. No matter what oath you took, you know your duty is to Germany, not one man. Disaster awaits at the end of the road we're traveling. Only you and a few other good men have the chance to avert it.

Please tell Fritz and Heinrich I'm safe and wish them nothing but the best. Keep Mother in your heart as you decide what to do.

Your son,

Gerhard

. . .

"You're encouraging them to rise up against the regime? Do you have brothers or sisters we could get this to?"

"I have two brothers—both committed Nazis. Heinrich joined the Party back in '28. He's risen quite high in the ranks now. Fritz is in the Luftwaffe. They've embraced the Nazis, but I know my father hasn't. If there were two or three more generals like him...."

"...they could march into the Reich Chancellery and arrest Hitler." Maureen ended the sentence for him.

"The military is what keeps him in power. Without them, he's just another blowhard racist."

"What about the SS and the Brownshirts? Wouldn't they rise up against the army and defend their messiah?"

"They wouldn't go down without a fight, that's for sure. But what's worse—a few days of fighting on the streets in Berlin, or a full-scale war in Europe?"

"That's no choice at all," she answered. "What happened to your mother?"

"She died back in '35. I haven't spoken to my father since the funeral."

"Why not?"

"You're full of questions, aren't you?" the young man asked. Maureen didn't respond. "He blames me for splitting the family apart. I refused to join the military. It was Christmas day in '34—the last time, apart from the funeral, we were all together. My brothers started an argument about my political beliefs and things got heated. Heinrich threw a glass at me, and punches soon followed. Mother hated the Nazis and couldn't take it. It must have been the stress of seeing us fight that caused the heart attack. My father drove her to the hospital, but a week later, she was dead. It wouldn't have taken much to drive a wedge between the members of our family. That was more than enough."

"I'm sorry."

"One more of a thousand stories of families torn apart by the Nazis." Gerhard stubbed his cigarette out on the bottom of his shoe and sat with his fingers clasped.

"But you still think he'd be amenable to our ideas of deposing Hitler?"

"I do. I'm sure he knows in his heart, Hitler is leading the Reich toward disaster."

Maureen weighed the idea of the Nazis being kicked out versus the bloody vengeance they would take on anyone who tried to move against them. "We have to at least try to get this letter to him."

"The problem is, as soon as he knows it's from me, he'll tear it up. I need someone he likes to give it to him. Would your father deliver it?"

"No. He won't get involved." Then an idea hit her like a lightning bolt. "Your father's a widower, probably a lonely man?"

"He and my mother were married for 42 years."

"Who do lonely old men listen to more than anyone else?"

"What are you getting at, Maureen?"

"My father isn't the one we need to speak to. The person we want is Lisa, my stepmother. She knows someone perfect for the job—someone who owes her."

12

Saturday, October 23

Paris's marvels were unending. The mundane seemed nonexistent here. Every street corner revealed new wonders that even a magnificent city like Berlin couldn't compete with. Lisa wore her best cream-colored dress and matching hat and didn't feel overdressed on the Parisian streets. Being a tourist was a new experience for her. She'd gone to the coast with her parents a few times as a child, but apart from that, hadn't been much further than the lakes or the forests surrounding Berlin. Marrying Seamus had opened up new worlds to her, and to be able to share this experience with Hannah was a dream. Being with the man she loved in this romantic city was food for her soul, and she soaked up every minute like she'd never be here again. With the threat of war hanging over Europe like the sword of Damocles, who knew what bombs and bullets would do to the beauty of this place? Lisa intended to enjoy it with her family while she still could.

After a boat ride along the Seine, they lunched in a café and sat on the street, watching the citizens of this enchanting city saunter past. People-watching was one of the most fascinating and amusing tourist activities, and the Ritter family engaged in it like a professional sport.

After a three-hour lunch, Monika took them to the Louvre, where they strolled around for much of the rest of the afternoon. Lisa marveled at artworks she wished she knew more about. Still, she enjoyed the mere sight of the thousands of paintings that adorned the walls of the old museum, and when they emerged into the crisp evening air, she felt like she was drunk.

Michael and his wife led them into the Tuileries Garden. An immense joy flowed through her as she and her family passed along the wide stone pathways lined with trees and shrubs manicured to perfection. Hundreds of Parisians sat on the benches and chairs around the fountains. Some sailed boats in the water there. It seemed as if she were in one of those stunning paintings in the museum. The beauty of that place came alive in everything that surrounded it.

Hannah ran back to a fountain to dip her hand in the cool water. Lisa watched her for a few seconds before she heard Maureen's voice in her ear.

"Can we talk for a few minutes?"

"Of course," Lisa replied. "Run along with the others. Catch up!" she said to her daughter, who ran on and took her stepfather's hand. The gratification she took from that sight brought a smile to her face. "This city is one of the most wonderful places I could ever imagine."

"Being here has dulled the pain of missing you and the others."

"Breaking up the family almost killed your father."

"The alternative would have been far worse."

Lisa wondered if Maureen ever thought about the man she killed as she herself did. Ernst Milch came only in her dreams and rarely now. She wished she could speak with her stepdaughter about her own experiences, but knew the impossibility of that.

"So, you're taking a trip to Switzerland on the way home?"

"Yes. Your father's obsessed with moving money out of Germany these days. He thinks it's the answer to getting the Jewish workers out too."

"I hope he's right."

Lisa thought to tell Maureen about Fiona and their plans to drop her off at boarding school in Basel, but again deemed telling the young woman too risky. They'd decided to keep it from Fiona until the last minute when they left her at the academy.

"So, are you and your brother glad you'll be able to buy an apartment in the city? Michael and Monika seem happy here too."

"Yes—I thank God for Monika every day. I don't know what my brother would have done during the last few months without her. The talent that he based his life on these last few years is gone. I'm just glad she is here to fill the void."

"He needs her."

"Agreed."

The rest of the family were 20 paces in front of them.

"This is for your ears only, Lisa, but I've met someone here whose father is a general in the Luftwaffe. He's convinced that his father isn't on board with the Nazis and would be willing to oust Hitler and the Nazis if he had the right support."

"You're trying to organize a coup in Berlin?"

"I think if certain generals were prodded in a certain direction, they'd be willing to bring their beloved Reich back to the days of the Kaiser. Democracy would be a step too far, but at least it would end the Nazi regime."

"How do we prod someone who's taken an oath of loyalty to Hitler? Would they really rise up against him?"

"The generals know they can't win a war against the Allies,

particularly when the United States joins against them." Maureen seemed determined.

"The Americans aren't too interested in the maelstrom over here right now."

"But the crusty old men in the German military remember the Great War. It took the Americans time to join then too, but when they did, the war was over in 18 months. Even a child in Germany these days knows Hitler is speeding the country toward war. Perhaps the generals care enough about the people they represent to avert that disaster. My friend certainly thinks his father does."

"My question about the oath of loyalty to Hitler remains."

"The Wehrmacht and the Luftwaffe will act if their generals order them to. The SS will never budge, but the other armed forces could overpower them."

"You make it all sound so easy," said Lisa.

"I'm not naïve enough to think it'll be anything short of a miracle if we can pull this off, but who are we if we don't try? My friend knows his father's heart. And he's powerful enough that if he can get a few others who think the same way to go along with him, we could rid the world of Adolf Hitler forever."

"And save Europe in the process."

"All we need is someone to deliver a letter to the general—someone who'll turn his head and cast a spell on him."

"Witches are hard to find these days."

"You told me Petra Wagner came to you seeking redemption. This could be it. She's one of the most beautiful women in Germany."

"And one of the least trustworthy. We'd all be hauled in by the Gestapo in hours." The mere mention of Petra's name sent shivers down Lisa's spine.

"Why would she come to you if she wasn't sincere? You saw her. Do you think she meant what she said?"

"No."

"What if she...convinces you?"

"It doesn't seem likely, but give me the letter. I'll think of something. If there's a genuine chance of getting rid of Hitler, it's got to be worth the risk."

"Thank you," Maureen said. "Don't mention this to my father. I don't want him passing on the letter himself. The less he knows about this, the better. He's too close to the situation. It would only put him in danger."

"I agree. Don't worry, I'll keep it to myself."

The two women picked up their pace and caught up to the rest of the family outside a beautiful gray-brick mansion lit up against the dark of the Parisian night sky.

Maureen waited until after lunch on Sunday, when the Ritters emerged from the Café de la Paix together. The splendid sight of the Opéra national de Paris brought a smile to Fiona's face. Maureen knew this was the time. Her sister had been quiet during their trip—enjoying the splendors on show, but seemingly maintaining something in reserve. She and their father spoke little, but Maureen hearkened back to herself at the same age and didn't see that particular behavior as abnormal. Maureen took her sister's hand. They still had a few hours before they left for Switzerland.

"Can we take a walk together?"

"Where do you want to go?"

"How about the Royal Palace gardens?"

Her sister shrugged her shoulders. Maureen took that as consent and told her parents she'd have her back to the hotel in plenty of time. Her father thanked her and let them go.

"Isn't Paris incredible?" Maureen began, having rehearsed this conversation in her head many times. It was vital to start slowly and build from there. Fiona loved Paris and where they were staying, so they talked about the food and the people for a few minutes.

"I love it here," Fiona replied.

"Could you see yourself living here, or somewhere else?"

"Other than Berlin?" Fiona asked. "I don't know. It's exhilarating to feel that you're in the most important city in the world. Rumor has it that the Führer prefers Munich, but he needs to be where the action is. I feel the same way."

"It's not so long ago we were living with Aunt Maeve and the girls in Newark. Do you reminisce about those times much?"

"When I'm angry with Father."

"So, pretty much all the time?" Maureen laughed.

Her sister smiled. "Pretty much. Living in that house was a symbol of not just his failings as a father, but of the entire economic system in America."

"You think it's better in the Reich?"

"You're joking, aren't you? We live in a mansion in Berlin, with two cars parked outside. Even Father has to acknowledge how much National Socialism has done for our family."

Maureen nodded as they crossed onto Rue du Quatre-Septembre. "You see the name of this street? It was the date the current government system in France was set up in 1870, when Napoléon III was deposed."

"And they're celebrating that?" Fiona said with a giggle.

"Do you think the method of governance in Germany is better?"

"How could anyone not? Look at what the Führer has done for the country over the last few years. The Reich is an international powerhouse once more."

"What about the role of women in German society?"

"As opposed to elsewhere? What do you mean?"

"Women aren't trusted to be judges or civil servants in Germany anymore. Half of the lessons you receive in school are to prepare you to raise a family, never to experience a fulfilling career of your own."

"But the government supports us. You know about the Law for the Encouragement of Marriage. When I settle down, the government will lend me and my husband 1,000 Reichsmarks, and we get to keep 250 for every child we have."

"And you're happy to bear children for the Reich?"

"Isn't that a woman's role in any society?"

"I think that we can be more than just a reproductive organ."

"Perhaps, but that's our role in the family. I can't wait to be a mother—it's what I was put on this planet to do. Harald and I are going to be married soon, likely after his six-month service to the state. We have no idea where he'll be sent, of course, but once he gets back and before he joins the SS."

Maureen was in shock. Each word hit her like a fist. She had no idea. "What? You're not even 16!"

"We can get a dispensation to be married. It won't be hard."

Maureen tried to think of who Harald was. She'd met him once or twice in passing, and now he was to be her brother-in-law?

"What do Father and Lisa say about this?"

"They're none too happy, let me tell you, but what can they do? Once we receive the dispensation from the government, we'll be free to marry."

Maureen searched for the right words, wary of pushing her sister further away. "Are you sure? It seems sudden. We don't know Harald. Has he said..."

"Not in so many words, but he's been clear enough with his intent."

They stopped at a crosswalk and people closed in around them. Maureen took the time to breathe in and out a few times. Perhaps Fiona was being misled. Better that than getting married to an SS recruit on her sixteenth birthday. They crossed the street and kept walking.

"I'm glad you told me about your plans. When do you think this will happen? I'd like to come home for the wedding."

"It's impossible to say right now, but I'll keep you informed."

Comforted by her vague answers, Maureen walked on.

They passed a boulangerie and stopped outside to stare at the immaculately presented cakes and pastries in the window. Maureen was eager to change the tone of the conversation. She couldn't afford to scare her sister off, so she brought her inside and ordered two pains au chocolat. They ate the delicious pastries as they walked.

"What do you think about my marriage plans? You didn't congratulate me," Fiona said as they finished.

"I think you're too young."

"I'm old enough to have babies."

"You need to live more of your life before you anchor yourself to the kitchen. Young women are being funneled toward it in Germany these days. I felt that way when I lived there."

"Perhaps that lifestyle wasn't for you."

"Perhaps it's not for many women who don't see themselves as having any other option because of National Socialist policies."

"I wondered when this would come. I knew this was why you wanted to talk to me," Fiona snapped.

"I wanted to spend some time with my sister. I wanted to see how you are. Your commitment to the Führer seems to have become a large part of your persona now."

"Did Father put you up to this?"

"Of course not. Is it really so terrible to walk these streets with me, eating sumptuous pastries?"

"I miss you."

Fiona's sudden admission startled her. "I think about you

every day."

"Why did you really have to leave? Did you kill that policeman?" My friends think it was your picture in the newspaper."

"No." The lie stung like a hornet. "If the picture looked like me, it was a coincidence."

"Well, anyway, I told them the gypsies must have killed him."

Maureen finished the pastry in her hand and led Fiona down the narrow one-way street of Rue Vivienne. "What about the camp at Marzahn? Hundreds of innocent people are still imprisoned there."

"Innocent? Come on, Maureen. Would the authorities go to so much time and expense to lock up harmless people? They must be guilty of something. You know the reputation those people have."

"Do you think the children there are criminals, or are they just locked up because of that reputation you just mentioned?"

"I'm no expert on that place, but I do know the streets of Berlin are safe for citizens now. Not like before the Führer came to power."

"That's because there was a virtual civil war going on between the Nazis and the Socialists on the streets of Berlin back then. If you remove one side from the hostilities, then the violence ends."

"So that proves it was the Communists who were behind it all. Who misses them?"

"You say the streets are safe now, but for who, exactly? Not for the Jews still living in the Reich."

Fiona didn't answer. Maureen quit waiting for a response after ten seconds or so. The atmosphere had changed, but she knew she had to press on.

"Is what's happening to the Jewish people in Germany fair? Tell me what you feel, not what the group leaders in the League of German Girls tell you. What's in your heart?"

"The Führer shares my heart with Harald."

Ignoring her sister's statement, Maureen proceeded. "Do you think Jews should be excluded from society, banned from marrying German citizens?"

"I don't write or interpret the laws, but I see what Germany is becoming, and that's because of the glorious revolution happening there."

"You've spent some time with Herr and Frau Bernheim these last few months, haven't you?"

"Yes. Father forced me."

"What kind of people are they?"

"Jews," she said dismissively.

"I heard about the attack on their house."

"I was wondering when this would also come up. I wasn't there, so I don't know anything about it. I'm sick of being accused of something I didn't do."

"I didn't accuse you of anything. I just wanted to ask you if you thought what happened to them was justified, or excusable in any way."

Fiona's face was tight as a snare drum now. "I don't know, because I don't know what they did to cause it."

"Do you think they deserved that because they're Jewish?"

Fiona shrugged. "Hard to say."

"What about Judith Starobin?"

"Who's that?"

"Father didn't tell you about her?" Fiona feigned ignorance and shook her head. "She was beaten within an inch of her life a few weeks ago, but her husband wasn't so lucky. Brownshirts kicked him to death on the street for no other reason than that he was a Jew."

"That's not my fault." A tear broke down Fiona's face. "None of my friends have to deal with this constant questioning from *their* families."

They reached the Jardin du Palais Royal. Maureen stayed

silent as they strolled through the entranceway, but neither sister was paying attention to the grandeur of their surroundings anymore.

"I think I want to go back to the hotel now," Fiona said.

"Can we talk a little more? I don't know when I'll see you next."

They walked to the park behind the palace and found a bench opposite the massive fountain.

"Fiona, you can't think it's right that people in Germany are killed because of the religion they belong to, or the ethnic group. What happened to the Bernheims, and especially to Judith and her husband, is awful."

Fiona remained silent, but Maureen took her hand and looked into her sister's eyes. "Just do one thing for me, please? Think for yourself. Use your heart to evaluate the things you see and hear. You're a wonderful young woman—the best sister I could ever ask for. You were always there for me when I needed you when Father was gone. And when Mother died, you were my north star. I don't want to lose you. I know what the League says to girls whose parents don't agree with their teachings."

"I'm not about to leave home unless it's to marry Harald."

"You might share the same roof as Lisa and Father, but you're not in the same place. All I'm asking is that you listen to them. They're not always right, but you know what? Neither are your group leaders in the League. Neither is Hitler."

Maureen feared she had gone too far with the last sentence, but her sister didn't react. "There might come a time one day when you have to choose between your devotion to the Führer and your family. Father and Lisa might not be able to stay in Berlin forever."

"Are they planning to move here, or to America?"

"No. Father's work in the Reich is too important to leave right now."

"It's an important mission. That's what I don't understand about him. He's so holier than thou with me about the Nazis and the League, yet he makes weapons. Who is he to preach to me? He was on a hunting trip with Herr Göring recently."

"Father is looking after the interests of his family, and his workers."

"It wasn't so long ago that you two fought like cats and dogs. What changed?"

"Maybe I matured. I think we both did, and you will too. I just don't want to lose my little sister along the way."

"I'm not lost, Maureen. I just miss you and Michael so much, and Mother too. I think about her all the time." Something seemed to break within Fiona, and she wept like a child. "Everyone's been lying to me ever since you and Michael left. They think I'm ten years old."

No, they know they can't trust you. She took her little sister in her arms and held her. "Just remember who you are—who our mother raised you to be. The answers to all your questions are in your heart, and I'm here whenever you need me. I'm so sorry I had to leave."

Maureen heard the echo of her father in her words. Fiona was finding refuge with a group of people who seemed, on the surface, at least, to value her.

"I never wanted to leave you," she said.

They sat holding one another on that bench until time ran out, and then Maureen walked her sister back to the hotel.

Monday, October 25: Basel, Switzerland

Seamus left Conor with a friend for the afternoon, promising he'd be back to pick him up at dinnertime. He went to meet with his banker, Ingo Varner, who lent him his car. Seamus,

Lisa, and Fiona set off for a trip he knew would define his relationship with his daughter for years to come. It was hard to believe it had come to this. He blamed himself—it was his responsibility to shield his children, and he had let Fiona fall prey to the greatest evil in the world.

Lisa insisted on coming along despite his protestations. He was glad of that as they sped through the pretty green countryside outside of the city of Basel. He reached over and took his wife's hand without saying a word. The sad, nervous look she exchanged with him mirrored his feelings, but they had no choice. Left to her own devices, Fiona would fall farther and farther down the Nazi rabbit hole, and if she married Harald, she might be lost forever. As much as this hurt, he had to do it. Lisa was in complete agreement, and if they'd told her in advance, she wouldn't have come.

She was curious about where they were driving to, of course, and lying was the last thing he wanted to do, but it was a necessary evil. This was about saving her soul, and if that meant her hating him for the rest of her life, it was a price he was willing to pay. It was a temporary measure until the chance arose to move back to America. He couldn't leave Germany yet, not while so many things were still undone. And even if he tried, would Hayden stand in his way? It was clear that a school in Switzerland was the only long-term option left to save his daughter.

Fiona was silent in the back of the car, reading a book. Seamus's hands were slick on the steering wheel. "Is this the house?" she asked as a black gate came into view.

"This is our destination," Seamus answered.

The boarding school was set among a glen, surrounded by luscious green fields. The school itself was red brick, with ivy growing up the walls. The scene looked like something from a painting set above a fireplace.

"This is a château?" Fiona asked, her chin jutting upward as she took in the view.

Neither Seamus nor Lisa spoke. They were through the black gates before Fiona could read the name, but she was no fool.

"What is this place? Answer me!"

A cohort of young girls was in the garden performing calisthenics while a teacher barked instructions through a megaphone. Lisa poked him, indicating he should answer. "It's an excellent school for young girls."

"What?! You can't do this!" she roared.

"We have a meeting arranged with the principal," Lisa said and turned to her. "Just give him a chance to speak. I think you'll see this is for the best."

"You can't do this!"

"We can. It isn't what I wanted, my darling," Seamus said, struggling to keep the tears in, "but it's for the best."

He pulled up outside the school, and a student was waiting in uniform as they got out. Fiona's face revealed her horror as Seamus tried to cajole his daughter out of the back of the car.

"No!" she shouted. "You can't make me!"

"People are watching," Seamus hissed as he reached into the car for her. "Just come take a look. This can be as easy or as hard as you decide, but make no mistake—you're coming inside with us."

"I'm to marry Harald! You can't take me away from the Reich." Fiona's hair was strewn all over her face, and tears poured down her red cheeks.

"Please," Seamus said, holding out his hand. "You're causing a scene."

His daughter grudgingly reached out and grabbed his hand. She climbed out of the car and dusted herself off, tears still flowing from her eyes.

"I'm not staying here. You can't force me."

"I've tried everything else. I love you far too much to bring you back to Berlin."

"You don't love me at all!"

The student at the door managed a watery smile before leading them inside. Seamus gripped his daughter's hand—as much to drag her along as to hold it.

The trio waited five agonizing minutes outside the principal's office before he greeted them. Principal Greitens was a small round-headed man in his 50s, and had obviously dealt with holdouts like Fiona many times.

"We have a lot of reluctant students, Fiona," he said. "They all come around in the end. This is a wonderful place. Your parents have sent you here only because they want the best for you."

Lisa patted her shoulder. "It's only until the end of the school year. Then we can reevaluate."

"This is the best thing," Seamus said. "You'll thank me one day."

"For ruining my life? I don't think so." She stood with her arms crossed.

"You'll soon settle in," Greitens said. "You have dozens of new friends waiting for you."

"And we'll be down to visit soon," Seamus said.

"Don't bother."

They left her there with the suitcase she had brought to Paris, promising to send her luggage on. Seamus wanted to hug her before leaving, but the rawness of her grief and hostility made it impossible.

An hour after they'd pulled up to the school with her, Seamus and Lisa drove away alone. He broke down as they passed through the gate. It was the first time she'd ever seen him cry—the first time he'd done so since Marie, his first wife, died.

13

Tuesday, January 11, 1938

Michael pulled his scarf over his lower face as plumes of white condensation cascaded from his mouth.

"Where are you off to?" his new colleague, Frederick, asked. Michael was comfortable enough with French to converse now, though he was delighted that he could perform the functions of the job his father had set him up with in German. It was an administrative role—mainly dealing with the mail—but it paid, and it was a start.

"My wife's waiting for me."

"Can I come along and say hello? I'd love to meet her," Frederick said in German.

Michael weighed the question for a few seconds. The old instincts from living in the Reich were ingrained within him. Could he trust this young man? He and Monika were attending an anti-Nazi meeting in a local hall with Maureen later.

"Sure, she'd like to meet someone from my new job. Come along."

Michael and the young Frenchman had met in late November when he began working in Roland Eidinger's Parisian office. They descended the steps to the Métro together and were at the café Monika and Maureen worked in ten minutes later.

"You'll get to meet my sister too," Michael said as he pushed the glass door open.

Frederick didn't have time to answer, as Monika happened to be serving a table at the front as they walked in. She finished taking the order and held up a finger to them before disappearing into the kitchen.

"Does Maureen have a boyfriend?" Frederick asked.

"I'm not sure anymore. There's one back in Germany, but it's been a while."

The two men ordered beer at the bar. "Where's your sister?"

"Don't get any ideas," Michael said reflexively.

The Frenchman laughed. "You said she would be here. That's all."

Michael looked at his watch. The girls' shift was ending in five minutes, and the anti-Fascist event was in thirty. "We're going to a meeting after this," he said. This was Paris, not Germany.

"What kind of a meeting?"

"An anti-Fascist gathering."

Frederick drew a packet of cigarettes from his pocket and offered one to Michael. Even now that he wasn't training anymore, the sight of them sent shivers down his spine.

"No, thanks."

His colleague lit up. "I've never been to anything like that. Can I come along?"

"Is it a topic that interests you?"

"Hitler and the National Socialist Party? It's all anyone talks about these days."

Monika whisked past them with two steak frites on her tray,

which she placed in front of the customers. She wished them *bon appétit* in her heavy German accent and walked to the bar. She kissed Michael before turning to the new man.

"I'm Frederick Denis." He kissed her on both cheeks. "I work in the same office as your husband. I trust you're enjoying your time in Paris?"

"I love it here. It's a privilege to experience the wonder of this city."

"We Parisians prize beauty above almost anything else."

Michael was beginning to have second thoughts about his colleague by the time his sister arrived. Frederick changed his act a little when he met her, but the themes were the same. His sister seemed less taken with his charm than Monika.

"I'm sorry, Frederick—we need to leave. Perhaps we can have a beer another time?" she said.

"Michael told me about the meeting you were attending. I'd like to come along, if I may?"

Maureen gave Michael a look that could cut ice before turning back to Frederick. "It's open to anyone."

Frederick didn't take the hint. "Perfect. I'll finish my drink. Where's the bathroom?" he asked and followed Monika's directions.

"What are you thinking?" Maureen said when he'd gone.

"He asked what our plans were tonight."

"And you told him about the meeting? Don't you remember what Father said about Nazis operating here?"

"I do, but think about it—there's going to be 200 people in the hall, probably more," Monika said.

"It's open to the public. We don't have to whisper in secret here."

"Maybe that's what we should be doing."

"He's been working for Herr Eidinger for two years. I'm sure he's no Gestapo mole. And if you're so worried, why are we going at all?"

"I need to feel like I'm doing something," Maureen said as the Frenchman returned.

"Time to leave?" he asked with a smile. Michael's sister offered a reluctant nod, and they set off.

Maureen greeted the attendant at the door by name. They exchanged a few sentences before he pointed to a section near the center of the hall, where there were still some empty seats. Monika was right—at least 300 people had piled into the large room. The walls were adorned with anti-Fascist material, highlighted by caricatures of Mussolini, Hitler, and Franco, their ally in Spain. The air was thick with cigarette smoke and the murmur of French, German, and Italian conversation. Chairs were laid out in neat rows, facing a stage upon which a lectern was set. Most people in the room were in their 20s or 30s, but some much older people sat in the crowd among their younger comrades.

The four took their seats, with Frederick on the outside beside Michael. He had a curious look on his face as if he wasn't sure what to make of the surroundings.

Michael was leaning over to ask what he thought of the place when a wave of applause interrupted him. Maureen's friend, Hans Richter, took the lectern, and a hush fell over the crowd.

"A sickness has infected Europe," he began. "The terror of Fascism, a system designed to subjugate decent working people, has Germany and Italy in its iron grip. Many of you here tonight have fled here to escape the yoke of tyranny, but where is the freedom when the Wehrmacht grows stronger by the day?"

A murmur of discontent spread through the crowd until Hans held up his hands for quiet once more.

"I spent six months in a godforsaken hellhole called Buchenwald. I was one of thousands imprisoned because of our political beliefs, or simply because of the religion we were born into. I had the good fortune to escape, but the souls I left behind weren't so lucky." He stood back from the lectern for a few seconds to let his words sink in.

"The horrors I witnessed there are something I'll never forget. The routine abuse we suffered at the hands of our SS guards—the so-called 'cream of the German military'—is beyond description. It haunts my nightmares to this day."

Frederick appeared rapt.

"For those of you in this room who haven't escaped a Fascist state, you may be wondering why these tales of misery apply to you. The reason is that Hitler, the overlord of Germany, has been clear in his writings that he intends to take the very ground you're sitting on tonight. The politicians in the National Assembly, and across the Channel in Westminster, may be in denial about Hitler and his armies, but be under no illusion: He means to take France and Poland, and eventually Britain and the rest of the world. Hitler is the ultimate gambler. He gambled when he marched into the Rhineland. He's doing it again in Austria, and in the Sudetenland in Czechoslovakia. Any card player knows that if no one calls his bluff he can keep winning, never revealing his true hand. And this is just what the Führer has done these last few years. The Allies haven't called his bluff, nor have they stood up to him. Some say they're not ready for war. In that case, why aren't they readying themselves? The munitions industry in Germany is churning out weapons of war at frightening rates, while the French and British, and even the Americans, sit idly by. I'm no warmonger, but it's time to accept the reality that Hitler will likely only respond to force. He will keep demanding more and more until the powers that won the last war come together to stand up to him. It's the biggest crisis we'll ever know—a national emergency—and I'm calling on everyone in this room to tell their parents and friends and cousins about it. But more than that, we need to pressure those in power to effect change and to construct an apparatus to counter the vile threats Germany and Italy pose to the civilized world."

A man stood up in the third row. Michael could only see the back of his head, but guessed he was from Munich by the sound of his accent.

"I don't think Hitler's interested in coming west. He has his eyes on the east to provide the 'living space' he promised the German people. The Allied powers won't declare war unless they feel threatened. Perhaps the only way to bring down the Nazis is to raise a force of free German fighters and march back over the Rhine and hang that wretch from a pole outside the Reichstag."

Hans answered, "That might have been a possibility four years ago, but now, no. Hitler might not be ready for war yet, but the armies he's building are a match for anyone. The Luftwaffe's air superiority would alone be enough to snuff out such an assault."

"But Hitler holds all the cards," the man said. "He'll only push the Allies far enough to declare war when he knows his armies are too strong to stop."

"I agree with your point. The Führer will attack when his armies are ready. Without preemptive action, our only hope is that the Allies will one day be organized enough to stop him."

"The Wehrmacht will be miles ahead by then."

"I fear you might be right," Hans responded.

Michael turned around to survey the others in the room. His sister's friend Gerhard was sitting a few rows back. He tapped Maureen on the arm and pointed him out to her.

"The first thing we need to do is convince the politicians and the public at large that war is coming. It's all too easy to believe we've learned the lessons from the horror that occurred in the four years leading to 1918, but that's a dangerous assumption to make. The fear of battle has led to reticence on the part of the Allies, and it's that same fear that will lead to a conflict like we've never imagined."

The speech continued for another hour, with Hans fielding questions about his time in Buchenwald. The hall buzzed with the debate about what the Nazis wanted. Frederick never made a sound the entire time. He was transfixed.

Hans's lecture ended with him urging the attendees to warn everyone they knew of the impending disaster Europe was sleepwalking into. Michael felt energized by his words. It was a long time since anything stirred his emotions like this—not since the Olympiastadion.

Another speaker stood at the lectern once Hans finished, but raised the same points in a less salient fashion and didn't receive the same ovation. The meeting broke up at nine, and the crowd filed out the back entrance. A terrible thought that the Nazis might descend upon them occurred to Michael as he lined up to leave, but he kept it to himself.

"Did you know Hans was speaking tonight?" Monika asked Maureen once they were on the street.

"I had no idea. But he's been meeting with other groups."

"He's climbing the dissident ladder," Michael said.

"I couldn't help thinking one thing when we were in there," Frederick said. The others turned to him as if they were surprised to hear his voice. "How many Gestapo agents attend those public meetings? You don't seriously believe they weren't among the crowd, do you?"

None answered, so he continued. "If something ever were to come from those talking shops, I'm sure the Nazis would know about it in advance."

"Nothing specific was discussed tonight," Maureen said. Her tone bordered on the dismissive. Michael's sister wasn't disguising her dislike for his colleague.

"Don't forget what happened to Carlo and Nello Rosselli," the Frenchman said.

"Who?" Monika asked.

"The editor of an anti-Fascist newspaper in Paris. He and his brother were murdered by some of Mussolini's thugs back in June, before you arrived here. Of course, there are limits to what Mussolini's men or the Gestapo can get away with in a free republic," Frederick said.

"Those murders created quite the scandal," Maureen said.

"Yes. The Commies and the Pinkos have newspapers with wide circulations, and they do love a martyr to hold up. Don't you?"

"I'm no Red," Maureen responded with vitriol.

"A Pink then?"

"I'm not a socialist either. Democracy is the only truly representative system."

"Your American roots are still strong, I see. You must think they'll protect you from the Nazis here in Paris."

Michael thought to apologize for his friend and end the conversation, but he was curious about where the man was going with it, and Maureen was well able to handle herself.

"I don't intend to get into any trouble here."

"I'm sure that's what all the poor unfortunates the Nazis drag into their torture chambers said before being taken."

Michael had his fill. "All right, Frederick, enough of that talk. We only came tonight to hear an earnest exchange of ideas."

Frederick continued as if Michael hadn't spoken. "Ever heard of Château de Bellecour? No? It's about 90 minutes from the city, south of the town of Pithiviers, where my aunt and uncle have a grocery store. Their daughter, Emily, has been working as a maid at the château for a few years. She's used to tenants coming and going, but recently some Germans have taken up a lease and moved in. She and her boyfriend snuck back to look through the fence one night and saw the men dragging two people from a car into the château, beating them as they went."

"Gestapo?" Michael asked.

"They were in plainclothes, but who else? Don't make the mistake of thinking the Gestapo and SS are here only as silent observers. They mean to snuff out any resistance in Paris before it materializes."

Maureen said, "God only knows the tortures they inflict on the poor souls who end up there."

The reminder that the Gestapo was watching was a sobering one. It was easy to think they'd left the Nazis behind once they fled Germany, but their tentacles stretched throughout Europe and all the way to America.

Maureen's interest in speaking to Frederick surged like oil gushing from a strike, and she suggested they all stop for dinner. The Frenchman was happy to oblige. They sat in the corner, wary of who might be listening in.

"My cousin goes in to clean the place twice a week. The owner, the Duke de Bellecour, is rarely seen there these days. It's his family's ancestral home, but rumor has it that he spends his time on the Côte d'Azur, with his mistress. Keeping these old homes in order is a costly business. Best to lease them out to someone with the funds to maintain them."

"And in this case, those people are Germans?" Monika asked. "How does she know?"

The waiter brought a carafe of wine. Frederick waited until he left to continue speaking.

"The German flags, SS men in uniform. It's attached to the embassy. They're not hiding anything."

"What about the people she saw dragged in? Any sign of them?" Maureen asked.

"Not a peep, but apparently the place is huge, and the help are on strict orders to stay away from the cellar."

"That must be some wine collection down there," Michael said.

"Indeed."

"Can I meet your cousin?" Maureen asked.

"Wait, you want to go to the château?" Michael asked.

"I'm not about to waltz up to the front door and ask for a personal tour, but I'd like to see the place."

"For what purpose?"

"To see what they're doing. What if the next person they drag down there is one of our friends?"

"And what would we do if they did?"

"I want to find out if there's anything we could do. Don't worry, brother, I'll be careful." She picked up her glass of wine and took a sip.

"I'll take you," Frederick said.

Michael wondered what his colleague's true intentions were, but his wife beat him to the question.

"Why are you telling us this?" Monika asked.

"I went along to your lecture because I was curious, but I don't want Hitler and the Nazis in Paris any more than you. Daladier and Chamberlain are leading us to the precipice of a cliff. Perhaps there's something we can do to stop my country from walking over the edge."

Frederick's eyes moved away from Maureen's, and he stared out the window at the darkened street beyond. "My father fell in the last war, along with his two brothers. I have no desire to die facedown in a field like they did."

Maureen raised her drink, and all four clinked glasses.

~

Friday, January 14

The light was fading as they drove out of the city. Michael and Monika were sitting in the back, her head on his shoulder. Trying to convince them to stay home had been futile. Maureen's brother seemed determined to keep an eye on her, and wherever he went, his intrepid wife followed. Still, it saved the awkwardness that would have arisen had she been alone with Frederick. It was hard to know if he was doing this to help the fledgling Resistance or trying to impress her. Maureen mentioned Thomas and the fact that she was still his girlfriend several times, but Frederick persevered.

"It must be difficult to keep in touch with a boyfriend living in another country," he said as they passed a sign for Pithiviers.

"That's the town you mentioned," Maureen said.

"We're close."

The château was in the south end of the quiet town, which had once provided the labor to run it. They drove along a nondescript road with residential houses on one side and a long gray wall on the other.

"That's part of the château," Frederick said. "The estate stretches back to vast gardens beyond."

He slowed down as they approached the entrance, and Maureen arched her neck to see through the iron gates. "Where can we get a better view?"

"My cousin knows."

He took a right and pulled up outside a small red-brick house, not three minutes' walk from the front gate of the residence that dominated the surrounding area.

"Stay here, you two," Frederick said to Michael and Monika in the back seat before motioning to Maureen to follow him. He rapped on the front door, and a few seconds later, a petite blond girl, about 18 or 19, opened it. Frederick greeted her with a kiss on each cheek before introducing his cousin Emily.

"Frederick told me about you," she said as she eyed Maureen.

"We wanted to check out the château. Your cousin told us we could take a look."

"Not anymore," the girl said. "They've tightened security the last few days. The only way to get in now is over the wall or through the back of the estate, but both ways have guards and dogs. Neither are friendly."

"Have you been to work lately?"

"Take me to dinner and I'll answer all your questions."

"Seems fair."

Emily disappeared back inside the house and returned with her curly blond hair neatly brushed. She greeted Michael and Monika with a smile, and ten minutes later, they were sitting inside a café in town. They sat in the corner—the only table left.

"Have you had any interactions with the new tenants?" Maureen asked in a whisper.

People were sitting all around them. The loud conversation in the room would have made it difficult for others to listen in, but Maureen wasn't taking any chances.

"Only one man," she said with her wine glass in hand. "But he's as German as Hitler himself."

"Have you seen uniforms?" Michael asked. "SS?"

"The guards are in uniform, but apart from them, no. I met one man, called Gunther, who does look like SS. Blond hair, angular face, cheekbones you could cut glass with."

"How many of you go in?"

"Two at a time. I usually clean the drawing room and the library. The cellars are off limits, but I don't know if maybe the place has ghosts, because I've heard noises from down there."

"What kind of noises?"

"Muffled voices. But they weren't there before the Germans

came in. And all those dogs wandering around are protecting something, or someone."

Dinner arrived, and the conversation slowed. Frederick insisted on ordering another bottle of wine. Night was drawing in outside.

Maureen went over the details of Emily's job to get some clue as to what the Germans in the château were doing, although it seemed evident that it was an extravagant prison.

"Do the police know about this place?" Monika asked as the crème brûlée Frederick arranged for the table arrived.

"What can they do?"

"No one's reported the people taken there?"

"Arnaud, my boyfriend, did, but nothing happened."

"The SS could have passed that off as someone who had too much to drink," Maureen said. "And they have diplomatic immunity through the German embassy."

"So they can act with impunity?" Michael asked.

"Yes, once they're past those gates—unless something obviously awful is happening," Maureen said.

The café was almost empty. They were just about to leave when two men stumbled to the counter, demanding beer. They were in their 20s and speaking German. Both stared over at the table with lusty eyes, and Monika nudged Maureen under the table.

"Are you German?" Monika asked.

Maureen noticed her slipping her wedding ring off under the table.

"We work at the château," one of the men said. "Where are you from?"

"My friend and I are visiting from Berlin," Monika answered. "These are our cousins." Michael wouldn't have been delighted with his role but kept his distaste hidden.

"They're determined to leave, but we wanted to stay for some more drinks," Maureen said.

"We have a table. Want to sit with us?" the other man asked.

"Do you mind?" Maureen asked her *cousins* at the table.

They nodded and shrugged their shoulders, though she was already on her feet before they gave their responses.

The two men seemed hardly to be able to believe their luck as Maureen and Monika sat down with them on the other side of the café. The two men introduced themselves. Gerd was blond with a handsome, square face. His colleague, Ullrich, was tall and lean with black hair. Both were blind drunk.

"Have you been working at the château long?" Monika began.

"It just opened. We just arrived a few weeks ago," Gerd said. He finished his beer in seconds. Without prompting, he told them he was from a small town in Bavaria, while Ullrich was from Chemnitz. Monika went to the bar and returned with another round to a chorus of cheers.

Maureen was sick of men like these and even more of having to pretend to enjoy conversing with them. The others were still sitting in the corner. Michael was seemingly doing his best not to stare.

"You enjoy it here?" she asked.

"Yes, I love it. Do you?" Gerd asked.

"For a few days," she replied. "But I'm tired of these pathetic Pinks, and the city is overrun with Jews."

"It's like a rat's nest," Monika added. "I long for the day the Wehrmacht rolls in here. Imagine this place rid of Socialists and Jews, and with someone to keep the French in line?"

"Sounds wonderful," Ullrich said and raised his glass for a toast.

"I have an embarrassing confession," Monika said. "I'm not much of a drinker. It goes straight to my head."

"Well, drink up, then, little one!" Gerd roared in laughter with his friend.

Monika was so good at this. Maureen let her go on for a few

minutes, biding her time for the next question. No one seemed to have noticed that she'd stopped drinking and only touched the beer when she held it to her lips. Monika began singing the Reich's praises and expressed her fascination for Hitler with a coquettish smile.

"You're not the only one to fall for the Führer," Gerd said. "Little surprise. He's the most brilliant man on the planet."

"Germany's savior!" Ullrich slurred.

"Paris is full of Reds and Jews and betrayers of all shapes and sizes," Monika said. "Tell me you're here to punish those swine."

"I could ask some of my friends in the city for names, if you'd like," Maureen said.

"We don't need any help when it comes to that," Ullrich said. "I'm grateful, but we have our own means of monitoring those vermin."

"That's comforting."

"What do you do to them after you bring them here? Take them back to Germany?" Monika asked.

"Sometimes... If they make it that far!" Ullrich exploded with laughter again.

The two SS soldiers could hardly keep their eyes open now. The smile on Maureen's face was beginning to hurt, but it was worth it. Young men were all the same in certain ways.

"I read an article that they mean to assassinate the Führer," Maureen said, testing the water.

Neither man took the bait. "I wouldn't worry about any ridiculousness like that, Fräuline. We have those fools in hand," Gerd said.

"I can't bear the thought that the Führer might be in peril. The scum plotting against the Reich must be dealt with. They're dangerous, and they're spreading lies about us, poisoning our good name," Monika said.

"That's what we're here for, my dear." Gerd moved his hand

to Monika's. She pulled it away and ramped up some faux anger.

"You're just watching them? They need to be purged!"

"There's only so much we can do in a foreign country," Ullrich said.

"You're afraid of some sneaking traitors hiding in slums? You should snatch them up and eviscerate each one."

Maureen wondered if her sister-in-law was going a little too far.

Ullrich laughed. "You've got some spirit." Monika didn't react. "We've done something like that a few times already. The scum that dares to sully the Führer's good name will live to regret it."

"Or maybe they won't," Gerd said.

"That's Gerd's job."

"I give them something they won't forget."

"The whip?" Maureen asked.

"Whatever gets the job done."

"And what about the women among the Reds?" Maureen asked.

Gerd shrugged as if he were trying to appear charming somehow. "They're just as dangerous as the men. We can't afford to treat them differently."

"Our commanding officers would crucify us if we appeared softhearted."

The two men finished their beers. Being this close to them was enough to turn Maureen's stomach, and she rose, proclaiming her need for the ladies' room. She wandered past the other table on the way back from the bathroom. Her brother knew not to ask questions and agreed when she told him to meet them outside in three minutes.

The two men were boasting about their athletic prowess when Maureen returned. Monika was doing her usual stellar acting job.

"We need to leave," Maureen said as she sat down.

The men howled like hyenas in protest. Monika pretended to be disappointed, but not so much as to lead the men to believe she actually might stay.

"We'll be here tomorrow night," she added. Giving them hope made leaving easier, and Frederick and Michael were sitting in the car with the engine running as the women emerged. They climbed into the back seat.

"We know what that place is now," Monika said. "A house of torture for any dissidents unlucky enough to be scooped up."

No one spoke for a few seconds. Frederick started the engine and pulled out.

"Take me back to the gate of the château," Maureen said.

The others seemed to realize the futility of arguing, and they stopped at the gates this time as they passed. Maureen got out of the car and peered in. The four-story gray granite building was floodlit and shone in the night. A silhouette appeared at one of the wide windows and then faded as quickly as it came. The door to the carriage house opened, and a night-watchman emerged.

"Can I help you?" he asked in French.

"Just admiring the house."

The man's harsh stare delivered his message, and she got back into the car.

14

Monday, March 14

Seamus had a meeting near their house later that morning, and Lisa sat with him, enjoying a leisurely breakfast. It was still too cold to eat on the porch, so they stayed at the dining room table as a light drizzle spattered the windows. The sound of the mailbox snapping shut brought Seamus to his feet, and he hurried to the front door, returning seconds later.

"Nothing from Fiona. Again."

"I'm sorry. At least her teachers say she's settling in."

"The news of Harald leaving to do his six months of service to the Reich seems to have cooled her anger a little bit, but it'd be nice to hear from her more than once in three months."

"Harald being away is nothing more than a stay of execution. She'll want to marry him as soon as he gets back."

"I'm hoping the puppy love fades. Hoping," Seamus said.

He threw down the daily newspapers. Lisa opened one with a now-familiar sense of foreboding. The Nazis acquired their latest prize the day before, when the Anschluss of Austria had occurred. The broadsheet was full of stories of the Führer's triumphant return and pictures of his motorcade in Vienna, and the adoring crowds that met it were splashed across the front page. The situation had come to a head two weeks before when, under immense pressure, the Austrian chancellor resigned. Once a Nazi puppet replaced him, "tourists" who had been visiting Vienna suddenly morphed into uniformed SS and occupied the city's public buildings. All night, Nazi mobs paraded through the streets, screaming "*Sieg heil*!" and the battle cry of Anschluss: *"Ein Volk, ein Reich, ein Führer!"*

The new government invited German troops into Austria to preserve order—which was the legality Hitler desired. At dawn, the Wehrmacht crossed the border and sped toward the capital. Later that Saturday, the Führer himself entered by way of the town of Braunau, his birthplace. The "liberated" people threw flowers in his path and hailed him as their savior.

But as Lisa read the story, her mind harkened back to the meeting with Petra Wagner a few months before. The name Ernst Rolfing was repeated several times in the newspaper article, and she'd read that name only once before—on the paper Petra had left with them five months earlier. She got up from the table without another word and climbed the stairs to their bedroom. The paper was in the safe, marked Top Secret, and it felt almost wrong to even look at it. The details mentioned in the letter—which Lisa had dismissed as a forgery when Petra presented it—had been borne out in the events in Austria.

Keeping the document in her hand, she ran downstairs to her husband, who looked up in surprise as she reappeared at the dining room table.

"It's genuine." She threw the piece of paper down in front of him.

"What is?"

"The secret letter Petra brought to the house. Look at it—it mentions Ernst Rolfing. It details the paid protesters and the plan to move the SS in when matters came to a head. That's exactly what happened in Vienna."

Her husband took a few seconds to read through it. "It's either genuine or Petra has a bright future as a fortune teller. You think she was sincere in what she said about turning over a new leaf?"

"Maybe. The thought of trusting her gives me hives, but she knows all the top brass—the generals and the politicians. They must eat out of her hand. If we could use her...."

Lisa stopped talking and walked to the window, staring out at the thickening rain.

"She seemed eager to please you. It might be worth talking to her. And look at this," Seamus said, holding up the sheet of paper. "The movie star wrote her phone number on the back. I don't know her much, but people change."

"Do they?"

"I did."

"Maureen wanted her to deliver that letter she's been sitting on for months to General Engel."

"Call her. Have her deliver it, and we'll see from there."

Lisa couldn't believe what she was about to do. "Ok. I'll tell her to come on Wednesday—the day Engel visits his wife's grave."

"Good idea. Don't give her too much time to think about it." She sat down at the table once more.

Her husband reached out and took her hand. "Just don't tell her any more than she needs to know." He returned to his newspaper.

~

Wednesday, March 16

The cab pulled up outside the mansion in Charlottenburg. Petra almost had to peel herself off the back seat, and her hands were wet as she handed the driver his money. Lisa's husband would be at work, and maybe she wouldn't be home either. She took a breath and strode toward the front door.

Lisa answered it and stood looking at her for a few seconds. Petra didn't blame her for being reluctant or even for judging her. It was up to her to change her old friend's opinion...and soothe her own tortured mind.

"Come in," Lisa said with a flick of her head.

Petra followed her inside, and they sat at the dining room table, same as the last time. The house was empty. Offering no pleasantries, Lisa started straight in. "You want to do something to earn the atonement you're seeking?"

"More than anything. But I can't go on like before. I refuse to make their movies and attend their parties anymore."

"No, that's what you're good for. Keep making the movies. Keep going to the premieres and the parties, but do it for something greater than your career. Help me. You're too valuable to quit."

"I won't do that anymore."

"You're an actress, so act! You can do it."

Lisa's face was granite, yet a dim hope lit in Petra's soul. "You know Himmler and Goebbels and all the high-ranking Nazis?"

"I've met most of them, and the generals too."

"How about Luftwaffe General Horst Engel?"

"I've met him several times. He's always keen to talk."

"I wonder why?" Lisa said. Her words stung, but Petra shrugged them off.

"I have a small job for you." Lisa looked up at the clock on the wall. "The timing should be just right."

"For what?"

"I'll explain in the car. Come with me."

The air of mystery regarding their destination lent the journey the feel of one of the spy movies Petra would have liked to have been making. Lisa didn't speak much as they drove, but she was clearly beginning to trust Petra.

They drove east through Victoriastadt, a part of Berlin she hadn't been to since she was a child. "My spinster aunt used to live near here," Petra said. "My father sometimes said she wasn't interested in any man. I didn't understand that when I was a child."

"We're going to Rummelsburg Cemetery. Is your aunt buried there?"

"No. She was laid to rest in—"

"I don't care where," Lisa snapped. "But you're going to need a cover story."

"For who, exactly?"

"For General Horst Engel."

"Of course. I met him just last week at a fundraiser for the new Focke-Wulf fighter. He and all the other bigwigs were there, swooning over Hitler and Göring."

"The usual, then. General Engel visits his wife's grave every Wednesday at lunchtime. He lays flowers and sits with her for an hour or so before returning to the Air Ministry on Wilhelm-strasse."

"You want me to meet him?"

"You're finished with Goebbels?"

"Yes."

"Good. We want to preserve the illusion that you're available."

Petra took a moment to digest what her former friend said as the car halted at the black gates of the graveyard. The sky above was gray, and a cold wind from the north rustled the Nazi flag at the entrance. It seemed like the perfect day to visit the dead.

"In case anyone asks, your cover story is that you're visiting your aunt's grave. Make sure the dates on whichever tombstone you choose fit your story."

Lisa reached into her bag and drew out an envelope. "Give him this. It's from his son, Gerhard, in Paris. Tell him you were there recently."

"Why do you want me to deliver it?"

"Because sometimes the wrapping is more important than the gift." Lisa paused before continuing. "He may accept something from you that he wouldn't take from anyone else."

Petra stepped out of the car and looked back at Lisa for a nod or word of good luck, which she didn't receive.

"Understandable," Petra said under her breath as the car sped away.

She pushed through the black cemetery gates, where the gravestones were laid out in neat rows. She studied the names as she wandered, searching for a grave that matched her alibi while also looking for General Engel. She found a woman who'd died the year before.

"Hilda Kuntz, you'll do the trick."

A few people passed her, but none gave her more than a cursory look. It was refreshing. The pressure of being a movie star seemed lifted here.

She rounded a bushy corner, scanning the plots until she saw him, dressed in a gray trench coat, bent over a grave with flowers in his hand. His dedication was endearing, but this was business. She strode toward him.

"General Engel?"

He looked up with dewy eyes. "Petra Wagner? What are you doing here?"

"I was visiting my aunt's grave. But to be honest, this is one of the few places I can come to get away from the baying crowds. It's so peaceful."

"I agree," he said with a pained smile. "I probably spend too much time here."

They both looked down at the grave. "I'm so sorry."

"I took a bullet in the back when I was flying in the Great War, but the pain of that was nothing compared to the loss of my Millie."

"I hope to boast of a love as strong as that someday."

"A beautiful young woman like you? You must have hundreds of suitors."

"None worth wasting my time over. Not yet, anyway." She pointed to a bench 20 paces away. "Shall we sit and talk a while?"

His eyes lit up. She'd seen that look in men's eyes since she was a girl—the "I can't believe she wants to talk to me" look. It had no age limit.

He placed the bouquet down and followed her to the bench.

"I've met you so many times, but never like this," she began. "What was your wife like?"

"She was an idealist, a dreamer. A funny match for an old soldier like me. We were so different. Perhaps that's why it worked between us, you know?" Petra nodded. "I remember the first time we met as if it were yesterday. She was the most beautiful girl I'd ever seen. She hated Hitler from the start. I'd beg her to come along to events with me, but she refused. My sons would have wild rows over dinner about him, with me acting as referee. It killed her in the end."

"What?"

"A heart attack, brought on by stress after one of those ridiculous blazing fights between Gerhard and the other boys. He's just like her, except even more stubborn. I haven't seen him since the funeral."

"I remember you mentioning that to me. Is that when he left the country to go to Spain?"

"It was the best thing for him. He needed to feel like he was doing something to counter Fascism. It was an obsession with him."

"He's in Paris now."

Engel looked at her with a raised eyebrow. "What? How do you know?"

"I was there recently, and happened to meet him." She reached into her bag and drew out a blank envelope. "He gave me this letter for you." She handed it to him.

He looked at it for a few seconds as if evaluating whether to take it or not. "Thank you," he finally said and tucked it into his jacket pocket. He stood up and bowed. "Can we meet again?"

"That would be wonderful."

The older man took her hand and kissed her on the knuckles before bowing again and taking his leave.

She waited five minutes on the bench before strolling back to the cemetery gates, where Lisa was waiting. Lisa didn't want to talk there and put her foot on the gas pedal and drove a few blocks. She pulled over on a nondescript residential street and turned to the actress.

"How did it go? Did he take the letter?"

"Yes. He didn't read it on the spot, but he wants to meet me again."

"Would you be willing to do that? To find out what he's thinking?"

"To what end?"

"I can't reveal that right now."

"What did the letter say?"

"Same answer, but my bet is that if you see Engel again, he'll tell you. When he does, recount to me what his thoughts are. If you want to help the cause, this is the best way."

Lisa pulled out and drove a few blocks as Petra digested what she heard. She had no more desire to start seeing Engel than any other man 30 years her senior, but if this was her key to redemption...

"The tram station is two minutes' walk," Lisa said as she pulled over to the side of the road.

"I'll do it. I'll see Engel again, if it's so important." Petra reached over and let herself out.

She was on the street when Lisa called through the open window, "Well done."

Petra smiled and pushed a pair of sunglasses over her eyes.

15

Wednesday, April 13

Engel was different. The general was a gentleman of the old school, patient and polite, whereas Goebbels was more apt to root in the mud with the other pigs. The Reich Minister for Propaganda was a savage troll who took what he wanted from the desperate starlets he preyed upon and was more than happy to pass them on once he'd had his fill. Engel wasn't like him at all.

Petra had met him several times in the preceding weeks, but the general had kept his gentlemanly composure. He knew she'd been Goebbels' plaything for a while, but he never mentioned it. He also never spoke about her movies, which was fine with her. They only ever met one-on-one and never in public. It was as if they were closed off from the rest of the world when they were together, and there was certainly comfort in that. She wasn't attracted to him but felt affection. Perhaps if he were 30 years younger, this might not have all been for show. It was so hard to find an honest man.

The general was on the balcony of her fifth-floor luxury

apartment overlooking the street. The day was fading, and night was drawing in.

"It's amazing up here, isn't it?" she asked.

"Have you ever been in a plane?"

"I flew to Munich last year for a premiere. It was incredible."

"I still remember the first time I saw an airplane." He smiled as she handed him a glass of wine. "I wasn't a child at the time, but that was how it felt. Something changed in me as I beheld it. The dream I'd harbored my entire life was realized in that moment: Men could fly like birds. I was a full-grown man, but I blubbered like a child and knew I'd never be the same again."

"That's beautiful," she said.

"I'm sorry about all this secrecy," he said. "It's just been so hard since Millie died, and you're the first woman I've seen like this since—and for the previous 35 years!"

"That's longer than I've been alive."

"You could say I'm a little out of practice." He smiled and stared out at the city.

She put her arm around his waist, and he did the same. They stood in silence for a few seconds.

"I thought a part of me died when my wife passed away, but you've brought me back," Engel said and kissed her. "I never thought I could feel remotely like this again."

"I've met so many toads. Many rich and powerful men who think they can buy and sell me. You're not like them."

The basis of truth in her words made acting them out far easier.

"We haven't talked about many things. You have three sons. I know where Gerhard is, but what about the other two?"

"I see Fritz most days. He works in the Air Ministry with me. He's a fine boy. Heinrich is in the Party, a civil servant," he said with little relish.

"And your other son, Gerhard? Did his mother's death hit him hard?"

The general reached into his pocket for a silver cigarette case and offered one to Petra. She declined. He lit it up before answering her question.

"He was always impulsive. His trip to Spain to fight for the Republicans isn't something I readily admit to my colleagues—certainly not to Air Marshall Göring. My other sons are both committed to the Führer."

They spoke about Göring for a few minutes. The general seemed to believe in his vision for the Luftwaffe itself, if not his methods. "He's industrious and driven, but also a blustering fool," he said with a joyless laugh.

"We're alone. You can speak your mind. No secrets here."

Engel smiled and put his hand on hers. "The investment in new technology is staggering. Soon we'll have the finest air force in the world."

"To what end? Is Hitler leading us down the path to another war?"

"It's not my place to ask questions such as that, my dear." He turned his body to face hers, resting an elbow on the railing around the balcony.

"But as a human being, you think that, don't you? We all do. It seems to me the gears of war began grinding the moment Hitler took power."

General Engel looked at her in surprise. "Be careful, Petra. If you express those sentiments in front of the wrong person—"

"But you're someone I can trust, aren't you? Someone I can talk to."

He nodded. "Of course."

"I'm scared, Horst. This country seems set for another disastrous war. Do you think we can win against the Allies?"

Engel took a long pull on his cigarette. "It's on my mind every waking moment. I read that book Herr Hitler wrote. I was like everyone else at first—delighted to see the back of the ruinous years of democracy—but war does seem to be ingrained in the Führer's mind. There's no other way to achieve his goals. The other countries in Europe aren't just going to give up their territories to us."

"Austria did."

"That was an exceptional case. Hitler has his eye on Czechoslovakia next, and Poland, and then France and Russia. Someone's going to call his bluff sooner or later. It's as inevitable as the sunrise."

"Do you think we can win?"

Engel looked at her. "Hitler certainly does."

"And you?"

"I think if we take Czechoslovakia and Poland, and somehow convince the Allies not to intervene—"

"But they will."

"The problem is the lack of resources. We don't have enough gasoline to fuel the tanks and airplanes, and horse-drawn artillery will only get us so far. If we don't capture the oil fields in Romania and southwest Russia, the Americans will crush us. This war won't come down to whose men are braver or more determined. It'll be won by the side with more resources."

"Does the Führer know this?"

"Hitler lives in a constant state of denial. In his mind, no army can possibly stand up to the master race. He's convinced we only lost the last war because the Jews stabbed us in the back."

"He really believes that?"

"Unfortunately. Russia is central to his plans. I can't help thinking of what happened to Napoléon when he tried to overrun the east. I'm not sure it's possible. The place is so vast that if Stalin dropped behind the Urals, he could pump out enough tanks and guns to crush our armies like grapes.

Winning might be possible on a small scale, but for what Hitler is suggesting? I don't see it."

Petra knew she was on dangerous ground. Any talk undermining the Führer was punishable by a trip to a concentration camp. She and Engel had already crossed a bridge of trust few would approach.

"Do any of the other generals feel the same way?"

"It's not an easy topic to discuss, but a few men I trust have expressed similar sentiments."

"What did Millie think of the direction the country has taken?"

Engel shook his head and stubbed out his cigarette on an ashtray. "My wife hated Hitler from the start. She and Gerhard were on one side, with my other sons pitted against them. I was the referee. It was during one of our fights that she suffered the heart attack that killed her. Gerhard refers to it in the letter you gave me. I heard her voice in that letter—it was his writing, but her words. I know you were curious about it and brought it along to show you."

He walked back inside, but she caught him by the hand. "No, you don't have to show me."

"I want to. I want to share everything with you."

The older man's jacket was hanging on a hook by the door. He took his wallet from the inside pocket and drew out the folded letter.

"Here." They sat down on her leather couch together. She read aloud.

Father,

I first want to say sorry because I know you blame me for Mother's death. The events surrounding her heart attack haunt me in my dreams. I wake up every morning

WISHING I COULD TURN THE CLOCK BACK, BUT I CAN'T, AND I HAVE TO LIVE WITH THAT.

I UNDERSTAND THE POSITION YOU WERE IN, CAUGHT BETWEEN MOTHER AND ME AND THE TWO BOYS. I'VE COME TO REALIZE IT'S NOT THEIR FAULT OR YOURS, BUT THE REGIME'S ITSELF. THAT'S WHAT TORE OUR FAMILY APART, AND IT'LL DO THE SAME TO THE ENTIRE CONTINENT IF NOBLE MEN LIKE YOU LET IT. NO MATTER WHAT OATH YOU TOOK, YOU KNOW YOUR DUTY IS TO GERMANY, NOT ONE MAN. DISASTER AWAITS AT THE END OF THE ROAD WE'RE TRAVELING. ONLY YOU AND A FEW OTHER GOOD MEN HAVE THE CHANCE TO AVERT IT.

PLEASE TELL FRITZ AND HEINRICH I'M SAFE AND WISH THEM NOTHING BUT THE BEST. KEEP MOTHER IN YOUR HEART AS YOU DECIDE WHAT TO DO.

YOUR SON,

GERHARD

"Always so like his mother," he said with a tear in his eye.

"He's suggesting...."

"I know what he's suggesting," the general said. "But perhaps he's right, that it's the only way to save the Reich. Hitler is hell-bent on a war that will destroy this entire country."

"Can you do it?"

"Maybe. I've been agonizing over the words in this letter ever since you gave it to me. It was like talking to Millie again, and it's made me realize something."

"What?"

"It might be up to me."

~

Friday, April 15

Lisa kept her eyes down as she walked. The angry skies had cleared the massive Tiergarten, now emptied of all but the hardiest of souls. Petra stood waiting for her under an oak tree with her signature sunglasses. Lisa wondered if wearing them would bring more attention than they would deflect, as it was raining now. But they were the only people around. This was the perfect time and place to meet.

The raindrops were falling in earnest now, and Lisa opened the umbrella she was carrying and raised it above her head. Petra ran and joined her underneath. They crossed an empty bridge over a slate-gray stream coated in water lilies and waited until they reached the other side to begin talking.

"I figured out what your mission with the general is."

"And what might that be?"

"You want him to overthrow the government." Lisa didn't respond. "I think he just might do it," Petra said with a smile.

They kept on, wary of passersby. But the few people they encountered seemed more concerned with staying dry than listening to their conversation. Lisa thought about whether to correct the actress or to throw up some kind of smokescreen regarding their reasoning for her reports from the general but decided against it.

"Our relationship is progressing," Petra said. "We've met several times since I last spoke to you."

"Where?"

"Always in private. In my apartment yesterday, and we made sure no one observed him entering or leaving. I saw the letter his son wrote. He seems profoundly moved by it. It was incredible," she said with a beaming smile. "He told me the story of his wife and family—how he was the referee between the two sides."

They spent the next few minutes reliving the conversation.

Lisa asked every question she could think of, and Petra seemed more than happy to answer each one. Her enthusiasm never waned.

"Engel doesn't think the Nazis can win the war Hitler is barreling toward," Petra said. "But this is only the beginning. The kernel of insurrection is within him. We just have to give it the attention it needs to make it grow."

"How?"

"He's falling for me."

"Why am I not surprised?"

"We have a real chance to achieve something. A government run by the military wouldn't be perfect, but it would be so much better than what we have now."

Lisa stared into her eyes. The sincerity was visible. "Ok. You meet him next week and report back to me in the way my husband suggested. If anyone brings you in, we never met."

"Of course."

Lisa wondered how the pretty actress would hold up under the harsh spotlight of Gestapo questioning. How would anyone react if hauled into an interrogation room and strapped into a chair with a bright light glaring into their eyes? The agents would take turns questioning her, not allowing her a moment's rest for days. At intervals, they would burn her flesh with cigarettes or jam slivers of wood under her fingernails to liven her up and make her more attentive. They had figured out the exact amount of pain and sleeplessness that would reduce the human will to impotence and turn anyone's mind to putty. How could anyone hold out?

"Be careful, Petra. The Gestapo won't care who you are or how many movies you've made if they get wind of this. Their retribution will be brutal."

"All the more reason to convince our new friend to move against them. He's closer than I ever could have imagined—he just needs a push. But Engel's no fool. He's not about to go back to the Air Ministry shooting his mouth off. He won't make a move unless he's sure he has the backing of enough powerful men to oust Hitler for good."

The rain stopped, and Lisa took down her umbrella, shaking it out. "Keep the pressure on him, Petra, and let me know when you next have news."

"I will. The next step is for him to find like-minded powerful men, and he seems confident he will."

They hadn't seen another person for ten minutes but still left the park separately. Lisa watched her former friend walk away, wondering if their plan might actually work. The clouds shifted, and a bright ray of sunlight broke through like a flaming sword. The light of hope ignited within her, bringing a smile to her face.

16

Tuesday, April 19

Seamus was in his office poring over the books. Business was growing at an exponential rate—the Reich's boundless appetite for munitions had created a gold rush like no other in modern history. A new class of megawealthy armaments kings had sprung up these last two years. Most were more flamboyant and outspoken than he and his cousin, but few had gained more. The Nazis' lust for war had saved Ritter Metalworks, taking a dying concern and turning it into a thriving business, and the money was obscene. Seamus's bank account was swelling like a river in a rainstorm. Helga must have been one of the wealthiest businesswomen in the country. The workers themselves had benefited little, however. Wage fixing was a feature of the Nazi system. Still, as employees of an armaments factory, the Ritter workers received bonuses every quarter, though the German Labor Front capped even these. With the abolition of trade unions, the employees were left with little opportunity to promote their interests. Most were just pleased to have steady jobs after years of economic uncertainty. The Nazi flags on the factory walls seemed to multiply by the day.

Seamus pushed the ledger of the latest orders for bullets aside and stood up to walk to the large safe he kept under the window. Instinct caused him to look around, but there was no one, so he dialed in the code. The metal structure opened with a soft creaking sound, and he reached for an account book on the top shelf that sat beside several wads of cash. He removed it and shut the safe. Helga was visiting the airplane factory, where she spent much of her time now. It was a model of Nazi production, without the impediments of the Jewish employees who still worked here. The atmosphere there suited her better.

Seamus sat back down and opened the ledger. Names were written along the left, and the amount in Reichsmarks they'd deposited was written in the boxes alongside. Seamus shook his head. Perhaps it was human instinct not to trust others with one's life savings, but the Jewish workers weren't taking advantage of his offer to move their money abroad and avoid the Nazi taxes. Almost six months after he gathered them in his office and shared his plan for them to escape the Reich, few had lodged more than a few hundred marks, and many had given over next to nothing.

He slammed the book shut, picked it up, and strode to Gert Bernheim's office. The factory manager was on the phone when he entered. He held up a finger before motioning to Seamus to sit.

"You don't look like a man with a thriving business," he said once he'd hung up.

Seamus held up the ledger and placed it on the desk between them. "The Jewish workers aren't lodging money with us."

"Times aren't easy for the working man. Most of them can't spare it right now."

"But the pressure the Nazis are exerting on the Jews is—"

"You're going to tell me about that?"

"Of course not, my friend. I just thought they'd jump at the chance to leave. Who knows what the Nazis are going to subject them to next?"

"It's been a slow trickle of laws subjugating us," Gert said and opened the ledger. "It's all too easy to pretend things might get better. Most people on this list have never been out of the country. The thought of moving, even to Palestine? I know there are other Jews in that far-off place, but it might as well be the moon."

"They don't trust me with their money, do they?"

"It's not that. We always knew it was going to be a slow process."

"I thought we'd have made more progress after almost six months."

"That trust you're speaking of will grow. Someone needs to take the plunge first, then the others will follow."

"What about you?"

"You trying to get rid of me?"

Seamus smiled. "I'm trying to make sure you and Lil can enjoy your retirement someplace where the sun shines."

"I'm running this scheme. No offense, Seamus, but the only reason they've handed over any of their money so far is because I've been prodding the workers to do it. I feel a responsibility toward them." He pointed down toward the factory floor.

"You need to look after your family first."

"I've given more money to your Nazi tax-evasion fund than most of the rest put together. I'll be ready when the time comes. We're thinking about joining Ben in Switzerland. Bern sounds like a beautiful city in his letters."

"We'll be sure and visit."

"I'll keep a spare bed for you."

"I have a meeting this afternoon with Gilda Stein and Leon Gellert. I'd like you to sit in on it."

"Of course. They're two of the few non-Ritter Metalworks employees on the list." Gert pointed to their names at the bottom of the second page of the ledger. "But look at their deposits." A zero sat beside each of their names.

"Lisa mentioned they're interested in emigrating, but they haven't shared any other details."

"A wise policy these days."

Seamus walked back to his office.

The call came about 30 minutes later, and Seamus's secretary showed Leon and Gilda into his office. The two Subversives took a seat in front of his desk next to Gert. They spent the first few minutes asking questions about Maureen. It was difficult to gain insight from the curt letters she sent, which were edited for the benefit of the censors. They also asked about Willi Behrens and his family, whom they had helped escape from the camp for Roma in Marzahn. Seamus had little information. The last he'd heard, they were settled in Sweden.

Gilda started. "Leon and I spoke a few months ago, after you and Lisa had us at your house. We came up with a plan of our own."

"We need your help," Leon said.

"I'm all ears."

"Perhaps it would be best if we showed you."

Seamus looked over at Gert, and then back at their two guests. "Now you have my full attention."

The men followed Gilda and Leon into the factory parking lot. A brand-new black Mercedes-Benz 540K sat shining in the sun.

"That's what I call a car," Gert said.

"We bought it together," Gilda said. "We pooled our money."

"And we want you, Seamus, to drive it to Paris," Leon said.

Seamus laughed. "So I can sell it and get your money back?"

"Exactly," Gilda and Leon said in unison.

"You'll never get back what you paid for it," Gert said.

"Whatever we get will be better than paying the Nazis 81 percent," Gilda said.

Seamus ran his hand along the smooth, honed lines of the car. "Can you help us?" Gilda asked.

She was alone. Her husband was murdered by Brownshirts several years before, but Leon had a wife and two daughters.

"Are you both ready to leave?"

"Yes," Leon said. "When can you go?"

"Soon enough, I'd say."

"We've been ready to leave for weeks," Leon said. "We have our exit visas in place—the Nazis are eager to see the back of us. We'll be waiting for you when you arrive."

Seamus shook their hands. Gilda hugged him.

Wednesday, April 27

Petra's body rippled with excitement when she saw the older man sitting outside the restaurant. He was beaming like a little boy, holding a bouquet as she approached. The town of Oranienburg, 30 minutes northwest of the city, wasn't somewhere she'd ever spent much time before. But they could escape the eyes of the press here and at least dine in public.

"This is for you," the Luftwaffe general said.

"Thank you." She kissed him on his bearded cheek.

An elderly woman ambled past and wished them both a good afternoon. She probably thought the general was Petra's father. They both scanned the area for anyone who might be listening in. The general led her inside to a more discreet table in the corner of the restaurant. No one could see or hear them. Engel held her chair, and she sat down.

"Wednesday is quickly becoming my favorite day of the week," he said.

"You're so sweet."

"My life used to be mournful and dour, but you're like a rainstorm in the desert. You bring life to where it seemed none existed."

"You've helped me through some dark times too."

The waitress came out and took their order. Petra laughed to herself as the general ordered the ultra-traditional schnitzel and sauerkraut, while she ordered a salad. The anonymity was liberating, but they kept the conversation neutral as they ate.

Petra was already thinking three minutes ahead but remained patient, waiting until they went for a walk through the countryside later on, to ask the questions burning through her.

"Are we any further along in our quest?"

Engel's demeanor changed. He dipped his head down to speak in a whisper. "I spoke to Generals Busch and von Reichenau. They're both good men, loyal to the Kaiser. They share my concerns."

"Are they ready to do their duty to free Germany?"

"They were prepared to discuss the idea, agreeing that we can't possibly win against the massed forces of the Allies. The question is, will we have to? They're not convinced the Americans will join in the conflict. The generals see them as overprivileged and uninterested in the European situation. But these men don't want war, and would relish a return to the more noble times before the Great War."

She reached down and took his hand, but didn't change the tone of the conversation. "Do they command the loyalty of the armies beneath them?"

"Absolutely. Only the SS and the Nazis themselves worship Hitler like a god."

"So, with their help, do you believe you'd have the power to arrest Hitler and replace him?"

"With their help? In theory, yes. The Nazis' gaze seems to be shifting toward the Sudetenland in Czechoslovakia now. My guess is that if the Allies stand up to him there, the generals will be more likely to act. No one has forgotten the last war. I tried to stress to Busch and von Reichenau that Hitler is determined to destroy the flower of German youth once more."

"Did they agree?"

"They did. It's been obvious from the start that war is Hitler's way to snatch everything he wants. He's obsessed by ideas that can only come about through conquest. Every high-ranking military officer sees that, but some are of the same mind as the Führer."

"How close are we to being able to make the move to depose him?"

"Hard to say. Perhaps as short as a few weeks. I promised the generals I wouldn't try to seize power myself. The thought of attaining it for themselves seemed to please them."

"But you'd make a wonderful leader."

Engel smiled. "I only want to fly planes. I'll leave the ruling to others."

"Are you sure you can trust them? One word to the Gestapo and we'll both be at the end of a rope."

"I am sure, and I'd never let them touch a hair on your head. I'll die in agony before I ever give them your name."

Petra appreciated the sentiment and took some comfort in his words, but saying he wouldn't talk and not bending under interrogation were two different things. The most important question remained, and she wasn't about to hold back.

"Are you determined to do this? Germany needs a strong man. You could be the most important person in the world today, General Engel." She put her hand on his and stared into his gray eyes.

"It's not a matter of if, but when. I'll get those men on board. They wouldn't have spoken to me if their hearts weren't leading them in the same direction. I'll get this done for you, my princess, and one day soon I'll dedicate a statue to you in the middle of Kurfürstendamm."

A spring of hope, unlike anything she'd felt before, brought a smile to her face. She grasped his hands in hers as a tear fell down her cheek. It was the first hopeful tear she'd shed in as long as she could remember.

17

Friday, May 6: Switzerland

Fiona sat on the edge of her bed, the letter from Harald in her hand. No one understood what it was like to be in love with someone so far away—not her classmates, not her teachers, and certainly not her father or Lisa. And now Harald was slipping away. The three other girls in her dormitory were asleep, Steffi snoring as usual. The glow of the moon through the window by her bed offered just enough light to read by, and her gaze returned to the words on the page once more, as if somehow rereading it would change them.

Fiona,

My time on the farm in Saxony has opened my eyes to what one person can do for the Führer and the Reich. I've never experienced the friendships I've made here, or felt so important in my role before. It's whetted my appetite to join the SS more than ever. I went to the recruitment

OFFICE IN TOWN LAST WEEK WHEN WE VISITED AND, AFTER SPEAKING TO THE OFFICER IN CHARGE, JOINED UP TO SERVE THE REICH. I'VE BEEN WALKING ON AIR EVER SINCE. I CAN'T BELIEVE I'LL SOON BE PART OF THE FÜHRER'S PERSONAL GUARD. TRAINING BEGINS AT THE END OF MAY.

I'LL BE HOME FOR A FEW WEEKS BEFORE I LEAVE, BUT I FEAR WE'LL MISS EACH OTHER, AS YOU WON'T RETURN UNTIL A MONTH LATER. THE POSSIBILITY THAT WE WON'T SEE EACH OTHER FOR A LONG TIME IS SOMETHING I'VE HAD TO COME TO TERMS WITH. I AM VERY RELUCTANT TO SAY THAT IF YOU NEED TO FIND ANOTHER TO BEAR CHILDREN FOR THE FÜHRER, PLEASE DO SO. DON'T WASTE THE FLOWER OF YOUR YOUTH PINING FOR ME. DO AS YOUR DESTINY URGES. THE COUNTRY NEEDS STRONG WOMEN LIKE YOU.

HARALD

The paper was wet from her tears, resulting from the love of her life slipping away like water through her fingers. Her father's plan to destroy her life was coming into clear view, and it was working. Her time in the school was more bearable than she first thought it might be, simply because, in her mind, it was finite. All school years ended, summers arrived, and she would be home with Harald and her friends again. But this! She could lose Harald forever.

She'd read and reread the letter so many times but couldn't figure out why her love would offer her the chance to have children with someone else. It was incomprehensible. She was sure talking to him would sort all this out. He was leaving Saxony soon—any letter she wrote might not reach him in time, and the school term would end after he left to begin SS training. It didn't seem like she had any choice.

She reached under the bed for a leather-bound box and put it on the bed. The letters from Harald and Helga were on top.

She didn't bother keeping the ones from her family, and didn't even open the ones from her father. Underneath was the money Helga sent, which was more than enough for the train fare back to Berlin. Her passport was locked up in the principal's office, but she could con the border agents with a few tears, or even say her parents left her behind by accident. Her League of German Girls' papers would help too.

The time had come. The rest of her life depended upon her actions in the next few days. She wasn't going to stay here while the future she had mapped out for herself went up in flames.

Her dormitory room window was locked, but she'd been filing away at the metal for weeks. The drainpipe along the wall would negate the drop to the ground, and from there, it was about an hour's walk into town. The first train to Berlin was at 6 a.m. She'd be on it before the teachers even noticed she was gone. Her family was visiting Paris again this weekend, so it was the perfect time to arrive at Helga's house. Time was too important to waste. This was about the rest of her life.

Friday, May 6: Paris

The top-floor apartment in Rochechouart was old and unkempt. The windows were grimy, and the sunlight streaming through exposed the cobwebs hanging from the rafters.

"This place could use a little love," Monika said. A puff of dust blew up from the threadbare couch as she sat down.

"It was my great-uncle's," Hans said.

"Do you have much French blood in your family?" Michael asked.

"On my mother's side. But I'd only been to France once, before I escaped from Germany. Being able to speak French made settling here easier, but I've no intention of living here forever. Once the Reich is liberated, I'll return."

Gerhard stood alone in the corner, glancing around at the dusty old space. Maureen walked over to him. "We'd better get cleaning this place before the meeting tonight."

The young man didn't answer. He just nodded, strolled back outside the apartment door, and peered down. "Do you know the neighbors?" His voice echoed in the stairwell.

"Old Madame Garnier across the way won't bother us," Hans replied. "She's half-deaf anyway. The ideal neighbor!"

"What's that trapdoor in the corner?" Gerhard asked. He walked over and put his hand on a small painted square in the ceiling.

"I'm not sure," Hans answered.

Maureen took a kitchen stool and placed it below the trap-door. It was painted shut, and she had to take a knife and cut the door out. She couldn't move it, so Hans put his full weight on the handle, and it opened with a loud *crack*. He reached up for a white ladder, which extended all the way down to the floor.

"It leads up to the roof," he said as he climbed it.

Maureen followed him up. The door at the top opened more easily, and a rush of sunlight greeted them. Gerhard climbed up next. The rooftops of the other buildings extended several hundred paces left and right. They walked to the front edge and put their forearms on the wall before leaning over to peer down at the street five stories below.

"Maybe we should have the meeting up here," Maureen said with a smile.

"It's some view."

Michael and Monika were next up the ladder, and soon Hans joined them. "I've never been up here in all the times I visited my uncle."

They stayed on the roof for a few minutes, basking in the spring sunshine. Gerhard and Maureen were last to descend. He took her arm before she reached the ladder. "Can I speak to you?"

The others had climbed back down to begin the job of cleaning out the apartment. The first meeting was to be that night.

"My father wrote to me!" Gerhard said with a light of excitement in his eyes. "I received the letter a few days ago. It's heavily edited and coded, but the message was clear—he values his country more than the oath the Nazi Party forced him to take."

"You think he might act?"

"He didn't say, but he's never been one for idle talk. I'm hopeful. It's all thanks to you."

"We need to stay calm. There's a long road ahead," Maureen said, but she felt what she saw in her friend's eyes: A genuine belief that emerging from the darkness the Nazis had plunged Germany into was finally possible.

He took Maureen aside once more when the apartment was ready. "I'm going to tell the other Resistance leaders at the meeting tonight."

"About your father?" Maureen asked. "Please don't do that."

"No—no specifics, but if they step up their leaflet production and target the armed forces, the generals may stir against the Nazis. It could improve the coup's chance of succeeding."

"I don't know. We've gotten this far keeping our ideas and plans to ourselves."

"And we need everyone's help to make it the rest of the way. Hitler's obsessed with retaining power. He'll crush anyone who stands against him. We have to do our best to motivate the troops who are going to have to stand against the SS. They're unreachable. To them, Hitler *is* the Reich."

"If you're sure...."

"I am. It's time to announce the beginning of the end of Germany's nightmare."

Cleaning the apartment Hans's great-uncle had left him took several hours. Monika had brought crispy bread and cheese, and when it was time for lunch, they sat on the roof with glasses of red wine to wash it down.

The apartment was ready by the middle of the afternoon after setting the heavy dining room table in the middle of the wooden floor. *Perfect.* Maureen was excited. *The first meeting of our new Resistance movement! It may be possible to achieve something even here, four hours from Paris.*

Maureen motioned to Monika and her brother. "We have to go. My father should be arriving in an hour or two."

"What's the occasion?" Gerhard asked.

"It was hard to tell by my stepmother's letter. Our code only extends so far, but it seems she's driving across with my father and stepsister."

"Good luck. I'll see you later. The meeting's at nine."

"I haven't forgotten." Maureen smiled. "We'll get dinner, and I'll be back after that."

"With Michael and Monika?"

"Yes."

"I look forward to it."

Maureen kissed him on both cheeks before the trio left.

Riding the new Autobahns in Gilda and Leon's powerful automobile was a pleasure. The up-to-date roads, which many said were built to allow Hitler to transport his armies to the border more quickly, were mainly empty. Not many Germans had cars, particularly outside the cities. With no speed limit, Seamus put the Mercedes to the test, and Hannah whooped from the back seat as they hit 110 miles per hour. The border crossing was as easy as ever. Lisa had nothing on her passport to denote she was half-Jewish, and with not much more than a bored glance from the border guards and a cursory search of their luggage, they crossed into France.

Gilda, Leon, and his family were already in Paris, having left Germany by train the day before. All their money was in this car, entrusted to him. Leon was waiting with his wife and daughters, but Gilda was alone, her husband murdered by SA men in the early days of the regime. No one was ever charged with the crime. He was just another dead Jew on the streets of Berlin, ignored by the authorities.

Lisa called out the directions Gilda had given her as they neared the city. The tiredness of the 13-hour trip washed away as new energy electrified Seamus's body.

"I'm so relieved," Lisa said when they saw the sign for Bagnolet, the eastern suburb of Paris where they had arranged to meet Leon and Gilda.

"Were you nervous? It was an easy trip."

"For us. But it wouldn't have been for Gilda or Leon."

"Just another stamp on our passports."

Hannah was asleep in the back, books strewn around her on the seat. She woke as they pulled up at the address where an old metal sign read Levi Nussbaum's Garage. Seamus parked the car in the lot, got out, and opened the doors for his wife and stepdaughter. Gilda emerged from the office with a beaming smile on her face. Lisa threw her arms around her as if they hadn't seen each other in years. Leon, his wife Jennifer, and their two daughters—both taller than their parents—jogged out after her. They took turns shaking Seamus's hand, and Leon picked Hannah up and threw her in the air. It wasn't hard to see why they were so happy. Driving the Mercedes over the border was simple, especially for a non-Jew who traveled frequently. But Seamus accepted the congratulations and plaudits without question.

"I have to confess, Seamus," Gilda began, "that we haven't been entirely truthful with you."

"What are you talking about?"

"Let me show you," Leon said.

A man in dirty overalls, who Leon introduced as the proprietor of the garage, handed the composer a blade.

Hannah stood behind her mother. Leon smiled. "Don't worry, sweetheart."

"Be careful. That's an expensive car," Seamus said as Leon approached the vehicle.

Leon bent down and sat on the back seat before plunging the knife into the red leather cushion beside him.

"You have to sell that!" Lisa said, but Gilda smiled beside her.

Leon drew the blade back to expose the cushion underneath, which brimmed out like foam over the edge of a coffee cup. He reached his hand in. "What do we have here?" He drew out a wad of banknotes and threw it to Seamus. It was thick with 100-mark bills.

"How much?"

"Five thousand," Gilda said and patted him on the shoulder. He handed her the money in disbelief as Leon dug for another wad. His wife brought a leather satchel, and over the next few minutes, Leon handed her about twenty wads of cash.

Seamus shook his head with a wry smile. "How much?"

"Between us?" Gilda asked. "One hundred thousand Reichsmarks. I'm sorry we lied to you. We knew you would have done it anyway, and figured you'd be less conspicuous if you didn't know about it."

"You're right," Seamus said with a bewildered grin. "But it would have been nice to know what I was transporting."

"We were confident you wouldn't be stopped," Gilda said.

"I never am."

Fifteen minutes later, the Mercedes was stripped of the cash they'd smuggled out, and the mechanic drove it into the shop to repair the upholstery.

"I should still get a good price for the car," Leon said.

"How are we going to get to our hotel? The 540K's wrecked!" Seamus said with a grin.

"I think we can afford a taxi," Gilda said.

Lisa hugged her friends. "Wait until Maureen hears about this!"

"So, where to now? Are you settling in Paris?" Seamus asked.

"We're going to try America," Leon said, taking Jennifer by the hand.

"The Land of the Free," Seamus said.

"I'm thinking about staying here," Gilda said. "I'd like to live somewhere so beautiful, it takes my breath away."

Two cars stopped on the road outside the garage parking lot, and five minutes later, they were speeding into the city, singing all the way.

Gilda dropped Seamus, Lisa, and Hannah off at the Hotel d'Angleterre in Saint-Germain, promising to meet them for dinner in two hours.

Lisa turned to Seamus as they strolled into the hotel with their bags. "They had us fooled."

"Did they ever!"

"Was I sitting on all that money on the drive here?" Hannah asked. "I wondered why the seat was so lumpy."

They all laughed as they pushed the door open and walked inside.

Michael picked up his stepsister and kissed her on the cheek. "You're getting huge!" he said to Hannah. "You'll be picking me up soon."

She giggled as he put her back down.

"How are the other children?" Monika asked as they left the hotel to walk to the restaurant.

"Conor's staying with Aunt Helga for the weekend," Lisa said.

"I dread to think what they'll get up to together," Michael said. "A Nazi rally, perhaps?"

"Conor wouldn't be interested in that. Helga loves him, though. She jumped at the chance."

"How is Fiona?" Monika said.

"I don't know. She won't see us, and only wrote one cursory letter. We're hoping she'll thaw when summer comes. Harald is getting out of his Reich Labor Service any day, so if she comes back and reconnects with him we might be back to square one."

"Would it do any good for me to write to her?"

"I don't know, Monika. I'll try anything at this stage, though."

"Perhaps it's time you left Germany?" Michael asked.

"You have enough money now, and you could sell the business. Helga might even buy you out," his wife said.

His father looked at Lisa as if she understood his thoughts. "It's not as simple as that. Our mission there isn't over," he said with an air of finality.

Michael knew his father wouldn't talk about it anymore, so he let it drop...for now.

Maureen was waiting on the corner of Quai de la Tournelle with Gilda, Leon, and his wife. She greeted Michael and the rest of the family before turning to wag a finger at her friends from the Subversives. "They told me about the car!" she said. "You're an international money smuggler now, Father."

"Not for the first time." The group laughed.

They proceeded inside the world-famous Tour d'Argent restaurant together, where Gilda and Leon treated them to a glorious meal. Michael dined on the famous pressed duck. His wife ate fish so fresh it must have been in a net that morning. Once dinner was over, Leon stood up to thank Seamus and Lisa while lamenting that fleeing Germany had been the only viable option for his family.

"It was too much. We tried to ride it out, thinking that common sense would eventually prevail, but we know now that doing so endangered our girls. And I can't wait to work again! Not being able to compose has been eating away at my soul."

"Since 1933," his wife added.

They raised their glasses to a new life in the United States.

"And the hope of revolution in the Reich," Maureen added as the time to leave came way too soon. "We have a meeting to attend now."

"All of you?" Hannah asked.

"We'll see you tomorrow morning," Monika said and cupped the little girl's cheek.

Michael, his wife, and his sister stood up. "Once a Subversive, always a Subversive," Gilda said with a smile.

They walked to the Métro with full, contented bellies and spoke about dinner and their family on the way to Rochechouart. Two men in flat caps were sitting on the steps to the apartment block and looked them up and down as they stopped.

"You live here?" one asked.

"We're here for the meeting." Maureen called out their names, and the man checked them from a list he drew from his pocket. With a tilt of his neck, he motioned them inside.

They climbed the stairwell in silence. Maureen used the secret knock, and the door opened. Gerhard led them inside, where Hans and two other men were sitting at the table. Each had a glass of wine in front of them. Michael knew there was only one more chair for a reason, and Maureen sat at the table. He and his wife went to the kitchen and sat by the counter.

Hans stood up to begin the meeting, speaking in German.

"Welcome, one and all. It's truly an honor to have all the heads of the main anti-Fascist groups in Paris in one room. It wasn't an easy task gathering you here. I realize we don't agree on everything, but the core tenet of our beliefs is the same: The Nazis must be stopped. I called this meeting in the hope that we could set aside our differences and begin a new era of cooperation. Only by uniting can we hope to tame the National Socialist beast."

"Who are they?" Arnold Sauer asked, pointing to Michael and Monika.

"Extra security," Maureen responded.

"I have that taken care of," he said and drew a pistol from his pocket.

The group waited until he put it away to begin again.

"Our political messages are disparate." Uli Brandt was a former social democratic politician from Munich. "With all due respect to my colleagues, I can't promote a Communist system in Germany."

"That's because you want the status quo to continue," Arnold said. He was in his mid-30s, with a thin black beard. He wore the hammer and sickle on his lapel and had headed up the German Communist Party in Paris since the previous leader was murdered the year before. "What use is a revolution in Germany if the working man doesn't profit from it?"

Maureen sloshed the wine around in her glass before bringing it to her mouth. The irritation was plain to see on her face. "Round and round it goes," she said. "When are you going to realize that the Nazis are united in their purpose and growing stronger every day? They're spending more money on armaments than the rest of the Allies combined, and developing the most sophisticated weaponry ever known while we argue about political policy."

"What about the Americans?" Uli asked as if Maureen bore responsibility for the lack of urgency in her birth country.

Maureen spoke of America and the thought processes of the people there for a few minutes until Gerhard interrupted her.

"I don't think blaming Maureen for the shortsightedness of her compatriots is productive. What we need to do is channel our resources. Otherwise, we're wasting our time here."

"To what end?" Arnold asked.

"To enlighten the German people, and topple the Nazi regime."

"Topple the Nazis?" Arnold looked at the others around the table and then back at Gerhard, seemingly waiting for him to explain the joke, but Gerhard's stoic look didn't change.

"And how are you planning on removing Hitler?" Uli asked. "With a strongly worded letter? The process of bringing Nazi evils to the attention of the German public will take years. The entire system is set up to prevent the people from learning the truth."

"And what system will replace the Nazis?" Arnold asked. "It's vital that what follows them empowers the working man."

Michael closed his eyes and shook his head. Monika motioned to him. "This is a waste of time," she whispered. "Why did Hans go to so much trouble to arrange this meeting? I don't understand."

Michael didn't answer his wife, but couldn't argue. They stood by the window. Night had drawn in, and the city's lights twinkled through the darkness. Michael opened the window to let in a breeze. No one objected. The leaders of the various anti-Nazi factions in Paris were too busy to notice, arguing about which political philosophy would best replace National Socialism in Germany.

Michael stuck his head out the window and angled his neck to peer down at the two men guarding the door. They were standing by the front step, smoking cigarettes. Michael brought his head back inside and turned to face the table once more.

Maureen cleared her throat to speak. "Enough of all this ridiculousness."

"You expect us to be dictated to by an American?" Uli asked.

"I'm as dedicated to this fight as anyone in the room," she said.

They exchanged more useless barbs for a minute or two before Gerhard brought his fist down on the table with a *thud*. The bickering died in an instant. "There is hope to oust the Nazis. We can discuss the merits of what government should replace them once the Führer is at the end of a rope."

Silence fell over the room like a cloak. He opened his mouth to speak. Maureen, who was seated beside him, put her arm on his.

"I don't think we need to discuss that right now," she said.

"What are you talking about?" Arnold asked. "If there's something happening in Germany, you need to let us know."

Michael went to the window again and glanced down toward the men at the door but saw nothing. Two cars were parked across the street in spots that were bare a few moments before. A truck pulled up behind them. Two men in dark clothes with caps on their heads jumped out and strode toward the building. Michael kept watching, waiting for the men to step out and challenge them, but nothing of the sort happened. An icicle of fear slid down his spine.

The Resistance leaders were still waiting for Gerhard to speak.

"What is it, man?" Hans asked. "If we can't speak openly here, where can we?"

Michael ran past his wife and yanked the front door open. At least six or seven men were running up the stairs. He slammed the door shut.

"They found us!" he said to the room. The Resistance leaders turned to him.

"Who?" Hans asked.

"I don't know, but they're on the way up the stairs. Get up!" He ran to the table. "Help me push it against the door."

Fear took over, and the Resistance leaders stood up. Together, they shoved the table against the door. Gerhard ran to the trapdoor in the ceiling, and he and Michael pulled it down.

"Monika, go!" Michael shouted as he pulled down the ladder.

The men were banging on the door now as Hans, Arnold, Uli, and Maureen held the door closed with the table. The sounds increased in volume.

"They have a battering ram!" Arnold screamed above the din.

"Get up the ladder!" Michael shouted to his wife, and she disappeared into the black after pushing the upper door open. She climbed onto the roof.

The apartment door was straining on its hinges, and the Resistance leaders were struggling to maintain enough pressure on the table.

"S'ouvrir!" came a voice in French through the door. "Open up! This is the police!"

Arnold was next up the ladder, but without his weight behind the table, the front door began to open. Hans climbed up, then Uli. Michael stayed with his sister and Gerhard, straining to give the others time to get away, but it became apparent their work would be in vain when the blade of an ax hacked through the wood.

"Get out of here!" Gerhard screamed.

Maureen tried to argue, but Michael shoved her toward the exit to the roof just as the door gave way. She hauled herself up. Men spilled into the apartment, five paces away.

Gerhard lunged at them but was met with a punch in the face. Maureen called his name, but the sound was lost in the mêlée.

Michael shouted at his sister, "Move!"

She did as she was told and he grabbed onto the ladder behind her. Gerhard struggled against the men holding his arms.

"*Schweinhund!*" one of them said.

Another snatched at Michael's legs. He kicked him in the face and the man fell back, giving Michael just enough time to scamper up the ladder. The rooftop was illuminated by the city lights and the moon above.

"We can't leave Gerhard!" Maureen shouted.

"We've no choice," Arnold said and shut the door as one of the Nazi agents climbed the ladder. "I'll hold it," he said, taking the gun from his pocket. "I'll—"

Several loud *cracks* interrupted him as bullets splintered the wooden door. A round caught him underneath his chin and his body crumpled to the ground in an ungainly heap. The pistol flew out of his hand and Uli picked it up. Maureen ran to the stricken man, but Michael knew it was pointless when he saw his bloodied eyes.

"Across the rooftops!" Monika shouted. More shots flew up through the now almost-shattered trapdoor.

She leaped across the gap to the next building. Uli hesitated, dithering at the six-foot opening between the two structures. Michael ran for his sister, dragging her away from Arnold's body. Hans seemed drenched in fear, frozen to the spot.

"Come on!" Michael shouted, and Hans seemed to snap into action. A rooftop door flew open ten paces away.

"They're coming through the fire escape," Hans shouted as several figures emerged holding pistols. Michael didn't wait and jumped to the next roof after his sister. Uli came next. Figures in black suits swarmed Hans, who screamed as they grabbed him.

Uli shouted back, but Maureen grabbed his arm, dragging him on toward the next rooftop. They ran through the darkness, to the next building in front of them. More loud *cracks* sounded, and bullets whizzed past Michael's ears. Three or four men were on the rooftop behind them and jumped across the gap. Uli held up the gun and fired a shot. It flew harmlessly past a Nazi agent, who took careful aim and hit the social democrat in the chest. With no time to mourn him, Maureen picked up the revolver and kept on.

"Keep going!" Monika shouted.

Catching up, Michael took his wife's hand. The next roof was only a few paces away, and they leaped over it together. His sister was beside them, and the Nazi agents were a few seconds back. They came to a halt. The gap to the next building was 8 feet or more.

"I can't jump that," Monika said.

Michael peered across and saw a long wooden plank against a wall. "Someone must have used that to bridge the gap. I can make it," he said.

"I'll hold them off," Maureen said and crouched down behind a chimney with Monika, firing at their pursuers. The Nazis scattered and took cover.

Michael kissed his wife and turned to Maureen. "I need to take a run at it. Cover me." She nodded and opened fire. The Nazi agents kept their heads down just long enough for Michael to run back a few yards.

He remembered the Olympiastadion in '36 and exploded into a sprint as bullets zipped around him. Hitting top speed in just a few paces, he launched himself across the gap and landed in a rolling ball on the other side. Picking himself up, he reached for the plank and laid it across the gap. It seemed brittle in his hands, but he hadn't time to check it. He shouted to the women, and Monika sprang to her feet. Maureen covered her sister-in-law with the one or two bullets left. Monika reached the plank and put her arms out to balance.

A Nazi agent took aim, and everything seemed to slow. He stood up to shout to his wife, and she turned back to her pursuers. The bullet struck the plank at her feet. Michael reached out as the wood splintered and broke. Her body fell like a stone. He threw an arm out and caught her hand. Her face burned with terror.

"I have you. I'm not going to let you go."

It took all his strength to haul her up and over the lip of the building. She collapsed on the concrete surface, panting.

Michael stood up. "Maureen?"

She looked across at him with her hands in the air. With no bullets left, she had no other option. She tried to smile as the agents swarmed her, like lions feasting on a fresh kill. One aimed at him across the gap they wouldn't be able to cross. Monika yanked him down, and the bullet whizzed over his head. Hot tears filled his vision. He collapsed onto his haunches. Impotent rage swelled through every cell in his body. The Nazi agents dragged her away in handcuffs.

Monika was pulling at his arm, saying something he couldn't make out. It took him a few seconds to regain himself.

"We need to get out of here. They could come up the stairwell of this building next," she said while shaking his arm.

Michael nodded. They kept low as they scurried across the rooftop. One agent was still taking shots at them, but it was too dark to see, and they pinged off the concrete five yards away. The fire escape was on the other side of that rooftop, and they descended to the street. The cars driving past offered some comfort, but they didn't stop until they reached the relative safety of a crowded café at the end of the block.

Slowing down, they walked inside. Michael wiped the sweat from his brow and asked the portly man behind the counter if they had a telephone. The call to his father in the hotel would be the most difficult he ever made.

Seamus arrived at the hotel at about 10:30. He held the door open for Hannah and his wife, and they proceeded into the lobby. The little girl's yawns quenched his desire to stay out later, and weariness from the long drive from Berlin was bringing itself to bear on his body, causing him to long for his bed.

"Excuse me, Monsieur Ritter," the man behind the desk called out as they passed. "There was a phone call for you." Seamus walked over. The desk clerk, a man in his 30s with a twirled mustache, pushed a piece of paper over to him. "It was your son. He's at this address. He asked you come pick him up. It seemed to be a matter of some importance."

"How did he sound?"

"Alarmed."

Seamus pressed him for more details he didn't have before asking about the address.

"It's a café in Rochechouart, about 30 minutes in a taxi. Shall I summon one?"

"Right away."

He walked back to his wife and child and explained the situation. Lisa made him promise to let her know as soon as he had any details and took the little girl upstairs to bed.

Seamus did his best to dismiss the grisly thoughts clogging his mind during the long taxi ride north, but he was in a cold sweat as the driver dropped him off. "Stay here and keep the engine running," he said, giving the driver a generous tip.

Dozens of patrons sat outside the café, basking in the evening air, sipping wine and beer. Seamus scanned the crowd in case Michael wasn't where the hotel clerk said he would be.

His son and daughter-in-law were at the back, hidden in a corner by the phone. Both looked pale and cold. Michael was shaking as Seamus hugged him.

"What is it? Where's Maureen?"

"They took her," Monika said.

"Who?"

"Nazi agents," Michael said. "They found us somehow."

"There must have been a rat in the house," Monika spat.

"They broke down the door and arrested Maureen, Hans, and Gerhard. The two others are dead. Their bodies are still on the rooftops," Michael said.

"Where did they take her?"

"I don't know. We barely made it out of there alive," Monika said.

"She saved us, Father. Maureen held them off so we could escape."

Seamus hugged his son again, though he could hardly raise his arms. His insides felt like they were collapsing, but he couldn't display his emotions. He had to be strong.

"Did the police come?"

"I think they're up at the building now. It's only two blocks away. Lots of people in here are talking about it," Monika said.

"Did you mention anything about being there?"

"No. I wanted to wait until you arrived. We don't trust the police," Michael said.

"Good man." Seamus put his hands on his son's shoulders, then gave him 20 francs. "The taxi I came in is still outside. Take your wife back to my hotel and call Lisa in the room when you get there. I'm going to see what I can find out before we make a plan."

"We have to get Maureen and the others," Michael said.

"I know. We probably only have a day or two before the Gestapo smuggle them back into Germany. We can't let that happen."

"I think I know where they took them," Michael said.

"You do?"

"A château south of the city. We were down there back in January. Maureen wanted to see the place."

"You're sure?"

"No, but they took other prisoners there," Monika said. "I spoke to two of the SS men at the time."

"Probably the same agents who came for us tonight," Michael added.

They stood and talked for a few minutes. Seamus peppered his son and daughter-in-law with questions about Maureen's captors and the Château de Bellecour. When he was satisfied, he shepherded the young couple through the restaurant and to the taxi outside.

"I'll be back soon—we have to act fast. Have Lisa call Leon and Gilda when you arrive. We need to meet with them tonight."

"Ok," Michael said as Seamus shut the door. He stood and watched the taxi drive away before proceeding up the street.

About 100 people had gathered behind the barriers erected on either side of the street. Seamus stood beside a man in a suit. "What happened?" he asked in English.

"Some Reds had their meeting interrupted."

"By whom?"

"Other Reds, or Pinks, most likely. They spend so much time fighting among themselves, their dreaded Nazis needn't lift a finger."

Seamus took a few seconds to evaluate the man's words, but remembered the one word Michael heard one of the pursuers say: *Schweinhund—German*.

Several policemen were standing by the entrance to the apartment building with notebooks in their hands. Two blood trails extended from the steps below the doorway across the street, where they disappeared. Seamus worked through the crowd to where a young uniformed policeman stood.

"Excuse me," he said in English once more. Paris was a city much like Berlin, where many people spoke his native tongue. "My name's Clayton Thomas. I'm with the *New York Times*." He held up his membership card to the Berlin Chamber of Commerce. The young policeman looked at the laminated card, but Seamus put it straight back into his pocket. "I'm in town writing a story about Nazi resistance in Paris. You think they had something to do with this?"

"A load of Reds met upstairs on the fifth floor. One or two are known troublemakers. Some of their rival factions must have got wind of the gathering and broke it up."

"What's with the blood trails?"

"Seems they took out the two guards on the door. Slit their throats and dragged them away."

"Don't you find that a little extreme for a feud between parties that are essentially on the same side?"

"Not according to the chief of police. He made a statement saying that we're looking for Communist agitators."

"You don't think Nazi agents operating in the city could have had anything to do with it? All their enemies in one place... Seems like they'd be interested in such a group."

"As I said, the chief of police was here a few minutes ago. He's already dismissed that notion."

"On what grounds?"

The policeman stared at him like he was about to use his baton. "You'd have to ask him that. What was your credential again?"

"*New York Times*. How many bodies?"

"Two on the roof, and maybe two more on the street, but we're still trying to ascertain that."

"Anyone else missing?"

"Missing? No. This was a hit."

"So the police think there were only two people upstairs at that meeting?"

"Others must have escaped across the rooftops. We have some men up there investigating right now."

Seamus nodded and thanked the man before melting into the crowd. Any help the police could give would come too late. His daughter probably had about 36 hours before they stuffed her in a car and drove her back to Germany. And once she was in the Reich, the only laws that existed were those the Nazis wrote to stamp out any dissension. A swift trip to a concentration camp would be the best she could hope for. *The best thing.* It was up to him to ensure she didn't make it that far.

He walked a few blocks before flagging down a taxi with a shaking hand. He struggled to hold in his tears for the duration of the ride.

A voice called out as he entered the lobby of the Hotel d'Angleterre. Lisa was sitting at a table in the corner with Michael, Monika, and Gilda. They greeted him with a hug before he sat down. Each was visibly shaken. He suppressed his instinct to berate his son for allowing Maureen to attend a meeting where the heads of the Communist and Democratic Resistance forces met. There wasn't time for that.

"So, tell me about this château. It's about an hour from here?"

"I work with a man called Frederick—his cousin is a maid there."

"Where is this Frederick? Can we get him here?"

"He doesn't have a phone. I'll try his house tomorrow morning."

"If she's not in this château, do we have any other ideas where they might have taken her?"

Monika's voice was low. "No, but I spoke to the SS men stationed there. I'm sure that's where they took Maureen. Why would they have two holding locations around Paris?"

"I don't see why they would," Gilda said. "Have you reported it to the police yet?"

"I spoke to a gendarme at the scene. Chiappe, the head of the Parisian police, has already made a statement blaming the Communists for the bloodshed."

"No surprise there," Michael said through gritted teeth. "The man may as well wear the swastika on his bicep."

"And besides that, what are the police going to do when the German embassy claims diplomatic immunity? They're not going to search Château de Bellecour unless they have strong evidence of wrongdoing inside."

Leon entered the lobby and pulled up a chair. Monika caught him up on what they'd discussed already before Seamus leaned into the center of the circle.

"This is up to us. We have a day and a half, maybe two, before they bundle her into the back of a car and drive her over the border. No one's going to check the trunk of their car because of that immunity you mentioned. Like it or not, we're Maureen's only hope."

He sat back, waiting for someone to break the silence. Monika was the one to do it. "Frederick told me the maid goes in on Saturdays, around lunchtime. I'll head down to Pithiviers and speak to his cousin, maybe get into the château. I might need some bribe money."

Her husband looked grim.

"As much as you want," Leon said. "I have over 100,000 Reichsmarks in my hotel room."

"I don't think we'll need quite that much, but thank you, Leon," Seamus said. "When are you going down there?"

"Now?"

"Wait until morning. I know it's impossible to sit still, but the people we need to see are all in bed now. They won't start interrogating her until she's exhausted, so they'll just keep her awake overnight. We have a little time. It's best we all try and get some sleep tonight."

"What about the grounds?" Gilda asked after a few seconds of silence.

Michael sighed. "The nightwatchman at the door isn't the friendly type, and dogs patrol the gardens at the back."

"Did you see armed SS?" Seamus asked.

"No, but that doesn't mean they weren't there." Monika said.

Lisa was sitting in silence, just listening. Taking a backseat wasn't easy for her. "So, we need to find a way into the compound, past the guards and the dogs, and into the house," she said.

Monika continued. "And then into the cellar. The maid said they were strictly banned from venturing down there."

"Then we have to find the cell, open it, and extricate her... without dying," Seamus said.

"I wish Maureen was here," Michael said with a sad smile. "She'd figure out what to do."

Seamus reached over and ruffled his son's hair. "We can do this. I'll try and locate a locksmith to get us into the building."

"How are you going to find someone like that in a day? And will you know if we can trust them?"

"That 100,000 Reichsmarks Leon mentioned should smooth the path toward everything I just mentioned. I have some contacts who might know where I can find one."

"What about the dogs?" Monika asked.

Gilda was ready for that question. "A vet. We can drug them, just long enough so that by the time they wake up, we'll be back in Paris. But that still leaves the problem of the guards."

"I was a soldier 20 years ago, and a good one," Seamus said.

"As was I," Leon said. "We'll do what we have to."

"What about Hans and Gerhard, the other men the Nazis took?" Michael asked.

"We'll see about them. My first priority is my daughter."

"One of them is a rat," Lisa said. "And I know who my money's on."

"What do you mean?" Michael asked.

"Oh, come on. You think it's a coincidence that the Nazis raided a meeting with three heads of different resistance groups in Paris? Hans was waiting for this opportunity."

"What are you talking about? He escaped from a concentration camp in Germany. He fled here," Michael answered.

"Wake up," his wife said. "Your father told us before that there are agents spending time in camps. We can't assume we can trust him because of his story."

Seamus nodded. "You're right, but that's not our primary concern. Go back to your hotel rooms and try to get some sleep. I know we all want to start now, but there's nothing to be done at this moment. We'll be in better shape after some rest. We begin tomorrow morning.

"Gilda and Leon, you sort out transport, masks and clothing, and the vet. I'll find a criminal. Michael and Monika, go down to Château de Bellecour at dawn and take another look. Find Frederick and his cousin, and get into that building."

"What about the SS men she met in the café in Pithiviers, the ones they probed for information? What if they recognize Monika when she's in the château?"

"I doubt they interact with the cleaning staff. If you do see them, Monika, be sure to keep your head down. Are you ok with taking that risk?"

"We need to be ready. This is the only way."

~

The truck rumbled on. The shackles on Maureen's wrists were so tight that her fingers began to go numb. She shifted her body to relieve the pressure on her hands, pressed against the side of the cabin. Hans and Gerhard sat opposite her. All three were blindfolded and had already been warned against talking. Maureen replayed being dragged down the stairs in her mind. *Surely someone called the police? Why hadn't they pulled the truck over already?* Once they reached the château, the Germans would use their diplomatic immunity to its fullest extent and the French authorities would be powerless.

She took a deep breath, wondering how she could play this. What words could she use to extricate herself? Gerhard never mentioned the coup during the meeting, and Hans didn't know about it. The Gestapo couldn't possibly be aware either, unless Petra or Gerhard's father told. Perhaps sending the Resistance leaders home might deliver an effective message to the others who dared stand up to Hitler, even from the apparent safe haven of a foreign city. Were the Nazis planning on roughing them up and releasing them?

Who am I kidding? The men who took them, whether they were SS or Gestapo or someone else, meant to find out whatever they knew. And if she or Gerhard couldn't hold out, the plot to overthrow the National Socialist regime would be hacked to pieces. Word would travel back to Germany at the speed of sound, and General Engel and Petra Wagner would be the next dominoes to fall. The movie star would sing like a lark once in the Gestapo's crosshairs. And Lisa had been Petra's contact... She was the one who introduced seditious thoughts into the actress's mind.

Maureen tried to remember where the guard was sitting. He'd spoken a few minutes previously and seemed to be a couple of paces away. The only sound was of the truck's engine. How long had they been driving? Thirty minutes? Forty? Maureen decided to risk speaking.

"Are you ok?"

Gerhard seemed to wait a few seconds to determine if it was

safe to answer. "Just a few bumps and bruises," he whispered. "So far."

"I'm sure they mean to bring us to the château I told you about."

"Just tell them everything you know," Hans said with an urgent hiss. "Don't try and hold out. It's no use. If it takes two hours or two days, they'll get the information they want."

"No," Gerhard said. "We can't just capitulate."

"No use in trying to be a hero," Hans whispered. "They'll beat you to within an inch of your life. Perhaps if you tell them everything you know, they'll let us all go."

"Be quiet!" the Nazi agent said. "No more talking."

"Where are we going?" Gerhard asked him. "You can't do this here. This is a free country—"

Before he could finish the sentence, Maureen heard the guard leap across from his seat and punch him.

"You'll soon learn what fate awaits traitorous scum like you," the man said.

Gerhard coughed and groaned, and the sound of footsteps signaled the agent returning to his seat. Maureen tried to control the shaking in her body as fear gripped her. These men would do whatever it took to find out what they knew, and there was no one to stop them. She was just glad Michael and Monika got away. Rather her than them. The pain of what she was about to endure was nothing to the agony she would have felt if Monika or her brother were the ones to be caught. She clenched her eyes shut, even though she had a blindfold on. Trying to regulate her breathing, she urged herself to be strong. *I can get through this. Someone is coming for me.*

The truck slowed and came to a halt. The sound of voices speaking in French outside was audible, and then the truck started again, but much slower this time, and it stopped again seconds later.

"Time to get out," came a voice in German, and she felt

arms on her. She moved her foot to step down, but someone pushed her in the back and she crashed down onto gravel. Luckily she landed on her side, so she wasn't badly hurt. More hands grabbed under her armpits and raised her to her feet. The time for resistance would come later. Her entire body was cold. She was under no illusions about what this would be and how important it was to hold out. *Someone will come.* The light of hope inside was all that was keeping her going, and she held on to it.

18

Saturday, May 7: 7:00 a.m.

Seamus woke from nightmare-plagued sleep as the clock on the wall read seven. Somehow he'd managed to grab a few hours' rest. His son and the rest of the team had been in the lobby until he sent them home after two o'clock in the morning. Everyone knew their jobs. With a concentrated effort—and a lot of luck—they'd have what they needed to attempt to rescue Maureen by tonight. From there, who knew? But he was willing to die trying.

The thought of what his daughter was enduring almost brought him to tears. The Gestapo men wouldn't have let her sleep a wink the night before, leaving someone with her at all times to ensure the light they shined in her eyes served its purpose. Perhaps they would question her sporadically over the first 24 hours, prodding her to see what she knew. That was about the best he could hope for. But if they got wind of the coup she and Gerhard were planning, their retribution would be swift and merciless.

Lisa was already up, sitting at the desk, scribbling on a piece of paper. Hannah was asleep on the cot by the window. Lisa would be able to do little to help her stepdaughter here, and the frustration was tearing her to pieces.

"I've made a list of everything we spoke about last night," she said as Seamus sat on the edge of the bed.

"Did you sleep?" She shook her head and held up the notepad. "I'm glad you got some, though. You're going to need it."

"What must Maureen be going through right now?" Seamus said.

Lisa approached him, putting her hands on his shoulders. "We can't afford to think like that. Keep your mind focused on the goal of getting her back. One thing at a time."

"Michael and the others will be downstairs in 30 minutes. Leon and Gilda will have the money with them. They need someone to lead them."

Seamus nodded his head, fighting back the tears. "You're right."

"Maureen needs you to be strong."

Her arms around him felt like medicine. They maintained the embrace for 30 seconds or more until it was time for him to get dressed.

"I was thinking about a locksmith," he said.

"To get into the cellar in the château? I think we need someone morally flexible."

"Well put." He said and slipped into his suit.

"Something kept me awake last night, apart from everything else we spoke about," Lisa said as he searched for his shoes.

"What is that?"

"Petra and General Engel in Berlin. If the Nazi interrogators extract the information about the coup from Gerhard or Maureen, they're the first people the Gestapo will scoop up."

Seamus closed his eyes. With everything that happened the night before, he'd never spared a thought for those they'd left in Germany.

"What do you propose we do? We haven't time to write a letter. The Gestapo will be listening in to any long-distance call. Did you develop a code with her?"

"We never had the need."

"Call her later this morning, but be careful. Don't identify yourself. If the worst does happen and the Gestapo do find out about the plot to oust Hitler, we won't be able to return to Germany."

"But Conor is with Helga in Berlin."

"I know. We could send for him...."

Lisa stayed silent for a few moments while Seamus finished dressing. She sat down beside her daughter, still sleeping. "What if they don't want to leave? Fiona in particular?"

"We have to make sure that never arises. The only way we can do it is to get Maureen out of that château tonight, and hope. But call Petra."

The meeting in the lobby was brief. Few had slept more than three or four hours. Leon and Gilda handed out envelopes full of banknotes to each person. Seamus hoped that the adrenaline of the day would sustain them. Gilda was going to need the most money. She was tasked with obtaining the transport they'd need to travel to and from the château.

"The harsh truth is that Maureen and whomever else we free will likely require medical attention. I've located some hospitals nearby, depending on how urgent the need might be."

Gilda's assertion was met with silence. It was time for Seamus to say something else no one wanted to hear.

"Breaking into the château will be dangerous. The men in there are fanatical Nazis for whom the war began the moment Hitler rose to power. Understand that you're risking your life here. No one will think any less of anyone who wants to back out, but now is the time to do it. We have too much to accomplish today."

Once more, the response was silence.

"No one?" Monika asked. "All right, let's get on with this."

Everyone knew what they had to do. They wished each other luck, embraced, and promised to meet back in the hotel lobby that night at nine o'clock.

Seamus watched them leave before walking to the line of telephones behind the front desk. He took a notebook out of his jacket pocket and reviewed some phone numbers. After a few seconds' consideration, he decided to call Hayden rather than Clayton. The spy doubtless had more underground connections than the journalist. It took 30 seconds for the operator to patch the call through, and when she did, Seamus heard the familiar clicking sound that signaled someone else was listening in.

Hayden picked up after the fifth ring.

"Did I wake you, my friend?" Seamus asked in English. Maybe not speaking German would provide them some additional cover.

"No, I was just resting my eyes. Are you still in Paris? How did your business progress?"

"Swimmingly. Not a bother in the world. Something else has arisen. My daughter has...." He struggled to find the words that wouldn't incriminate either of them. "She has need of someone skilled in the arts of breaking and entering. You know how it goes—she's locked out of her house."

Hayden took a few seconds to answer.

"Do you know anyone who could help with that in the city? I know you're familiar with this place," Seamus said.

"I know a man in Bastille—Edouard Durand. Not the type to bring home to Mother, however."

"Sounds like my man."

Seamus wrote down the address and thanked his friend. "Be careful," Hayden warned and hung up the phone.

Seamus returned to Lisa and Hannah in the hotel room, knowing men like Durand didn't take meetings at ten in the morning. He had breakfast with his wife and stepdaughter, fending off the little girl's multiple questions during the meal about what was wrong and why they both looked sick.

Waiting for the opportune time to make the trip to Bastille was torture when every moment could have been Maureen's last, but noon rolled around, and he set off.

It was an overcast, gloomy day in the city, a perfect reflection of his mood. The taxi dropped him off at the address Hayden gave him, a tiny cobbler's store on the corner of Rue Trousseau and Rue de Candie—not an area tourists flocked to. The acidic stench of rotten trash filled his nostrils as he stepped onto the street. But even here, the buildings exhibited a dilapidated grandeur, like an aging beauty queen whom time had finally defeated.

It was just after midday when Seamus entered the store. The back wall was crossed with cubbyholes, each holding a separate pair of old shoes with tags on the laces. A man in his 20s wearing dirty overalls stood behind the counter, but didn't raise his head as Seamus approached. The smell of oil and leather was so thick he almost had to bat it away from his face like a mosquito.

"Is Edouard Durand here?" Seamus asked in his best French.

The man sneered a little before replying. "Who's looking for him?"

Seamus drew a 20-franc note from his wallet and placed it on the counter. "I am."

The young man put his hand on the bill and pocketed it swiftly, as if someone else would snatch it from him. "He's in the back. Give me a moment." He disappeared through a door behind the counter.

Two minutes later, the young man emerged and motioned for Seamus to walk through the gap in the front counter. He led him to a small office where a tall, lean man in his early 50s sat behind a desk piled high with shoes.

Seamus stood until Durand asked him to sit in front of the desk. The younger man nodded and left.

"So, why did you pay my son to see me?"

"Are you Edouard Durand?"

"And you are?"

"Call me Seamus. You speak English or German?"

"Some German," he said, switching.

Seamus switched languages. "I heard you're a man who knows how to break locks."

"Who told you that?" Durand asked.

"A friend." Seamus thought of Maureen and knew he had no time to waste. "My daughter was taken by Nazi agents last night."

"Gestapo?"

"I don't know. I have an idea where they took her, but I'll need someone with the skills to get past security." He took an envelope containing enough to buy the Mercedes he'd driven to Paris for Gilda and Leon and placed it on the pile of shoes. Durand's attempt to mask his shock at the amount inside was only partially successful. "As you can see, you'll be compensated generously."

The cobbler thumbed the cash for a few seconds before placing the envelope back on the shoes. "No use being rich if you're not alive to spend it. What's the security situation?"

"It's a château in Pithiviers."

"The Bellecour?"

"The Nazis have taken the lease and are using the place for their Parisian headquarters."

"Is it a consulate? Did they hire it through the embassy?"

"I believe so."

"Then it's officially German soil. Technically, we'd be trespassing in a foreign country."

"Hence the overly generous compensation."

Durand reached for a pack of cigarettes and offered one to Seamus, who accepted with thanks. A few seconds later, they were both puffing away.

"It's been a while since I took on a job like this," the old thief said. "What's the security situation?"

"Guards and dogs. We're working on getting something to put the latter to sleep."

"We'll need something for the former as well." Durand billowed smoke into the air. "What do the Nazis want with your daughter?"

"She was one of several Resistance leaders they snatched from a meeting last night."

"Is she a Red?"

"No."

"Do you have anyone on the inside?"

"I'm working on getting my daughter-in-law into the château as a maid. Once she's inside, she can grease the wheels for us."

Durand moved forward. "When is this happening?"

"Tonight."

The old crook laughed and then started coughing up smoke. "You can't be serious?!"

"What do you think the Gestapo are going to do to my daughter? I can't leave her there a minute more than I have to."

"What hardware do you have?"

"I was hoping you could help me with that."

"Come with me."

"You get this upon completion of the job." Seamus said. He picked up the envelope and deposited it in his pocket.

Durand strode out of the shop and turned down the street. They walked together for a few blocks until they came to a bar, the interior of which was dark and reeked of stale beer. A young barmaid was sweeping the floor. Durand asked her something in French, and she pointed to a door. Seamus followed him to it and waited as he knocked. A man with a thick black beard greeted Durand like an old friend and brought the men inside.

They spoke in French, the words coming like bullets from a Gatling gun. Seamus couldn't follow them exactly, but got the gist. He wasn't surprised when the new man opened a drawer full of handguns.

"What are you prepared to do?" Durand asked.

"Whatever it takes." Seamus reached into the drawer to pluck out a pistol.

8:30 a.m.

Monika stopped her husband outside a boulangerie in Croulebarbe, two blocks from Frederick's house. She'd never seen him like this, even during his recovery from being shot at Marzahn after the games in '36. Every move he made was cautious and considered. His hand was sweaty and wet, and she broke away from him.

"What are you doing?" he asked. "We haven't got a moment to waste."

"Are you ok? Are you ready for this?"

"It's just like what we did at the camp at Marzahn for Willi and his family. Except without Maureen this time."

Trying to hold his emotions in was causing his face to crack like a frozen lake in wintertime.

"It's ok to be scared, Michael. We all are."

"We have to get to Frederick's house," he said and began running.

Realizing she couldn't reach him, Monika quickened her pace to a sprint. He didn't stop and dashed the rest of the way to Frederick's parents' house. Monika caught him at the door, where he had already rung the bell.

His colleague appeared a few seconds later and opened it with a smile on his face. It melted in seconds. "What are you doing here? What's wrong?"

"Can we come in and talk?" Monika asked.

They followed him into the simply furnished living room, where his mother offered them coffee. Michael declined with thanks, having no time for niceties today. He explained the situation in a few sentences, and the blood ran from the young Frenchman's face.

"And you think she's down in the château my cousin works in?"

"Where else would they have taken her?" Monika asked.

The young man had no answer to that. "We have to get Monika into the château today with your cousin," Michael said. "She can check out the inside—draw a map for us. We can't go in blind."

"You mean to break into the place and rescue Maureen?"

"Yes, before they...." Michael said and ran his hands through his hair. "Time is of the essence. Every hour we wait could be deadly."

"I understand."

"Get dressed and let's drive down to Pithiviers. My sister's life depends on what we do these next few hours."

Michael's words seemed to have the desired effect. Frederick nodded and told them to wait a few moments in the kitchen for him to get dressed.

They sat making small talk with Frederick's mother until he returned to tell her that he was visiting the countryside for the day and would need the car. Monika defused the argument she saw was about to occur by thanking Frederick's mother over and over for being so kind as to allow them to have the car. Three minutes later, they were on the road.

The Frenchman had a thousand questions about the night before, most of which they were able to answer.

"What time does Emily start work in the château?" Michael asked.

"At about one. We should have plenty of time to intercept her."

It was just after 10:30 a.m. when they arrived in Pithiviers. Frederick seemed to realize not to broach any other topics apart from the rescue from that moment, and a determined silence fell in the car those last few minutes of the journey. They parked outside Emily's parents' house and got out of the car together. Monika almost had to hold her husband back.

"Let Frederick do the talking—at first, anyway."

The young blond maid greeted them with a surprised *whoop* and kissed each on both cheeks before leading them inside. An awkward moment followed when she introduced them to her parents, who didn't seem like they cared much for their nephew. Michael was almost leaping from foot to foot during the exchange. After five agonizing minutes, they finally got Emily alone in the living room.

"Do you want coffee?"

"No," Michael snapped.

"He means no thank you." Monika slapped her husband's hand.

"Why are you here?" Emily asked, her goodwill slipping away.

"You remember my sister-in-law, Maureen?"

Emily nodded. After 15 minutes of hushed explanation, the

young Frenchwoman was rooted to her seat, the blood drained from her face. "I knew this was going to happen sooner or later. I knew someone like you would ask me to do something like this."

"Can you get me inside the château?" Monika asked.

Emily hesitated.

"Those Nazis pigs are probably torturing my sister and her friends as we speak. If we don't free her soon, they'll drive her back across the border to Germany, and there won't be anything we can do. She'll spend the rest of her life in a concentration camp."

"This can't rebound on me," Emily said.

"What do you earn in there in an hour?"

"A little more than a franc."

Michael reached into his pocket and drew out a wad of banknotes. "We'll give you 1,000 francs to bring Monika in. You won't ever need to go back."

"You can move to the city like you always wanted," Frederick said with a smile.

Emily was white, her lips tight as a scar on her face, but she nodded.

"Ok, when does Monika need to be ready?" Michael asked.

"In about an hour."

"We'll need another of those 1,000-franc notes for one of the other girls. The Nazis will ask questions if a new maid turns up, so we need to pay one of the regulars off. And I know who."

They walked out to the car, and Emily directed them to a house on the other side of town. "I need the money now," she said as they pulled up outside a small gray house with chipped paint flaking off the shutters. They watched as she walked to the door. A small woman answered, and Emily disappeared inside. Ten minutes later, she emerged with a smile on her face.

"Françoise has wanted to leave her husband for years. Now she can!"

Frederick insisted on bringing them to a local café to eat lunch before Monika went to work with Emily, but no one finished their food. It was the first time Monika had ever seen her husband not clear his plate. She tried not to show her nerves, endeavoring to control them with deep breathing.

Time drew out like a blade, but the hour finally elapsed and they returned to Emily's house, where she lent Monika her spare uniform. It was a plain black dress, stained by past use, covering her legs down past her knees—not the traditional French maid's outfit she'd envisaged.

"Time to go to work," Emily said, and they left the bedroom together.

The young maid outlined what they were expected to do when cleaning the rooms and where the Germans forbade them from venturing.

Michael sat beside his wife on the back seat. "Please be careful. I don't want you to be the next one hauled into the cellar."

"Some of the girls wear these to protect them from the dust," Emily said and handed Monika a mask from her bag.

"That should help," Michael said.

Frederick dropped the two women off a few hundred yards from the entrance to the château. They strode together in silence. A Frenchman in plain clothes answered the gate as Emily announced their arrival.

"Who's this?" he asked, looking her up and down.

"A new girl," Emily said. "Françoise quit."

"I don't see her name on the list," the man said, holding a clipboard.

"We're short-staffed as it is. I found her last minute. If you turn her away, we might as well all leave."

Monika stood in silence, just about able to follow the conversation.

"What's your name?" the man asked.

"Jeanne DuPont," she responded in her best Parisian accent.

The man motioned them to keep walking, and the gates closed. The building was of gray granite, four stories in height, and big enough so that the royalty who'd built it could entertain their friends inside. Its expansive windows were all shut. Monika noted the ones closest to the outside walls as she walked. Two cars sat parked outside the château. Emily knew where to enter the building and led her to a service entrance around the side. They were greeted by a middle-aged woman who asked the same questions as the man at the gate, though in German. This time Monika spoke for herself. The woman seemed under pressure and relented in seconds before leading the two young maids inside the house. They entered a massive kitchen and walked down a hallway to a high-ceilinged French drawing room with elaborate frescos and gilding. The cleaning supplies were laid out in the middle of the floor.

"Don't dawdle," the woman said and left them.

Monika put on a mask, picked up a duster, and walked to the bookshelves at the back of the room. She observed every detail for as long as she deemed necessary and then pushed the door open.

"Where are you going?" Emily hissed. "We're not allowed to clean other rooms until they tell us."

"I won't be long." She closed the door behind her, the feather duster still in her hand. A massive portrait of Hitler hung on the back wall of the foyer she had just entered. The rug was an enormous swastika. Loud footsteps on the marble floor startled her, and a man in full SS uniform—shiny black boots and the death's head insignia on his hat—turned the corner. Monika had just enough time to duck behind a statue of a long-dead king and crouched down as the SS man passed. He walked out the front door and Monika emerged again. She waited until she was sure no one was coming. She ran across the foyer to the next room and pushed the door open.

It seemed to be a music room, with a concert-sized piano dominating the center. Several violin cases were stacked against the wall, and the bookshelves were again lined with books, this time of a musical variety. *Nothing in here for me. Got to find the cellar.*

She scurried to the door again and opened it just far enough to peek out. The coast was clear, and she steeled herself to venture out, keeping Maureen in her mind. The risk was worth it. Two hallways diverged from the foyer. She chose one at random and kept close to the wall as she hurried along. The sound of men speaking in German made her heart skip, but she stopped and began to clean the frames of the paintings in the hallways. Two SS men were walking toward her.

"What are you doing back here, little girl?" one of the men asked in German.

"Cleaning," she answered. "I was ordered to dust all the way to the entrance to the cellar."

"Well, then," he said, "you'd better hurry over to the end of this hallway, hadn't you? You're at the wrong end of the building. Silly girl."

"Thank you," she said and did a curtsy that made the two men laugh. They walked on.

Monika waited until their voices faded to head back the way the man pointed out. She stopped every few seconds to dust more picture frames as she went, avoiding another man, this time in civilian clothes. The cellar door came into view as she rounded the corner at the end of the hallway. It was black, constructed from thick oak, and locked with a bolt held in place by a large padlock. *Seems doable for the right person.* She thought to press her ear to the door but dismissed the move as too risky. Her heart felt like a rock in her chest as she contemplated Maureen being tortured behind it. But she'd done all she could and hurried back down the hallway to the foyer, where she almost bumped into Gerd, the drunken SS man she and Maureen had questioned.

"Watch where you're running, little lady."

"My apologies, mein Herr."

She kept her head down, not daring to make eye contact. "I should get back to my duties." She started back toward the drawing room.

"Wait a minute," came his voice over her shoulder. "Have we met before?"

Monika turned back. "My cousins live around here also. Some people say I look like them. If you'll please excuse me, I need to use the ladies room."

Without giving him a chance to answer, she hurried back into the drawing room, where Emily was still cleaning the floor.

"Did you find what you needed?" she whispered. "Then help me clean."

They finished the drawing room and moved into the music room and the foyer. When they were discharged for the day, the middle-aged woman from the service entrance came back to lead them out.

3:40 p.m.

The impotence of Lisa's role was frustrating her, along with the fact that she'd not been able to connect with Petra. The act of pretending everything was ok and that the only worry Lisa had was what amazing sight in Paris to see next was starting to wear her down. It was imperative her daughter didn't find out anything about what they were doing, but she longed to tell someone.

"We're going back to the hotel," she said.

"What?" Hannah asked. "I want to go to the gardens and play with the boats again!"

"Later."

She blocked out Hannah's whines and flagged down a taxi. Doing anything that constituted leisure felt wrong while Maureen was still in captivity.

Twenty minutes later, they arrived back at the hotel. The young man behind the front desk raised a finger to attract her attention.

"An important phone call for you," Madame Ritter," he said. "Please call this number at your earliest convenience." He handed her a slip of paper with Helga's number on it.

"What is it?" A stream of panic ran through her.

"I don't know any details."

"Can you bring my daughter to our room, please, while I make this call?"

"Certainly," he said and took Hannah upstairs.

Lisa ran to the public phone and picked up the receiver. Helga picked up. "You called?" Lisa said. "Is Conor ok?"

"Yes," her husband's cousin said. "Conor's fine. He's here with me, but so is Fiona."

"What? Fiona's there?"

"She left the boarding school and hopped on a train to Berlin."

"Why did she come to you?"

Helga hesitated. "We've been writing to one another. I had no idea she was planning to leave the school, and I swore I'd keep our communications secret, at least until she broke for summer."

Lisa could barely spit out the words. "Is she there? Put her on the phone."

"She's with me but says she won't speak to you—only her father."

Lisa repeated the command and heard the young girl

shouting that she'd only speak to her father in the background. Fiona wasn't Lisa's daughter, so she decided to back down.

"Can I speak to Conor then?"

The young boy came on the line.

"Did you know about this?"

"Not a thing. She says she can't take being away from Harald anymore and that she wants to live with Helga until she marries him."

"But he's still away."

"No, he's back," Conor responded.

We'll deal with that situation later. "Your father's away for the weekend with some business clients, but he'll be in touch in the next few days when he can. Look after your sister for us," she said and hung up.

Lisa stood in the phone booth for a few seconds, wondering what to do now. All they could do was send Fiona back to America, but would she even leave?

She was about to return to the room when she decided to try Petra one more time. No answer came, and Lisa stomped back to the room in frustration, vowing to keep trying.

4:00 p.m.

Frederick and Michael drove around the perimeter of the château, probing for weaknesses like lions circling a pack of wildebeest. The extensive gardens connected to the main house were ringed by a wall, little more than five feet tall. Getting into the grounds wasn't an issue, but reaching the château in one piece surely would be. The two men parked the car on a quiet road to the eastern side of the compound. A farmer driving a wagon heaped with bales of hay greeted them with a tip of his cap. Michael entertained the thought of asking him if he knew an effective way in, but decided it was too risky. They waited to approach the wall until the stranger disappeared around the corner. It wasn't difficult to peer through the thin foliage at the house in the distance. Michael calculated that he could sprint the distance to the château in about 40 seconds but that the dogs patrolling the gardens could cover the same distance in about 20.

Frederick pointed to the line of kennels beside the old building. Judging by the lack of wear and tear, they were new. Several were open, and they could clearly see three or four dogs wandering around, sniffing flowers or basking in the warm sunshine in the garden.

"Six kennels," Michael said. "How are we going to drug all six dogs? I can imagine one or two, but six?"

"What about the guards?"

Two men in SS uniforms were chatting on the back steps of the château. Michael and Frederick were hidden by the trees that lined the property—it was hard to tell from their vantage point if the soldiers were armed.

They stood peering over the wall for 10 minutes. The dogs patrolled the gardens, but a fence kept them out of the front of the property. With few changes to their incomplete plan, they returned to the car to wait for Monika to finish working inside.

5:30 p.m.

"We only use the pistols if we absolutely have to," Seamus said to Durand.

The picklock smiled. "I'm not a hitman. I haven't used one of these things in years."

"But you have used one?"

"Never with one of these." He held up a silencer. "Handy if

we get cornered. Getting in and out of a place like the château is all about keeping as quiet as possible. One bang and every SS man and Nazi torturer in the building will leap out of bed, armed to the teeth."

The conversation died as they left his friend's bar with a briefcase full of deadly weapons. Seamus flagged down a passing taxi. The two men hopped in and sped back to the Hotel d'Angleterre. It was almost time for the evening meeting before the group left for Pithiviers.

Leon and Gilda were waiting in the lobby as Seamus arrived with the criminal he'd promised to deliver.

"Let's not speak here," Seamus said, and his two friends nodded and followed them up to his room. Lisa and Hannah weren't there, but a note left on the desk by the window informed him that she'd gotten a hold of Petra at last. She wasn't sure if the actress understood the full gravity of the situation, but there was only so much warning she could give without implicating them both. Seamus tore up the note after reading it and tossed the pieces in the trash can.

"Give me good news," he said as Gilda and Leon sat on the bed.

"I will as soon as you introduce us," Gilda responded.

"This is Edouard Durand—a man who knows how to pick a lock." Durand shook their hands before Gilda began.

"We went to a used car lot in Saint-Denis. I bought two reliable cars for cash—we didn't want to risk renting them. I have black clothes and balaclavas for the job too."

"And enough tranquilizers to put a herd of elephants to sleep," Leon said. "I went to a vet who told me what I needed—all available over the counter. I also have steaks in the back of the car, big juicy ones we can embed the pills into. The dogs will gobble them up in seconds."

"I have something I need to show you." Seamus laid the

suitcase on the bed beside them. Their eyes bulged as he revealed the pistols.

"What are those separate barrels?" Gilda asked.

"Silencers. It's not my intention to mow down every Nazi I see," Seamus said.

Gilda smirked. "Why not? The world would be a better place. That scum murdered my husband."

"I just want to rescue Maureen, but if some SS guard is standing between me and the door, I won't hesitate. My daughter's life is at stake."

No one argued. They were packing up to leave when Lisa opened the door. Seamus introduced her to Durand before she took him out to the balcony. "Please be careful, my love," she said and put her arms around his neck.

"I will."

"Bring our girl home."

They embraced on the balcony for a few moments before he broke away. "We have to get to Pithiviers. The longer we leave it...."

"I know," she whispered.

He kissed Lisa one last time and returned to the others. He hugged Hannah, told her they were going to the countryside for the night and led the others downstairs.

Gilda drove one car, and Seamus and the other two men traveled in the other. The hour spent traveling down provided the perfect chance to run through the plan. They needed to be ready when they met Michael and Monika.

6:30 p.m.

Maureen spat blood, her head spinning. A glob of saliva dribbled from the side of her mouth as her head rolled back. *The light. The light!* It seemed like it had been there all her life, hanging above her like a ball of fire. Her eyes ached from it, but not like her jaw from the punches. Her left eye was swollen, making it hard to see through it. But what was there to see here? The light shining through her? The gray walls of the cell? The wine racks were empty—a reminder of what this place had once been, and that the person who built this cellar never meant it to be used as a torture chamber.

She was alone, except for the SS guard, who was always there. His job wasn't to beat or question her—that specialized role was given to another. The guard's role was a particular kind of torture. He was there to make sure she didn't fall asleep. It had only been one night without rest, tied to this wooden chair, but it felt like a dozen. Every muscle in her body yearned for the escape of sleep. It seemed like nothing in the world could have been more wonderful at that moment than to crawl between the sheets of any bed and pass out. She daydreamed of the bed in her father's house in Berlin and the softness of her pillow. She remembered dinners with her family and walks along the beach at Wannsee with Thomas as the sun faded to orange along the lake's shimmering waters. She tried to keep anything but this place in her mind, for she knew her torturer was coming back soon. He was growing angrier by the hour.

It was hard to know how long she'd been here, in a cell only about the size of the bedroom she shared with her siblings in Aunt Maeve's house in Newark when her father was away riding the rails. She couldn't help laughing. At the time, she thought being in that room every night with her siblings was the worst torture imaginable. Time was proving how wrong she'd been.

"Can I have some water, please?" she said to the silent SS guard. "I'm so thirsty. Please."

The SS man glanced up for less than a second before

returning to the book he was reading. She pleaded once more, but he didn't react.

Maureen was just about to try to appeal to him as a fellow human being when the sound she dreaded more than any she'd ever heard echoed in her ears. The lock on the wooden door rolled back, and her torturer strolled in, dressed in a full black SS uniform with sleeves flecked with fresh crimson stains. It was Ullrich, the drunken fool she and Monika had questioned in the café a few blocks from here back in January. It was impossible to know if he recognized her or not. He hadn't said a word. Perhaps he was too drunk that night to remember, and her face escaped him like water through his fingers.

Her entire body tensed with fear as he shut the heavy door behind him and approached.

"I've been talking to your friends, Hans and Gerhard. Both German. Why's a nice American girl fraternizing with the likes of those thugs?"

He grabbed her by the face with one hand. His fingers were like a vise. He squeezed her cheeks, already raw from countless slaps, and she yelped in pain.

"Please," she said. "I'd never met those men at that meeting before. I—"

"I know your lies. You were an innocent bystander. You just happened upon a meeting of illegal Resistance scum, planning to murder the legally elected leader of the greatest nation in the world."

He let her face go, pushing her head backward.

"I don't know anything. I'm just a tourist."

"You see, there's a problem. Your lies don't match your friends' lies."

Ullrich unleashed a fearsome punch that landed just below her left eye. Her head snapped back, and she heard herself scream like a little girl. When was this going to end? Perhaps she should just tell. Anything to stop the pain.

"What's the big idea to bring down the Reich?" the SS torturer asked.

A dagger of horror sliced through her chest. "What? What are you talking about?" *How does he know? One of the others must have broken.* "I don't know what you're talking about."

"At the meeting, one of your friends mentioned a coup to replace the legal, internationally recognized German government. Who is discussing this? Give me the names of these criminals and all this will end. Please don't force me to play rough, because it'll make what's happened to you so far seem like a picnic in the countryside."

Hans is the only one who doesn't know the names. It must have been him.

"I don't know anything about it. Please, I'm not who you think I am."

Ullrich stood back and shook his head. "I must say, I'm disappointed."

He punched her in the chest. The pain was like a bomb exploding inside her rib cage. The world faded to black for a few seconds, but when she opened her eyes again, the SS man was still there. *What is the use? How can I hold out?* She thought of Petra and Gerhard's father in Germany. She had to be stronger than she ever thought possible.

"This is a mistake," she said when her breath returned. "I don't know anything. Please! You don't need to do this!"

Ullrich flexed his fists, stretching out his bloodied fingers.

"I'm going to have dinner soon. I believe the chef has whipped up steak, with sautéed potatoes. I'll wash that down with a few glasses of Bordeaux and get a good night's sleep. Then, tomorrow morning, I'll come back and unleash misery on you most people could never dream of. I'll make you talk in ways you never contemplated in your worst nightmares. And you will tell me everything I want to know because that's the only way it'll end. Unless you have something to divulge right now?"

"I don't know anything."

"Ok, we can play it that way. Maybe I'll visit one of your friends before I retire tonight. I want to warm up for you. You will be my *pièce de résistance*, as our French hosts might say."

"Please," Maureen whispered.

"Make sure she doesn't get a wink of sleep," the SS man said and stormed out.

19

Saturday, May 7: 8:30 p.m.

Despite it being a warm, dry evening, the cloudy skies would obscure the light of the moon and stars above their heads. The conditions couldn't have been better, and they had everything they needed. Michael and Monika were waiting at the meeting spot on the edge of town, about ten minutes walk from Château de Bellecour. Gilda was already parked as Seamus pulled up, and she, Michael, and Monika stood with stoic faces. He embraced each of them and then introduced the new man.

"This is Monsieur Durand. He'll get us past any locks we might encounter."

With no hotels in Pithiviers to rent a room and nowhere else to go, their meeting place was an old abandoned farmhouse outside town that Frederick told Michael about. Although he was eager that Maureen knew his role in rescuing her, the young Frenchman had left a couple of hours before, after swearing secrecy.

Monika had drawn maps of what she knew of the interior. She handed each person one, and they stood in the fading light as Seamus began to speak.

"We'll wait until dark. Believe me, I am as eager as any of you to get inside, but we don't know how many SS are in there. The more of them who are asleep, the better."

"So what time do we go?" Michael asked.

"Midnight."

"We studied the perimeter while Monika was inside," Michael said. "Frederick and I walked around, looking for the best spot to hop over. The wall itself isn't an issue—it's not more than five feet tall most of the way around. The problems start once we're inside. The place is crawling with dogs. We counted six." He took a map of the perimeter and laid it on the hood of one of the cars. "If we enter the compound here, we'll avoid most of the gardens," he said, pointing to a spot near the house. "These trees behind the road lead to the wall."

"That's where the kennels are," Monika said.

"That won't matter if the dogs are asleep," her husband replied.

"So we leave the cars on the road?" Gilda asked.

"Plenty of room to park them," Michael answered. "And it's quiet. I didn't see one other vehicle in the 20 minutes I was there."

"How long will those drugs take to put the dogs to sleep?"

"Ten to twenty minutes," Leon answered. "I think it's best if we throw steaks over the walls at several different points," he said, using his finger on the map. "Then we wait for the German Shepherds to take a nap."

"The guards are going to notice their dogs falling asleep all over the gardens. We'll have to time it just right," Seamus said.

"What about the guards themselves?" Leon asked. "We can't feed them raw steak."

"If only," Gilda said.

"They seem to stick to the house, mainly on the balcony overlooking the gardens at the back," Michael said. "I didn't notice them in the gardens."

"Can we enter here," Seamus asked, "and then tiptoe around the house, below the guards, to the service entrance?"

"That's where I went in," Monika said. "It's around the other side. You'd have to make it all the way past the guards on the balcony, and then go in through the kitchen."

"What kind of lock is on the door?" Durand asked.

"An old-fashioned one with a large brass keyhole. Same as on the cellar door."

"Will that present a problem?" Seamus asked.

"Not in the slightest," the old thief said. "Have you any idea about the doors inside the cellar?"

"I didn't make it that far."

"I'm sure they won't present a problem," he said.

Seamus let the others talk for a few seconds and opened the car. He drew out the briefcase from Durand's friend and placed it on the hood. Silence fell upon the group as he opened it.

"This is serious business," he said, making sure to meet each gaze. "Leon, Edouard, and I are trained to use these. I'll say this one last time: If anyone needs to leave, we won't think any less of you."

No one flinched. "Good. Gilda and Monika, you stay by the cars. Be ready, because we might come bounding over the wall with the SS on our tails."

"We will be," Monika said.

"There's something I forgot to mention," Leon said and took out a rifle. "The car dealer gave me this."

"A free rifle with the car, eh?" Monika said.

"I asked where I could buy one. He agreed to part with his own for a few francs," Leon said.

"I don't think we'll need that, but good to know we have it," Seamus said.

"I have directions to a hospital nearby," Gilda said.

"What if the Nazis follow us?" Monika asked.

"They won't dare," Leon said. "Not on French soil. Inside the safety of the château, they can do as they please, but out here, the law applies."

"Not so much in Paris," Monika said.

"They won't snatch Maureen out of a hospital bed," Seamus said.

"Who's going in?" Michael asked. "I've never handled a gun like that before—"

"And you won't be starting tonight," Seamus said. He saw the rage about to boil over in his son and pulled him aside.

"Father, I'm fitter and stronger than anyone here. She's my sister!"

"Exactly. I'm not losing any more children to this place." He took his son's face between his hands. "You've done so well. I'm even more proud of you than when you ran in the Olympics. I didn't think that was possible, but you proved me wrong. You're a vital part of the team, but I can't let you inside the château. I have no idea what we're going to face in there."

"But you trust Leon? He's older than you! And who's this French crook? We don't even know him."

"He's experienced, and willing to work for the money. I have faith in him. And Leon might be older than you, but he's faced down danger before."

"In the war? That was 20 years ago."

"Wait with your wife, son. We need you at the wall when we leave." Seamus walked away, putting an end to the conversation.

Gilda handed out balaclavas, black pants, and sweaters for each of them. She also handed out miniature flashlights to the men breaking inside. Once ready, they got into the two cars and drove to the road by the château wall at the location where Michael suggested they enter the perimeter.

Seamus crouched at Durand's side as they hid in the scrub between the road and the château walls. Leon and Gilda stayed by the road with the cars. Michael and Monika went to the wall, peering over at the silhouettes of the dogs in the garden and the guards at the house. It was only ten thirty, and though it was dark already, they would wait.

"Have you ever dealt with somewhere like this before?" Seamus asked Durand.

"I've broken into a lot of houses and picked just about every kind of lock you can imagine, but I've never been on a job quite like this. A château full of Nazis? I can't believe what this country's coming to. I have the distinct feeling I'll be seeing a lot more of Hitler's crew in the days and months ahead."

"I wish I disagreed."

Durand paused. "In case something happens to me—"

"Nothing's going to happen."

"Just promise me you'll deliver the money to my son. He's a good boy. Better than his father."

"You have my word."

The two men stopped talking. Any everyday details they might have chatted about were out of bounds. The less they knew about one another, the better.

Seamus crawled back through the scrub to the cars and sat down with Gilda and Leon. His hands were shaking as he lit a cigarette.

11:30 p.m.

Terror flooded Maureen's veins as the door creaked open. *What time of day or night is it? Has morning come already?*

The night's respite Ullrich had promised earlier didn't seem like it would be happening. He hadn't been gone more than a few hours. The SS torturer strode to her and bent down so that he was inches from her face. His gray eyes were on fire. His breath smelled of onions.

"Petra Wagner?" The SS man shook his head. "I saw one of her movies last year. She's quite the dish—the perfect Aryan woman, or so I thought."

Maureen's entire body tensed. "Who?"

Ullrich made a show of laughing in her face. "I think you're more than aware of who she is. I doubt you made many trips to the cinema to catch her movies, but I'm sure you approve of her involvement to depose our beloved Führer. I'm surprised your friend broke before you."

"I don't know what he's saying. You torture someone long enough and they'll tell you who started the Great Fire of London, but that doesn't make it true."

The SS man slapped her across the cheek, but her skin was so numb she barely felt it.

"She and General Horst Engel of the Luftwaffe will be receiving the justice they deserve soon enough. It's disgusting—a high-ranking member of the German military beguiled by a scheme like this. It's amazing what a pretty face can achieve. Yes, you've probably had that same effect on men since you were a girl, but that ends tonight. You lied to me, and I'm angry. The Führer is the greatest man in the world, perhaps in the history of the human race. I take any threat to him personally."

Maureen raised her head. "I don't know who any of those people are. You've got the wrong person. I don't know what the others said."

"Oh, you keep on with your lies. They won't save you."

"Why don't you just kill me and get it over with?"

"Kill you?" he asked with a mirthless laugh. "No, I'm not going to kill you. But you won't be pretty anymore when I'm done with you. Then I'll drive you back to the Reich and dump you off in a camp myself. Plenty of dissidents and Jews to keep you company there. You think about that for a while. I'll be seeing you soon."

He slammed the door behind him.

20

Sunday, May 8: 12:05 a.m.

The sounds of the dogs in the gardens had faded to nothing. Seamus was able to make out the figures of four of them sleeping, with fresh meat in their bellies. Nothing else was moving. Two guards were playing cards on the balcony at the back of the house, seemingly oblivious to both the steaks thrown over the walls and the fact that the dogs were no longer doing their jobs. Their raucous laughter echoed against the house. They sounded drunk.

Seamus, Leon, Durand, Michael, and Monika were at the wall, hidden by the scrub around them. "I'll go first," Seamus said. "Then Durand, then Leon."

"We'll keep watch," Monika said and hugged Seamus.

"Good luck," Michael said.

The trio approached the wall. Each carried a pistol with a sound suppressor attached to the barrel. The balaclavas over their faces hid everything but their mouths and eyes, and their black clothes must have made them almost impossible to pick out from a distance...at least, Seamus hoped so. He took a deep breath and climbed over the wall, keeping low as he moved. The empty dog kennels were on his right, the château perhaps 30 paces away. He hid by a bush trimmed into the shape of a perfect sphere and waited for the others.

Durand came next and hurried to the bush beside him. Leon was last. The composer was about 50, but lean and fit. He leaped over the wall with impressive athleticism. Seamus could hear the guards talking on the balcony behind him. The steps up to it were about five yards from where Seamus and Durand were hidden. One man was mocking the other for his lack of prowess with French ladies.

Leon hunched over, moving with deliberate care across the lawn that separated him from the bush Seamus and Durand were hiding behind. That's when they heard the snarl. Leon came to a halt as the figure of a German Shepherd emerged from behind a row of bushes. The composer stood still, trying to hush the dog. He reached into his pocket for one of the remaining steaks and threw it to the dog, but it paid it no mind and launched itself at him. Leon turned and ran back toward the wall, the dog barking now. The guards ran to the edge of the balcony to investigate. Leon beat the guard dog to the wall and hurled himself over. The dog leaped against the concrete barrier, rebounding off it as the guards arrived beside it.

"What's going on, girl?" one SS man said.

Seamus was still hiding with Durand, the guards a few paces away. Both SS had handguns drawn and were facing the wall.

"Did you hear something? What's gotten into Gertie?" He slurred the words.

Michael and Leon were beyond the wall the SS men were walking toward. One of the guards grabbed the dog by the collar.

"What is it, girl? Was it a rabbit?"

On his feet, Seamus drew his pistol. Holding the weapon in

two hands, he walked up behind the men. The dog smelled him first. Seamus raised his gun as the SS guards turned around and put a bullet in each of their chests. Their bodies collapsed to the ground, but the dog, now free of the SS man's grip, turned to attack Seamus. With only milliseconds to react, Seamus fired at the German Shepherd, but the silent bullet sailed past it. The dog leaped at him as if in slow motion. Its weight knocked him off his feet, and he raised his arm to protect his face. The dog began to bite his forearm, but the sound of silenced gunfire cut her off before she could sink her teeth in. The dog fell limp on top of Seamus. Michael stood behind him, holding Leon's pistol in his hand. He reached down and pushed the German Shepherd off his father.

Seamus stood up and held a finger to his lips. "Back over the wall," he whispered. Durand emerged from behind the bush to join them.

"We can't leave the bodies here," the lockpick said.

They took the dog's corpse. "I'm sorry, girl," Seamus said. "It wasn't meant to be like this."

The pain from her bite radiated up through his arm, and black droplets of blood stained the wall as he lifted the dog over. Leon was lying on the ground just behind, holding his leg. Seamus and Durand went back for the SS men and dragged their corpses behind a well-tended hedgerow near the wall.

The three men climbed back over and hunched down.

"My leg. I think I twisted it when I jumped over the wall. I can't walk." Monika was beside Leon and gave him some water from a canteen she was carrying. "I don't think I can do it, Seamus."

"I'll come along," Michael said. "We need three."

"You're not—"

Michael cut his father off. "We have about five minutes to get inside before someone notices the guards are gone. We don't have the luxury of arguing this point."

Seamus peered at his son in the dark. He'd never seen him so forthright before.

"I can do this, Father."

"Ok," Seamus said. "We need to go now. Same plan as before."

"How's your arm?" Monika asked.

"Fine. I don't have time to worry about it."

Seamus took the lead again and climbed back into the garden behind the château. The three men crept past the freshly killed bodies of the SS men and kept close to the back of the house as they made their way around toward the entrance. Durand had his small suitcase with him and reached into it at the kitchen door.

"Give me a few seconds," the Frenchman said and stuck what looked like two metal levers into the lock. Seamus and Michael stood waiting, the only sound that of their breath.

The deadbolt shifted back with an audible *click*, and Durand pushed the door open. "*Et voilà*!" he whispered.

Seamus drew Monika's map out of his pocket and proceeded into the dark, old-fashioned kitchen. His flashlight illuminated the sideboards, ornate marble floor, and the next door. The other men inched behind him. Seamus stood back and let Durand open the door. The old thief used the handle.

"Unlocked!" he whispered. A dark hallway lay before them. Michael was last out of the kitchen and left the door open in case they needed to leave in a hurry. The house was silent. A dull light at the end of the hallway served to show them where they were headed.

The entrance to the cellar was on the other side of the house. Seamus took the lead again. Each step was silent and considered. Time was of the essence, but not arousing the attention of the likely dozen or so sleeping SS men upstairs was also paramount.

It took the three men five minutes to traverse the château.

The rooms were empty, the place quiet. Seamus took a deep breath as the cellar door came into view. Durand stepped forward to pick the lock.

"Can you do it quietly?" Seamus whispered.

"Of course."

The Frenchman placed his bag on the floor and reached in for a different set of tools. Seamus and Michael stood back, keeping watch as the thief worked in silence. Two agonizing minutes passed before the deadbolt rolled back, and the door opened.

"This is it," Seamus said. He extinguished the flashlight in his hand and held up the pistol. Stone steps led down in a spiral. Seamus took each one with slow care, the other two men behind him. They came upon a stone hallway lit by two lightbulbs suspended from the ceiling. An SS man sitting by the wall stood up with wide eyes as he caught sight of the silent intruders. Seamus raised his pistol and put two bullets in him before he had the chance to draw his. His body collapsed on the stone floor.

Two wooden doors were built into the stone wall on either side of the cellar. The fetid odor of dirt, blood, and sweat hung in the air. It was unlike anything Seamus had smelled since the war.

Michael put his ear to the first door. He pointed, nodded, and pushed the handle down. Seamus ran the five steps to him as the door opened. An SS man in a chair in the corner stood up. Seamus pulled his trigger, but the Nazi was too fast, and the bullet only caught him in the shoulder, spinning him around.

Michael was on top of the SS man in seconds, directing punches at his face. The soldier got on top of him, but Durand put his gun against the Nazi's temple.

"Enough of this." He pulled the trigger.

Maureen sat in the middle of the room. The chair she was

tied to seemed the only thing keeping her upright. Seamus ran to his daughter, lifting her head with his hand.

"Father?" she asked in English. "You came for me?" He had to strain to hear what she was saying, even from just inches away.

"You didn't think I'd leave you here, did you?" Tears flowed down his face.

His daughter's face was a bloody mishmash of cuts, swollen to the point that he hardly recognized her. And he noticed some of her fingernails were missing.

"Cut those ropes!" Seamus whispered.

Michael cut through the ropes, and Seamus caught her, taking her full weight in his arms. Maureen's head rolled back as he picked her up. Her body was weak and limp against his.

"Gerhard and Hans. We have to get them," Maureen mumbled. "They know. Someone talked."

"They know what?"

"About the coup," she whispered.

The soft words hit Seamus like a fist, but he didn't have the time to mourn their plan—or the lives of Petra Wagner and General Horst Engel.

"Is she ok?" Michael asked.

"We have to get her to a hospital."

"Not without Hans and Gerhard."

Seamus took a second to contemplate and nodded. "Try the other doors."

Michael ran to the first door and shoved it open to reveal an empty space with a single lightbulb suspended above a chair.

Seamus followed behind, his daughter in his arms. The next room was the same. The door to the last was locked, and Durand picked the lock. Gerhard was slumped over in a chair bolted to the ground.

"He's alive," Durand said after checking his pulse. They cut him loose. He was in worse shape than Maureen and groaned in pain as Michael picked him up. He remained unconscious.

"I can carry him," Michael said and heaped him on his back in a fireman's lift.

"Let's go," Seamus said, all too aware that getting in here had been the easy part.

"Where's Hans?" Michael asked.

"Not here. Dead already?" Seamus said.

"Ullrich. We have to get Ullrich," Maureen said as if in a dream.

Seamus ignored her and carried on toward the stairs. Durand took the lead now, and he was at the bottom when another SS soldier appeared with a drink in his hand. He dropped the glass and drew his gun as Durand fired. One shot echoed in the narrow chamber, and both men fell. The Nazi on the steps tried to raise his pistol again, but Seamus shot him in the chest.

"Durand!"

The old crook smiled. "Get the money to my son."

"You have my word."

The Frenchman's eyes closed as he exhaled his last breath.

"That gunshot is going to bring the entire house on us," Michael said.

"We have to go now!" Seamus ran up the stairs with Michael just behind, but both men were hindered by the bodies they carried. They came to the top of the stairs as two men came down from the top floor with rifles, barring their way to the kitchen. The SS couldn't see them.

"Out the front door," Seamus whispered, and they ran to the front of the house. Michael pushed outside, and Seamus followed, doing his best to cover them. His son ran around the side of the house. Seamus was a couple of seconds behind Michael.

The SS guards appeared just as Seamus rounded the

corner. The rounds they fired hit the wall, but he knew they'd catch him on the other side of the house. Michael, with his amazing speed and strength, was streaking ahead. He was going to make it, but Seamus knew he and Maureen never would.

He carried his daughter around the back of the house and saw his son push the wounded man over the wall. Every muscle in Seamus's body was screaming, and the SS men were gaining. He steeled himself for the bullets that would soon rip through him. He looked back to see the SS soldiers at the corner five paces behind.

He stopped to try to surrender, but the SS guards wouldn't accept it. They raised their rifles. *Cracking* sounds came from the trees, and the Nazis dived for cover as bullets impacted the brickwork above their heads. Seamus began running again.

Leon was at the wall, the rifle poking out over it. He fired again.

"Come on, Father!" Michael shouted.

He reached the wall, and Michael helped his sister over. Gerhard was lying against a tree, his eyes closed.

"I'll stay behind to cover you," Leon said.

"No chance," Michael said. "You can't run. You'll never make it."

"And you can't shoot," the composer responded.

The younger man grabbed the rifle. "The Hitler Youth taught me well. I'll follow you."

Monika helped Leon as best she could while Seamus ran ahead and laid his daughter's unconscious body on the back seat of the car. "Be ready to leave in about 30 seconds," he said to Gilda, who was sitting behind the wheel.

"Yes, I heard the shots."

Seamus helped Monika with Leon, and soon they were in the car with Gilda.

"Get them to a hospital," Seamus said and slammed the

doors shut. The car careened off down the dirt road. Seamus ran back toward his son and Gerhard.

Michael still had the SS pinned down, but several more had joined them. Their shots slammed into the wall, causing fragments of rock to fly in the air.

"I'm almost out of bullets," Michael said.

"Count to ten after I leave, and follow me," he said as he picked up Gerhard.

Seamus was back on the Western Front, a wounded man over his shoulders and running from the Germans again. The trees were dark and thick, and he struggled to find his way through. He heard one last rifle shot, and his son was beside him in seconds.

"Get the car started," Seamus shouted. "They'll be right on our tails."

Michael sped ahead as bullets started striking the trees around them. Seamus felt his breath thundering in and out of his lungs—Gerhard's dead weight on his shoulders felt like a rock. The clearing opened, and Michael was in the car, the back door open.

Seamus threw Gerhard's body onto the seat and jumped in after him. The figures of SS soldiers appeared through the scrub.

"Go! Go!" Seamus shouted, and Michael pressed down on the accelerator. A bullet struck the back window and the glass shattered, but Michael kept his foot down. The car raced away. Seamus looked back at five or six SS men firing after them, but it was too late. They were gone.

~

4:10 a.m.: Berlin

Petra Wagner woke from a troubled sleep to the sound of the phone beside her bed ringing. She reached over and picked up the receiver, pushing back the silk sheets Goebbels had given her. Her fifth-floor apartment was pitch-black, and she turned on the light at the same time.

"Hello?" she gasped.

"It's your friend in a foreign place," said Lisa. Her voice was sharp and laden with stress. She sounded as if she was about to cry.

"Why are you calling at this—"

"I've been trying all night."

"I just got home less than an hour ago."

"It might be time for you to join me. Our friends have found out about our holiday plans." Lisa's voice broke. "They're coming to pick you up. I'm sure of it."

Petra's heart melted, and a tear ran down her face. "How do you know?"

"It's time to leave, old friend."

Petra heard a screeching sound on the street outside and walked to her balcony door. She pushed back the curtains, the phone still in her hand, and looked out.

"I think it's too late," she said. Several men jumped out of a car and ran into her apartment building. "They're already here. Coming up the stairs."

"I'm so sorry," Lisa said, sobbing now. "Someone cracked. I only just found out."

Petra was shaking so much that the phone almost fell out of her grasp. "I just wanted to do something to make a difference."

"And you did," Lisa said. "For what it's worth, you've more than paid your debt to me—many times over."

"Thank you." Petra hung up the phone.

The sound of someone hammering on the door erupted

through the silence of the apartment. Petra felt her breath catch in her throat. The phone clattered on the marble floor. The door was shuddering on its hinges, and the voices of the Gestapo men behind it were bleeding through. Petra tried to block them out and, still in her pajamas, pushed the door to her balcony open to behold the city she loved. A massive Nazi flag hanging from the building across the street billowed in the gentle breeze.

"It won't always be this way," she whispered.

The lock on her front door gave, and the Gestapo men spilled inside. She glanced back and climbed up onto the railing. Petra took one last look around before stepping out into the night. The *whooshing* of the air around her was the last thing she heard.

21

Monday, May 16

Seamus slipped on one of the two suits he'd brought and stepped out of the hotel room. Staying away from Berlin was torturous, but he couldn't leave while Maureen was still in the hospital. Helga assured him that Fiona was safe and acting rationally, so he trusted his daughter to stay with his cousin until he got home. Then the fireworks would begin.

He waved to the receptionist at the desk in the hotel lobby before walking out onto the street. It was a bright, sunny morning, and the streets of Paris were alive with color and sound. Well-dressed people sauntered along as if they had nothing more to concern them than where to order their next coffee. Seamus joined a line at the newsstand on the corner and picked out a German newspaper from the day before. The headline at the bottom of the front page sent a chill through his spine, and he folded the paper in half and returned to the hotel.

Lisa and Hannah were in the restaurant on the bottom floor

of the hotel having a breakfast of café au lait and croissants. He kissed them both and took a seat.

"Look at this." He showed Lisa the newspaper:

Luftwaffe General Found Guilty Of Treason Executed

His wife threw the broadsheet on the table and put her head in her hands. "It's over." The story of Petra Wagner's suicide was still rocking the Berlin social scene. No one could work out why one of Germany's biggest up-and-coming movie stars would take her own life.

"Is this our fault?"

"It's no one's fault but the Nazis themselves," Seamus replied, aware of his young stepdaughter's presence at the table. "There's nothing we could have done to prevent this from happening. They moved like lightning."

"Are we going to visit Maureen again today?" Hannah asked.

"Right after breakfast," Lisa said.

"Did they ever catch the nasty person who ran my sister over?"

"The police have their best people looking into it," Seamus said and placed his hand on hers. She finished her croissant and drank her orange juice in silence.

"Do you think Gerhard saw this?" Lisa asked.

"I don't know. He's not in good shape. Perhaps the nurse read it to him, but it could well be up to us."

Lisa shook her head behind the coffee cup and took a sip. Seamus lit up a cigarette and sat back, unable to eat anything. He stared out the window at nothing for a minute or more before he spoke again.

"We had a chance, didn't we? To make a difference?"

"We still do, my love," Lisa answered. "Hayden's expecting us back in Berlin in a few days."

"Hannah, can you go upstairs and fetch my hat from the room?" Seamus asked and handed his stepdaughter the key.

He reached over and took his wife's hand once the child was gone.

"Have you decided anything about Fiona?" she asked.

"Not yet, I need to see her first. I haven't had any breakthroughs. We could take her out of school and have her work at the factory. At least I could keep a close eye on her there."

"But she'd still be subjected to Nazi propaganda. How about sending her back to America to live with Maeve again until we're able to join her?"

"I don't think she'd go." The following words were even more painful to utter. It took him a few seconds to muster the strength to say them.

"I've been thinking about us returning to Berlin. Much as it pains me to say so, I think you and Hannah should stay here in Paris." He took a drag on his cigarette. "With everything that's happened, it's too dangerous for you in Germany. I don't have the luxury of choice. Conor and Fiona are still in Berlin, so I need to go back for them. I have my commitment to Hayden, and my workers."

Lisa let his hand go. Her face contorted as if she were about to get angry, but then she seemed to relent. "The newspaper stories never mentioned anyone other than Petra and Engel. We don't know that the Gestapo have any reason to suspect me."

"We don't know anything. Gerhard has no recollection of what he told them, and we don't have any notion of the circumstances around Petra's death."

"She jumped from her balcony. I spoke to her just a few moments before."

"Yes, but how do we know the Gestapo didn't question her first and then throw her over? Her suicide is a neat ending to what could have been a nasty scandal for the regime. Perhaps they questioned her in the apartment and then killed her once they had the information they needed."

"What are you saying, Seamus?"

"That you should stay here, or somewhere else safe, until I wrap up my business in Germany and join you."

"How long's that likely to be?"

"A few weeks. A few months. I don't know."

He stubbed out his cigarette and took his wife by the hands. "Believe me, this is the last option I would have chosen. The thing I want most in life is to keep us all together, but my workers... I can't abandon them. Most of the Jews in the factory are letting the everyday business of living their lives obscure the great danger they're in."

"And you're going to save them?"

"I don't know, but I have to give them one last chance at the scheme Gert and I proposed. I can't abandon them."

"And what about Hayden?"

"I don't know how happy he'd be to just let me go back to America now. I'm one of his most valuable contacts."

"What could he do to stop you?"

"I'm not sure, but the US State Department would be a powerful enemy."

Lisa let his hands go and picked up her coffee again. "Is Paris safe for us after what just happened?"

"I don't know. Perhaps Switzerland might be better."

"Don't make us wait too long, Seamus. You have a commitment to us too, and you know I don't care about the money. We have enough in the bank in Basel already."

He looked around the bright dining room. "I just need a little time, and we'll be together again."

Hannah arrived with Seamus's hat, and they stood up to leave. The Métro journey to the hospital was one they knew well. Maureen had been moved to the bigger hospital in Paris after a day in Pithiviers. It was strange having her recuperate only a few minutes from the château, and Seamus was relieved when the doctors discharged her to the city. Gilda was right—

the Nazis didn't come for her or Gerhard, but Seamus sat at her bedside all day and night while she was in Pithiviers to make sure.

Lisa kept hold of Hannah's hand as they walked into the hospital. They moved through the hallways in silence, only speaking as they greeted the nurse at Maureen's door.

"How is she?" Seamus asked before they went into her private room.

"Better," the young nurse said. "She slept through the night."

"Good!" Lisa said.

"We were also able to take the stitches out of her scalp." She seemed to sense Seamus's mood. "She's going to be all right, Monsieur Ritter."

"Thank you," Seamus answered.

Maureen was sitting up in bed as they entered. The light from the window streamed in, bathing the room in glowing white.

The bruises on her face had healed, and the stitches were gone, but her skin was pallid and dull. Concern over internal injuries had faded to the point where the doctors said she could leave the next day. She would have scars to remember her time in the château for the rest of her life. He supposed they all would.

"How are you feeling?" Lisa asked as they approached the bed.

Maureen turned to them with a beaming smile. "Much better. I'm not peeing blood anymore, so that's a good start to any day."

Her right arm was in a sling—the SS torturer had broken her clavicle. She held up her other hand. Her fingernails were starting to grow back in.

"Imagine all the money I'll save on manicures now too."

Seamus tried to laugh but felt a dagger of pain instead.

"One of the nurses told me Gerhard is sitting up now. I can't wait to see him."

"He's a strong young man," Seamus said. He hadn't the courage to tell his daughter about her friend's scars and multiple broken bones. Gerhard was an example of what would have happened to Maureen just hours later had they not rescued her when they did.

"How is Leon?" Maureen asked. "I'm so glad he and his family came to say goodbye."

"They should be somewhere in the middle of the Atlantic by now," Seamus said. He had tried to reimburse the composer for the money he spent on the cars, clothes, and weapons. Maureen's fellow Subversive only took a fraction of what he offered, but Seamus made sure to pay Durand's son himself.

"Gilda was in here yesterday. She told me she wants to live in the south of France."

"Yes, in a warm place," Lisa said. "We owe them so much."

Seamus had the German newspaper under his arm and held it up. "I saw the headline I was dreading. General Engel was executed." He didn't hand the broadsheet to his daughter, instead giving her a moment to digest the news.

"This is all Hans's doing."

"You're sure?" Lisa replied.

"I am."

They stayed with her, waiting until Michael and Monika came in before lunch to tell all the young adults about Lisa and Hannah. They sent Hannah downstairs to the lobby with a book as they talked by Maureen's bed.

"You're going back to Berlin alone?" Michael asked.

"We don't know how much Petra told the Gestapo before she died. I can't risk Lisa being picked up."

"And you don't think they'll come for you?"

"I have no direct link to any of this. Lisa was Petra's contact." Seamus put his arms around his wife's neck from behind. "I'll miss all of you more than I can say, but it won't be forever. I have some loose ends to tie up, but I should be able to leave by the start of 1939."

"Have you decided what you want to do?" Maureen asked her brother.

Michael smiled and put his arm around his wife. "I can run again. The strength is returning. It's hard to explain, but somehow, I feel whole again."

"He ran under 11 seconds yesterday!" Monika kissed her husband on the cheek.

"I think we might need to book our tickets for the games in Helsinki in '40!" Lisa said.

"But I can't run for Germany again. I wouldn't."

"We have our steamer tickets to America, and I've been practicing my English," Monika said in her husband's native tongue.

"We wanted to wait until we were all together to tell you," Michael said, returning to German.

"It's the right decision. I just hope we'll all be together in America soon," Seamus said.

"Back where it all began," Michael said.

"Speak for yourself," Monika replied.

Michael and Monika took his parents and Hannah to lunch after their visit. Seamus and Lisa left Hannah with them for the rest of the afternoon as they returned to the hospital to spend what would be Maureen's last day there.

Seamus strolled hand in hand with the woman who'd taught him that love never dies—it just gets passed on.

"This is the last thing I wanted," he said as the imposing beauty of Notre Dame emerged. "All this. Everything I've striven for these last few years has been with the end goal of keeping my family together. But I failed. We're going to be scattered all over the world."

"You haven't failed, my love. They're making their own choices now."

"I can't stand the thought of being away from you."

"I already miss you. This feels like a memory to me, not something happening now."

Seamus stopped walking and kissed his wife. "I'll never let you go. We'll be together again soon."

"What about Maureen?"

"Maureen's an adult who can make her own way. I'll ask her to join you in Switzerland when she's well enough to travel."

They continued walking. "What if she refuses?" Lisa asked.

"She's a grown woman now. I can't force her to do anything. I can only trust her judgment and be there for her."

"When she needs to be rescued from a Nazi torture chamber?"

"Hopefully not that again." He smiled. "I need to get back to Berlin. I should leave tomorrow, when Maureen gets out of hospital. Fiona and Conor have been with Helga too long."

The atmosphere between them changed as the realization of what was to come descended on them like a hammer.

Wednesday, May 18

The train to Berlin Hauptbahnhof was late in arriving. Seamus alighted from the carriage alone and walked along the platform crowded with SS and Stormtroopers. A line of massive Nazi flags fluttered in the breeze outside the station as he flagged down a taxi. Leaving Lisa and Maureen and the rest of his family behind was like a millstone around his neck, but the thought of seeing Conor and Fiona again kept him afloat.

The streets of Berlin were the same bustling, maddening, exciting mix as ever. People's attitudes, dress sense, and customs differed here from those prevalent in Paris or elsewhere. But people were more or less the same here as in France or America. Most Germans weren't diehard Nazis. They were just trying to live their lives and do the best for their children. They didn't thirst for war or conquest, just a chance at prosperity and a higher quality of life. He hoped Hitler and the world's leaders would be able to see that before the coming storm finally hit. He wished he could make his own daughter see it.

The late train upset his plans to meet the children after school, and he was forced to direct the taxi to Helga's mansion, which was only a mile from his own. The driver dropped him off with a kind word, and Seamus jogged to the door with his suitcase in hand. Helga's butler, a well-mannered man from Bonn in his 50s, answered the door and took his luggage and hat. The house was new, and completely refurbished. Seamus's shoes clacked on the Italian marble flooring as the butler led him inside. Conor sat at the table with Helga, doing his homework, but jumped up to run to his father as he saw him. Seamus picked up the young boy. Helga stood waiting.

"I swear you've grown since I left," Seamus said and put Conor down.

"Where's Lisa and Hannah?" Conor asked.

"They had to stay in Paris with Maureen to help her recuperate after her accident. We'll see them soon, I promise."

"You mean it's just you, me, and Fiona for now?"

"For now."

He spoke with Helga about Maureen's health and the bogus hit-and-run they'd blamed her injuries on before he asked for Fiona.

"She should be home any second," Helga answered.

"Thanks for keeping the business running when I was gone."

"I expect you to make up for your absence in the coming weeks."

"I will, but I also have some important conversations I need to have with you."

Helga seemed just about to ask what they were when the front door opened, and Fiona walked in, dressed from head to toe in her League of German Girls uniform.

Seamus had to stop himself from asking her why she was wearing it to school. He suppressed his anger in the hopes of forging a lasting peace. They hadn't seen each other in months.

"I'm home," he said.

His daughter's face dropped, but the tsunami of anger he expected came only as a trickle. This was all his fault, not hers. He never should have brought her to Berlin. She should have been in America, worrying about getting on the cheerleading squad, not attending mass rallies of Hitler Youth.

"I didn't know you'd be coming back today." Fiona cut him off before he could speak. "I wasn't going to leave school early. Something came up."

"Harald," he said.

"Yes. He's beginning SS training in a week. I had to see him."

"How did it go?"

"With Harald?"

"Yes."

Fiona shook her head. "I never knew you were so interested in my social life."

"I'm fascinated by you. By everything about you."

A look he hadn't expected to see crossed her face, a painful grimace. "He said he doesn't want to settle down yet. Perhaps in a year or two. His focus is on his SS training right now."

Seamus resisted the temptation to be delighted. "I'm sorry." He walked over and put his arms around her. He held on for as long as she allowed him—about three seconds—before he led her to the balcony overlooking the perfectly manicured garden. He explained everything he'd just told his son and Helga. Conor joined them once he was done with his homework.

"I understand you must have a thousand questions."

Fiona walked to the edge of the balcony and turned around to face her father. "When are you going to tell us the truth about what's going on?"

"I don't know what you mean."

"We're young, not stupid," she said. "My troop leader is an expert at telling when people are lying, and she taught me a few tricks. She says I'm a natural."

Seamus stood staring at his daughter for a few seconds, wondering how he ever let it come to this.

"Pack up your things. We're leaving here in ten minutes."

~

Friday, July 8: Paris

Gerhard was sitting alone drinking a beer when Maureen arrived. He immediately called the waiter over and asked for the bill.

"You back on your feet again?" she asked.

"Just since yesterday."

His crutches were gone, but he still wore a sling to support his left arm. His face was red, and scars extended down his jawline from his ear past his neck. His hair had grown back in patches, and the stitches in his head were still visible. Now skinny, his hands shook as he held the beer glass to his lips. His rugged handsomeness had all but vanished. She just hoped the torture hadn't diminished her the way it had her friend.

"Let's go." They stood up to weave their way out of the crowded café. "Whose car is this?" he asked as they reached the curb.

"The same one that whisked you away from the Château de Bellecour."

"You have everything?" he asked as they sat in the car.

"Yes. You're sure they're there?"

"I've been following him for three weeks now, sitting outside that godforsaken château on my own. I'll never forget that face as long as I live."

"And his voice."

"It's him. It's both of them."

Maureen started the car. Going back to Pithiviers felt like returning to the scene of a crime. Gerhard directed her along the route he'd driven many times in the past few weeks. It was dark when they arrived, and he checked his watch. He nodded to Maureen, and they pulled on the balaclavas she had brought. The silenced pistols were in a bag in the back, and they reached in for them and checked the clips. Then they waited.

Emily emerged from the café across the street at 10 p.m., precisely on time. Maureen rolled down the window as she approached.

"Inside on the left."

"Anyone else nearby?"

"No. Should be clear."

Gerhard produced a map of the interior of the café, and Emily pointed out the table before walking away alone.

The former prisoners got out of the car, concealing their weapons in long coats as they crossed the street. Maureen's breath was booming in and out of her lungs as Gerhard pushed the door open. They raised their pistols and turned to where Ullrich, the SS torturer, and Hans, their former friend, were sitting. The two men realized what was happening too late, and Maureen and Gerhard brought them down in a hail of silent gunfire as they reached for their own weapons. Her only regret was that the Nazis didn't know who pulled the triggers.

The job done, the two Resistance fighters returned to the

car. Maureen pulled out, and they drove into the night. It wasn't revenge. It was justice. The guilt she suspected might come never materialized. Why would it?

This was war.

The End

ALSO BY EOIN DEMPSEY

Standalones

Finding Rebecca

The Bogside Boys

White Rose, Black Forest

Toward the Midnight Sun

The Longest Echo

The Hidden Soldier

The Lion's Den Series

1. The Lion's Den
2. A New Dawn
3. The Golden Age
4. The Grand Illusion
5. The Coming Storm
6. The Reckoning (Coming Soon)

ACKNOWLEDGMENTS

I'm incredibly grateful to my regular crew, my sister, Orla, my brother Brian, my mother, and my brother Conor. And thanks to my dad for instilling the love of story telling in me. Thanks to my fantastic editors. Massive thanks to my beta readers, especially Carol McDuell and Cindy Bonner. And as always, thanks to my beautiful wife, Jill and our three crazy little boys, Robbie, Sam and Jack.

Made in the USA
Las Vegas, NV
27 June 2024

91556906R00164